Praise for Rene Lyons' *The Daystar*

5 Literary Nymphs "...deeply emotional and extraordinarily creative...Ms. Lyons is a talented writer with expert characterization and world building skills. The detail that accompanies each facet of her story makes for easy visualization and an exceptionally pleasurable reading experience."

~ *Water Nymph, Literary Nymphs Reviews*

The Daystar

Rene Lyons

A SAMHAIN PUBLISHING, LTD. publication.

Samhain Publishing, Ltd.
512 Forest Lake Drive
Warner Robins, GA 31093
www.samhainpublishing.com

The Daystar
Copyright © 2006 by Rene Lyons
Print ISBN: 1-59998-352-4
Digital ISBN: 1-59998-148-3

Editing by Angie James
Cover by Scott Carpenter

First Samhain Publishing, Ltd. electronic publication: November 2006
First Samhain Publishing, Ltd. print publication: May 2007

Dedication

Angie: Well, we've gotten through another one. I hope I continue to be worthy of your belief in me.

Amanda: Thank you for all you do. It doesn't go unnoticed or unappreciated.

Andrei: Your generosity and kindness is an inspiration. Thank you for everything.

Mandie: What a pair we make. The window-licker and the helmet-wearer—a match made in heaven! Without you, we'd never know how Constantine felt. I couldn't have done this without you.

Ann, Bianca, Donna, Rowena, Nicole, Marivel, and Sylvia: My Sanity Squad. Your love and humor never fails to keep me sane.

Frankie: with you by my side I've touched the moon. I thank God for every day I have with you. This one is for you.

"World of Shadows"

By Jeff Holmes of The Floating Men: From the CD Tall Shadows

Don't say a word

Words won't change things

Cause if I thought it was right, you could stay every night from now on

I don't need a friend

And you ain't gonna save me

You can romanticize and fantasize at night but some things you can't own

You're so damn young

Thrills come so easy

When you've been kicked around the underground like I have you might turn to stone

Don't swallow the lies

The hallow glamour

Cause if you think it's all handshakes and earthquakes, girl you got it wrong

Don't you fear the darkness?

Let your dreams be dreams

You don't need what you want

I don't know how to make you go home

How do I turn off what I never meant to turn on?

Go spend all your time out in the sunshine

Girl, you don't belong here in my world of shadows.

Don't get me wrong

I know how love feels

And if I couldn't care I wouldn't dare pretend that it's time to move on

You might be strong

But you're never strong enough

See, I was born with the clean heart of a child but now look how I've grown

Chapter One

Wiltshire, England—Draegon Castle

September 1293

Constantine Draegon scurried down the length of the great hall, his hands thrown over his head in an attempt to protect himself from the brutal blows raining down on him. He dared to steal a peek to the right and saw, as always, she was watching.

Her beauty made him want to weep.

She wore an ornate tunic the color of rich wine. Her hair, the color of new wheat, hung in a thick plait down her back. She stood with arms crossed over her bosom as her cold blue gaze took in the scene in the hall. By the way her arching brows were drawn together in a deep, disapproving frown, Constantine knew it would get worse before this finished playing out.

"I will not tolerate a weak son." Her tone held no affection.

"Nor I," Henry Draegon thundered. He stopped for a moment to regard his wife. "This wretch can be no spawn of mine."

Aislin rolled her eyes heavenward. "God's teeth, Henry, not that argument again."

By this time Constantine, a mere eight years of age, had made it to the doors. He pressed himself against the wall and eyed the huge metal-banded double doors of the main entrance.

So close that if he dared, he could attempt to escape this beating.

Lack of bravery wasn't what kept him frozen to the spot. For a young lad he already possessed an abundance of courage. What kept him from running was trail by error. He'd tried running in the past. Bones were broken in punishment. He'd not risk such pain again.

When his father gave him a hard kick, Constantine grunted from the impact and fought back tears. He prayed vehemently for the strength not to cry. Tears were not permitted in Henry and Aislin Draegon's hall—especially if those tears came from the eyes of their only child, Constantine.

"You have yet to explain what you were doing in the stable with young William all those years ago."

"That, dear Henry," Aislin drawled, "should have been obvious even to you."

Henry grabbed him by one arm and hauled him off the floor. Constantine dangled like a bruised and bloody rag-doll in Henry's grip. "My seed could not have spawned this."

"Believe me, the boy most certainly is yours." His mother passed a frosty look over Constantine. "I should have cleansed my womb of him before he came screaming out of my body."

"Yes, well, too late for that now, wife." Henry's mix of regret and disgust was palpable as Constantine was tossed aside. "We can only hope Ulric will beat the manhood into him. Lord knows I've tried."

"One can hope. Though I doubt anything can turn the sniveling creature into anything more than what he already is." Unfurling her arms, Aislin stalked from the hall, her long legs carrying her up the stairs. Before she reached the top, she turned and regarded Constantine from head to foot. "Two more years with Constantine will seem like a lifetime."

She spun with the grace of a queen and disappeared in the shadows. Constantine knew the only place she would go was her chamber, where she spent much of her time with whatever young soldier she could lure there with her beauty.

After Henry took himself out into the courtyard and the servants hurried away, Constantine let out a breath of relief.

He bit back tears and puffed out his chest with false bravado. "I am not weak," he whispered, but there was no one left to hear him.

I am a dragon.

Now, if only it were true. Maybe then his father and mother wouldn't hate him. Maybe he would feel his mother's arms wrap around him and hold him close as a mother should. And maybe, his sire would ruffle his hair and give him an affectionate clap on the shoulder as they walked off the lists, as he'd seen him do with his knights.

"I am a dragon."

He needed the strength of a dragon, he told himself. He willed it to be so. Dragons didn't cry because their fathers beat them and their mothers hated them. Dragons were strong and thus far in his short life, Constantine learned he'd need such strength in order to survive.

"I am a dragon," Constantine repeated as he pushed himself off the floor.

He skulked from the hall, past the courtyard and down to the rolling stream cutting through the dense forest. It sat on the edge of his sire's land. This was the place where he found his strength even as he washed away the blood. Here, he imagined the days to come, when he would be a knight and fierce enough to keep his sire from hurting him.

His body sore and bleeding, Constantine sank down on the bank of the stream. He fisted his hands in the damp earth and squeezed his eyes shut as he sent a silent prayer to God. He begged his Lord for courage. But most of all, he implored God for his father and mother's love.

The only answer was the dull ache in his heart God refused ease.

Chapter Two

September 2005

Raphael de Vere watched as the lithe brunette passed in front of them. She did a double take before stopping dead in her tracks. Arching a brow in appreciation of Dragon's dark and dangerous looks. The tip of her tongue peeked out from between blood-red lips. Such was the usual reaction of women when it came to Constantine Draegon.

Dressed in baggy charcoal pants, complete with an array of chains dangling from them, and a black tee that read, *You laugh now... But you won't be laughing when I crawl out from under your bed,* Constantine looked every bit the Goth-God.

Black hair, an ashen complexion, and a black leather collar with razor-sharpened spikes around his neck completed the look. If Raphael had dared that getup, he'd look like he dressed early for Halloween. Even here at The Gate, a gothic themed club in Scranton, Constantine stood out among the like-dressed crowd. He just had a look about him that screamed, "don't fuck with me".

Over their clothes, both he and Constantine wore ankle length black trenches. One was forced to wear such a coat when one was strapped to the fangs with weaponry.

A quick glance at Constantine warned Raphael this night was going to be hellishly long. The expression on Dragon's face was downright murderous, never a good thing when they were on the hunt for food. The woman appreciating Constantine either didn't notice the look he wore or else she chose to ignore it.

Sauntering toward them, her hips swaying seductively, the woman had no idea the trouble she was courting by approaching Constantine. The unflattering black velvet gown hid whatever curves might lay hidden beneath it. She gave Constantine an alluring grin as her gaze raked over him. Raphael almost saw her mentally stripping Dragon of his clothes. The moment she noticed the wicked scar that cut down the left side of Constantine's face her step faltered. She regained her composure and continued her advance. When Constantine gave her one of his more vicious of scowls, she smartened up and hurried away.

Raphael muttered a curse under his breath. "Jesus Christ, Constantine, is this what we're doing tonight? Scaring off potential females?"

"Leave off, Rogue. I'm in no mood for your shit tonight."

"I just want to know if you're going to snarl at every women who comes near you." Raphael ignored the nasty scowl Constantine directed at him. After seven centuries of dealing with Dragon's attitude, he was used it to. "I don't want to waste more time here than necessary, that's all."

Looking around the club, Raphael released a dramatic sigh. He hated it here. He'd avoid it altogether if this wasn't the easiest place to feed.

If not for their god-awful pasty completions, the crowd of vampire-wannabes would blend in with the black decor. If they wanted to know what a real vampire looked like, all they had to do was look at him and Constantine.

"What part of 'fuck off' didn't you understand?" Constantine's glare intensified. "And I'm not throwing around attitude."

"Obviously not," Raphael retorted when Constantine sneered at him.

Constantine looked away with a grunt. He fingered the long, jagged scar that ran down the left side of his face—a "gift" from his past. "It's the scar. I can't help it if it scares the women away."

Raphael sincerely hoped Dragon didn't think he believed that bullshit. Hell, all Constantine needed to do was crook a finger at a woman and she'd come running. He had the whole badass thing working in his favor. The ladies seemed to love it, which made feeding relatively easy for him provided he was in the mood to *make* it easy.

Tonight clearly wasn't one of those nights.

"Balls," Raphael snorted. "It's that puss of yours. Do you even remember how to crack a smile?"

Constantine leveled him with a droll stare. "My face would break if I tried."

Raphael rolled his eyes. "I'm doomed, aren't I? I'm forever to be surrounded by brooding bastards."

"Shut the hell up before I'm forced to *shut* you up."

Any retort Raphael might have shot back was put on hold when the bartender inquired for the fourth time if they wanted drinks. The way Constantine sent him away ensured it would be the last time the man bothered them.

They might be sitting at the bar, but it wasn't for the drinks. Here, they had a clear view of the entire club, which was always a good thing when one had as many enemies as the Templars did.

With time being of the essence, they couldn't linger here all night. They needed to feed and get the hell out of there and continue their hunt for the vampires responsible for the recent rash of murders. True, no other women had been murdered since the night Lucian disappeared, but until they found the Daystar, they had to assume more humans would be sacrificed in the quest for the ancient Druid relic.

No one wanted out of the club more than Constantine did. He eyed the brunette, who was still giving him looks from over her shoulder. He couldn't bring himself to act on the hunger and be done with it.

He'd never hesitated to feed. When it came to his body's needs Constantine sated them without any qualms and devoid of remorse. Any willing woman would do as far as he was concerned. He usually forgot them as soon as he finished with them.

The brunette looked back over at him. The feel of her gaze made his skin crawl. The smell of her desire would have gagged him did he still possess such a reflex. If it weren't for the scent of her blood coupled with his growing hunger, he would have put her out of his mind completely.

"Fuck it all." He pushed away from the bar. "Hurry up and find a female. I want out of here as soon as possible."

As he strode away he heard Raphael mutter, "It's about time."

He stalked toward the brunette as if he were heading into battle. When he reached her, she gasped with surprise even as she smiled with pure sexual excitement. He grabbed her by the arm and hauled her out of the club. Her friends gaped in shock as they watched him drag off their friend. Yet not one of them made any motion to follow after her, especially not when Raphael joined them and made a move on the remaining three women. Rogue would have them all if there were time.

Constantine had every intention of taking her hard as he drank her blood. Hard enough to drive the haunting imagine of Lexine Parker clean out of his mind. Unfortunately, like everything else when it came to him, it didn't work out as he'd planned.

CRℰD

To bring beauty to Seacrest, Tristan had called in the best landscapers. They'd created a beautiful haven of flowers to break the austere feel of the dreary gray castle. It helped to bring life to the otherwise bleak fortress. Lexine Parker knew he'd done it for her, since he'd lived here for centuries without it.

Sitting in that garden, hidden behind the keep, the night crawled over Lex. Restlessness and anxiety festered in her. The chronic itch above her navel was driving her insane and added to her unease. As much as she ignored it, the truth was, it grew worse every day.

Though she welcomed the night, since it was the only time she saw Allie and the Templars, lately the sun and her soul seemed one entity. Its glory infused her with so much energy it charged her entire body. When the sun slipped below the Adirondack Mountains, it was if a part of her went with it.

Unable to leave the castle alone, her days were spent out in the courtyard basking under the loving caress of the sun. Come the night, she threw herself into learning all she could about vampires and the Knights Templar. She poured over books and spent long hours lost in history and folklore on the computer.

Some nights, however, when she secured herself an escort, she went out on ghost hunts.

Though she didn't quite pick up where Allie left off, Lex took up the job now that Allie was a vampire. Thus far she'd gone on four hunts, each of which Raphael accompanied her on. Of those hunts, she'd detected the presence of two spirits, both of which had run from her as if she were the baddest thing this side of Hell.

The ghosts hadn't disappeared or refused to show themselves. No. They ran from her as if a vampire had invaded their territory. Though Lex made a lame attempt to explain it away by telling herself it was possible some of the Templars' energy rubbed off on her, she knew better. The truth was, a spirit would sense her lifeforce and know she was of the living.

With another investigation set for tomorrow night, Lex promised herself she'd quit her newfound occupation if such an event occurred again. The last thing she wanted was to torment an already tortured soul by driving it out of its sanctuary.

A cool breeze passed over her and Lex shivered. Late September always brought with it the first breath of winter here in the mountains. How different life was in Damascus than it had been in Florida. Life was slow here and though she was surrounded by death, Lex was more alive now than ever she had been living with her parents.

Though glad she'd stayed in Pennsylvania, this wasn't exactly the best place for a person who worshiped the sun and despised winter. The summers were short and the winters brutal. And yet, this was where Lex knew she belonged. Something had pulled her back to Damascus and compelled her to stay. As much as Allie assumed it was Lex's fascination with the mysteries of the night, the truth was, there was more to this rural area than the Templars dared to admit.

When Allie attempted to bribe her into staying a month ago, Lex had to assume the last thing Allie had anticipated was for her to be thrust into the Templar's world rather than eased in. What Allie hadn't known at the time was, Lex and Constantine had met the night before they'd gone to Seacrest.

Standing over six feet tall, with a mess of spiky black hair, tattoos and piercings, Constantine had stopped her dead in her tracks as soon as she'd emerged from the church. His scars, and he had plenty of them, somehow only added to his appeal.

From that first night, though he never outright ignored her, Constantine kept his distance from her. Allie explained that Sebastian had behaved much the same way toward her when they'd first met. Not that it helped in easing the pain of Lex's broken heart at Constantine's rejection of her.

Voices broke the silence of the courtyard. Lex didn't bother to look around for the source of the chorus of female voices. They were in her head, a jumble of sounds too loud to discern one from the other. Lex slapped her hands over her ears in a futile effort to block them out.

Crazy people heard voices; especially with the clarity Lex heard these. And yet, she knew she was sane. The voices came to her from someplace out of her scope of understanding. They invaded her mind with growing frequency over the last months, their voices louder, becoming almost urgent.

When she was younger, she'd heard them the few times she slipped away from the path of purity. She'd never told anyone. Not even Allie. Lex had kept this to herself since she was a kid. She'd suffered in silence, as a child fearing people would think she was a crazy. When she got older, she realized how right she had been to never talk about it to anyone. She'd witnessed how people treated her sister and it was awful. Lex knew she lacked the thick skin her sister possessed. Where Allie was able to shrug off people's harsh opinions of her, Lex wasn't able to do that.

Today was a good day, Lex realized, when the voices quieted as fast as they'd come. She dropped her hands and almost wept with relief at how short this episode was. Sometimes, it would last for nearly an hour.

With a glance at the closed portcullis, Lex stood and quit the garden. As she walked through courtyard she looked toward the massive gray stone keep. Even now, after being here for the last month, she still found it unbelievable that this was "home". It amazed her that she lived in an exact replica of a medieval castle surrounded by creatures most humans believed fictional.

Life had certainly taken a turn for the surreal.

When Lex entered the keep she smelled the delicious aroma of baking cookies. Chocolate chip, if she weren't mistaken. One thing about Anne, the grandmotherly woman who took care of the castle and its inhabitants, she cooked like no one's business.

After two decades of having no one to cook for, Anne more than made up for it with Lex. If she kept on stuffing her the way she did, Lex was going bust right out of her clothes. Given the tightening of the waist of her jeans, maybe she'd eat only two cookies tonight instead of the entire dozen. Though she doubted it.

Glancing at the empty hall, Lex was reminded that not only had Constantine gone with Raphael to search for information on the Daystar, but they went to feed as well. Though she had no right to be jealous, she was. After all, she was only human.

After going directly into the den, Lex powered up the computer she shared with Allie. This was the only contact she had with the outside world. She attempted to keep up with her friends through phone calls and emails. But those calls and emails grew fewer and farther between as each day passed.

Settling into the lush black leather chair, Lex opened the media player program and selected the special edition of the Enigma album, *MCMXC A.D.* The haunting beat took her mind away from the here and now.

Dark, mysterious and medieval, the music reminded Lex of Constantine. Her eyes slid shut as "Sadeness" overwhelmed her. Her body hummed to life as she imagined Constantine's calloused hands and unyielding mouth on her. Having never experienced the touch of a man, she ached for her first kiss to be with Constantine.

Without realizing it, her hand went to the itch. The skin was raw from the damage made by her nails and hurt when she passed her fingers over it. When the hum of energy began to vibrate through her, coherent thought fled. She was transported to a dark and peaceful plane of sub consciousness. All Lex heard and felt was the music pumping from the speakers and the electricity shooting through her body. The rest of the world faded away.

Leaning her head back against the chair, Lex surrendered herself to the sensations coursing through her and let the music mix with the energy. The power took her away, where there was no death and no fear. For a blessed moment she was relieved of the worries of her life and the nagging grief of losing her brother, which was something she had yet to work through. But then, Lex assumed that the loss of a sibling was something a person never truly got over. There were days when the loss of Christian was so keen, it choked her, making it difficult for Lex to breathe. His death had drawn Allie and her even closer, since all they had now were each other. God knew their parents were completely worthless.

Right then, however, all of that faded from her mind, leaving the imagined sensation of Constantine's touch upon her body. She gave over to the sensation, believing it was as close as she'd come to knowing what it would be like to be touched by him.

Chapter Three

As soon as Constantine entered the keep, the mix of the rhythmic beat of Enigma's music and the sweet scent of Lex had his body growing so damn hard it hurt. He found himself in this painful state often since she came to live here. Each night it became more difficult for him to hold on to the civility he'd fought for centuries to maintain.

There wasn't a part of Lex's body Constantine didn't burn to touch—with both his hands and mouth. Hell, he wanted to bring other parts of himself into play as well, but that train of thought was best left unexplored.

The fact of the matter was, he couldn't be in the same room with her without wanting to haul her up to his chamber and lay claim to her body once and for all.

Even knowing this, Constantine walked to the den and leaned his hip against the frame. He crossed his arms over his chest and watched Lex. She looked so at peace. Lord knew such a state was a rare thing for any of them these days.

He remembered the night they'd met and had to bite back a groan as his desire for Lex intensified. He'd never believed he would come across a being of such purity until Lex. She'd stepped from the church like a beautiful dark angel. He'd been enraptured by the innocence of her, yet one touch had told him she was Allie's kin. That knowledge alone was all that had saved her from being dragged away from the church and taken in every depraved way he could imagine—and when it came to the darker side of life, he had a *very* vivid imagination

When he'd touched her, an odd frisson of energy had passed between them. For a moment he was given a blessed reprieve from the cold and the hunger that were his constant companions. When Allie had brought Lex to Seacrest Castle the next night, Constantine had known his existence would never be the same.

Pushing aside those memories, Constantine sniffed the air. The sweet aroma of honeysuckle wafted from her. He wondered if her sun-kissed flesh would taste as sweet as it smelled.

Something told him she would taste even sweeter then he imagined.

Constantine found having a conscience was a real bitch when it came to Lex. The damn thing had snuck up on him when he wasn't looking.

The evil bastard in him wondered what Lex was thinking, yet he didn't attempt to invade her mind. Somehow, she managed to block his telepathy when not many other humans could. Well, Allie had possessed the same ability, but she was a stubborn wench and he expected nothing less from her. Allie was so thickheaded he doubted a jackhammer could crack that skull of hers. Yet that was part of her appeal. It was what made her blend in with the Templars, long before Constantine had brought her over to this side of death.

Still watching her, Constantine marveled at the strength of Lex's lifeforce. It shone with a light that cut through the night like a blade, a tangible force in a world of shadows and mist.

As if Lex sensed him, she turned her head toward the doorway. When she opened her eyes and pinned him with her profound gaze, Constantine grunted as if punched in the gut.

She offered him a lazy smile. "Hi."

"Where is everyone?" With his need for her riding him, the question came out harsher than he'd intended.

Lex shrugged and Constantine sensed her relief. "I didn't expect you back this soon."

He didn't like her interest in his comings and goings—especially his *comings*. "Neither did I."

He found the way she licked her lips fascinating. "Did you feed?"

He nodded and stepped into the den despite knowing he should turn around and walk away. "I did."

Which is why I'm not tearing into you right now, elf.

Though Constantine had sated the bloodlust, his body's needs were far from met. He knew he should have taken the wench he'd fed from. He should have used her body to slake his sexual needs and been done with this torture. At least then his body wouldn't be screaming for release. Yet, something told him what he needed, only Lex could give him.

As he approached her, Constantine heard her heart racing. Her breathing grew erratic, causing her breasts to rise and fall with each hard gasp of air she dragged in. He relished the sound of the rush of blood through her veins. The metallic scent of it filled him, waking the monster in him.

When he stood before her, Lex reached out to him. Constantine engulfed her small hand with his branded one. He tugged her up from the chair and bit back a groan when she stepped into him. The moment her body pressed against his and her arms wrapped around his neck, everything savage in him came to the forefront.

Constantine let out a hiss as energy rippled through him. It reached every recess of his body. Though he'd experienced it before, it hadn't been as strong as it was now. He'd explained it away as nothing more than a powerful lifeforce. Now, it packed a punch that damn near felled him.

Constantine shoved Lex away and narrowed his eyes on her. "What the fuck is that?"

She shook her head, feigning innocence. "I've no idea what you're talking about."

Lex, he realized, was a horrible liar.

He gripped her shoulders. Again, the energy surged through him. This time he was prepared for it, welcomed it when it infused his being with heat. The sensation was the same after feeding, only this was a thousand times more intense.

"Don't lie to me, Lex." He gave her a small shake, letting her know he wouldn't tolerate her playing dumb.

A fleeting look of fear crossed her face but she hid it behind the annoyingly serene expression she went around wearing. "I don't know what it is."

He gave her another shake. "You're lying."

Her mouth worked but she said nothing. Constantine surmised she was picking her words with care. That was something she did often and it infuriated him.

"I swear I don't know what it is, Constantine."

Constantine let her go. As soon as he did, the cold rushed back into him, a result of being soulless. "How long?"

She looked away guiltily. "A while."

He cocked a brow at her, resisting the urge to shake the hell out of her again. "That's not a bloody answer, Lexine."

Inwardly, Lex cringed at the determination in Constantine's tone. This wasn't something she was ready to talk about, yet judging by the look on his face, Constantine was going to get an answer out of her one way or another. She didn't relish finding out what the "other" way would be.

"Since I was a kid," she whispered, Lex's hand went instinctively over the raw patch of flesh on her stomach. When she noticed Constantine's gaze following her hand she moved it away.

His hands came at her and Lex backed away. Constantine had the speed of his vampire's body working in his favor. He slapped aside her hands and yanked up her shirt. When she tugged it back down, he growled. She let go and let him do his thing.

Lex went up in flames of mortification when he knelt before her. His face was only inches from her stomach as he examined the chaffed skin.

"What is this?"

Lex shrugged. "Nothing. Just a rash I think."

Though she knew Constantine sensed her lie, he let it pass without calling her on it. "They have to be told."

Lex knew who "they" were and she wasn't about to say a word to them yet. The Templars didn't need the worry of her to add to the burdens they already carried. And Allie—well, she was the last person Lex wanted to worry. Her sister had been through enough. She didn't need this heaped upon her shoulders as well.

"Please Constantine, don't say anything. Give me some time to work this out in my head before the others find out."

Expecting him to reject her plea, Lex was surprised when he agreed to keep her secret. "I'm telling you now, woman, I'm not giving you long to sort this shit out."

"I know."

On the rare occasions she'd tried to tell Allie about it, the words had stuck in her throat. After a while, she'd given up and accepted this was something she'd have to suffer alone.

With Constantine's hands dancing over the sensitive flesh of her stomach, Lex knew the surge of heat flooding her had nothing to do with the energy raging in her. Her heartbeat raced as if in time with the music as his feathery touch woke her body to desire. When his nostrils flared and he let out a very low growl, it was obvious he smelled her arousal. Lex wished the floor would open and swallow her up even as she dared to hope he'd give her body what it craved.

He glared at her for a good long while before he reached to touch her hair. Obviously rethinking the action, he dropped his hand. "Why do you want me?"

Clearly he didn't realize how gorgeous he was.

Although she wanted to evade his question for her pride's sake, Lex knew he'd never leave her to her silence. "Because I've never known a man who affected me the way you do."

He brought his face close enough that their noses nearly touched. Lex shivered with a delicious fission of excitement. The beats of the music washed over her, made her imagine what it would be like to lay beneath him and have him pump into her in time to it. Oh God, she wanted to kiss him. Kiss him and then do so much more...

"And how do I 'affect' you, elf?"

Unable to resist the urge to touch him, Lex placed her hands on his chest. Since no heart beat there, it was eerily still. His body warmed under her palms and he sucked in a hard breath. His chest didn't rise or fall with the action, but hers did. Her own heart pounded wildly and her chest rose and fell with her frantic breaths as she ached for something she knew only he could give her.

"What do you want to hear, Constantine? Do you want to know that every time I'm around you I can barely breathe? And that all I want to do right now is have you kiss me?"

She lowered her eyes, more embarrassed than she'd ever been in her life. When he fisted his hands in her hair and forced her to look back at him, Lex saw the hunger reflected in Constantine's silver eyes. His upper lip curled back and she was met with the terrifying, and vastly erotic, sight of his fangs.

"You don't ever lower your eyes."

She blinked at him as a wealth of emotion stole the breath right out of her. "You make me lose myself, Constantine."

"You shouldn't want me."

He ground that out a breath before he lowered his head and took her mouth in a brutal kiss. Everything within Lex came alive as Constantine laid claim to her using nothing but his lips and tongue—and occasionally his teeth. The hypnotic music playing in the background added to the spell of raw desire wrapping around her and pulling her down into a place she'd never thought to go. A place where the world around them failed to matter and it was just the two of them.

Her limited imagination couldn't have envisioned her first kiss to be so barbaric. The chaste, gentle kisses she'd always imagined paled in comparison to the demand of Constantine's mouth. She gripped his waist and held on as he kissed her with a force that robbed her of breath and reason.

When he pulled his mouth from hers, Lex whimpered at the loss of contact. Constantine fisted a hand in the hair at the nape of her neck and forced her head back. "I should have fucked that woman tonight." His fangs flashed as he spat the words at her. "But I couldn't get you out of my goddamned head."

He released her hair and straightened, breaking the spell he'd woven around her with his kiss. Lex didn't want to envision him taking the blood of another woman, yet the image invaded her mind with sickening clarity. Her relief that he'd refrained from doing more knew no bounds. From what she'd seen of him so far, he was not a man who abstained from anything—except for her.

Balancing on her tiptoes, Lex caressed his face. She spared a brief glance at the scar that cut down his left cheek before placing a soft kiss on his lips. She pulled away and smiled at his frown.

"Thank you."

"For what?"

"For being you."

Constantine groaned as he grabbed for her. He slammed Lex against his chest and wrapped his arms around her to hold her there. His lips caressed her throat as "Sadeness" ended and "Mea Culpa" began. He ran his tongue over the pulsing vein, pulling a rasping breath from her, the sound more seductive than Enigma's rhythmic beats.

He palmed the back of her head and moved her so that his mouth settled over hers. With his other hand, he grasped her chin and forced her mouth open. With a primal need that rocked her, Constantine made her body melt into his as he kissed hard and deep. All of his restrained passion was there in his kiss, so much so that Lex had to hold fast to him to keep from being felled by the force of it.

He ground his hips against her in time to the beat. She groaned into his mouth and dug her nails into him as her entire body sparked to life. Constantine opened her to receive anything he wanted to do to her. He broke through years of suppressed sexuality, bringing it all to the forefront as his body slid into hers. Lex moved her hands down his back until they settled over the taut muscles of his ass. She pressed him against her and thrust forward to meet his hips.

Lex didn't stop it when her mind opened to him and her every thought was laid bare. He hissed against her lips when the flood of thoughts flowed from her to him. Though she had a limited imagination when it came to sex, she knew enough to know what she wanted—and what she wanted him to do to her and what she wanted to do to him played out in vivid detail.

He pushed Lex aside with a vicious curse. She stumbled, but righted herself by gripping the edge of the desk. "What's wrong?"

"Everything," he ground out, barely able to hold onto his control.

"Constantine..."

"Go away, Lex."

Though dizzy and disoriented from his sexual assault, Lex was smart enough to hear the warning in Constantine's tone. So though she didn't want to leave him, she knew it was best for him if she did.

Lex said nothing more as she stepped around him to leave the den. When their arms brushed, Constantine hissed a moment before his teeth snapped as if he needed to bite something. Well, not merely something. It was clear he wanted to bite *her.*

God forgive her, but she wanted to know what it would feel like to have Constantine take her blood.

He must have been reading her mind, since he let out a sound horrific enough to chill her blood. She'd almost reached the door when his voice cut through the quiet.

"Lex," Her name was a harsh curse falling from his lips. She stopped and turned back to him. "Lock your door."

When Lex heard Tristan and Raphael in the hall, she thought she'd die of shame. They *had* to know what they had been doing in here. If they didn't hear what had gone on—which Lex was sure they had—they'd sense it since the Templars were connected in mind and body.

With a curt nod, Lex left the den and raced up the stairs. She burst like a storm into her room. After she slammed the door closed, she touched her fingers to her swollen lips. Delicious warmth spread through her and she was grateful her first kiss was with Constantine.

Stepping away from her door, she crossed the room and flopped down on her bed and fought to control not just the frantic beat of her heart, but the power surging through her.

She didn't lock her door.

CR&SO

With a grunt of frustration, Constantine turned off the computer, ending the rhythmic beat of Enigma's music.

Lex's energy continued to throb within him, making it damn difficult to regain his control. Whatever was going on inside of her was strong enough to heat his body, which knew only cold since the time when Michael had ripped his soul from him.

All those centuries ago he woke bleeding and burnt raw on the sands of the Holy Land, left to make the long trek back to England as his body raged with needs that cut through him like a million blades.

During his relentless journey, the sun had come close to destroying him at least a dozen times. By the time he'd touched

English soil he'd been nearly mad with hunger and his mind ravaged by memories.

After what had seemed like an endless journey through Hell itself, Constantine had made it to Seacrest Castle in Northumberland. There, the other Templars waited for him, and all in as bad a condition as he was. Lucian, however, was much worse off then them all. He'd been damn near raging mad. It had taken years for him to break out of his stupor and come to some sort of acceptance of his actions after he'd gone back to his ancestral home of Penwick Castle. After what he'd done there, he'd found his way to Seacrest, as they all had. They'd gone there to heal and for refuge. Even now, centuries later, both Seacrests were their only havens.

They all knew the rules they were to exist by and what they needed to do in order to earn redemption. With their souls at stake, and the threat of Hell a constant companion, they'd learned to fight hunger and take only what they needed from humans in order to survive.

Unlike renegades, vampires who prowled the night unfettered by God's laws, Templars were forced to uphold the Ten Commandments. The Templars had made an oath to God in exchange for the chance of redemption. Renegades had not. They were without morals and conscience. They tortured and slaughtered the living with gruesome abandon. Should Templars veer from their path to Heaven, they'd be thrown down into Hell, where they would rot for eternity.

The fear of such a fate had even Constantine resisting the nature of the creature they were damned as.

As he paced the length of the den, Constantine shook off the affects of Lex's energy. He had a damn good idea what it was inside of her. Yet he'd keep her secret. He wouldn't betray her trust in this.

Not only did Constantine live by the code of God's law, he had his own set of rules that governed him. Twisted as it may be, he'd not betray Lex by telling the others until she was ready. This wasn't his secret to tell and, as one who knew all about secrets, he wouldn't force her into a situation she wasn't ready to face. All he could do was watch over her and make damn sure no renegade got to her.

"I thought you'd still be out."

Glancing at Tristan, who stood in the doorway looking haggard, Constantine sensed the bloodlust was upon him. "Obviously I'm not."

Tristan cocked a brow imperiously. "You're playing a dangerous game, Dragon."

Constantine leveled a chilling look at Tristan, who wasn't moved in the least. "Stop the cryptic bullshit and say what you came here to say."

With a shrug, Tristan got right to the point. "Raphael saw you kissing Lex."

"Well good on him." How the hell had Constantine missed sensing Rogue? "Did he like what he saw?"

"Don't be a bloody arse, Dragon. You know damn well you're playing with fire."

"Last I heard my father gave the devil his due when that piece of shit died and went to Hell. I don't need you to step in and take his place."

In a flash of movement, Tristan came at him with fangs bared. He grabbed a fistful of Constantine's shirt. Constantine's fangs slammed down into his bottom lip when Tristan gave him a hard shake.

"Hurt Lex and we'll all take turns making sure you spend the rest of your miserable existence regretting it."

With a vicious growl, Constantine knocked away Tristan's hold. "Fuck you."

Constantine brushed past Tristan and stalked from the den. Though they crossed swords on the lists countless times over the centuries, he'd never done so in anger. He refused to do battle with a man he'd thought of as a brother. Not even he was that much of an asshole. Although, there were nights when Tristan came dangerously close to hitting that mark of complete and utter bastard.

Tristan watched Constantine storm from the den. He heard him leave the keep and drive off. He hadn't meant to threaten Dragon, yet he wouldn't stand by and risk Lex being hurt.

"He cares for her, you know."

Tristan looked to see Raphael filling the open doorway. "Of course I know. Why the hell do you think I want him to keep away from her? She's too bloody innocent for a man like him. You *know* what he's capable of."

Raphael moved to the hearth and tried to steal some of the fire's heat. "It is what it is. And personally, I'm glad. Constantine needs her. If anyone is going to cleanse him of his past, it's going to be Lex."

Tristan joined him by the fire. "She's too innocent."

"Tristan, leave this alone. Don't you think Constantine deserves a bit of happiness?"

"Of course I believe he deserves happiness. By God, when I think of all he's suffered..."

Raphael clapped a hand on his shoulder and offered him a reassuring smile. "Then step back and let things be. He won't hurt her. If anything, he'll hurt himself."

"That's what I'm most afraid of."

Chapter Four

Winter 1295

"You are no dragon, you miserable wretch," Henry ground out.

Constantine, exhausted beyond measure, dropped his arm. So sore, the limb shook, he wondered how he'd managed to continue fighting for as long as he had.

The blade of the sword scraped the ground, cutting a deep line in the frozen dirt. Constantine's warm breath came out in puffs of white smoke when it hit the cold air with each rasping breath he took. Knowing this day was far from finished; his body rebelled at the notion of lifting the sword—which was nearly as long as he was tall—one more time.

Fifteen hours had passed since he'd come out to the lists just before dawn. With the night upon them, the mid-winter frost had set in. The garrison had long since taken to the hall, escaping the cold of the December night. Constantine, the young soldier he fought and the lord of Draegon remained out in the cold long after all others had migrated to the warmth of the hall.

Constantine's stomach constricted as it begged for food. His muscles burned. Each ragged breath he dragged into his lungs was an experience in pain. His legs were long past the point of
36

having the strength to hold him. He remained upright out of sheer willpower and fear of his father's wrath should he dare falter.

Hands numb from cold were barely able to grip the sword. Constantine realized the numbness was a blessing when he chanced to glance down at his bleeding knuckles. The pain was nothing but a mild bother.

With his father looking on, Constantine knew if he gave in to the exhaustion and the pain, he'd suffer Henry's wrath for it. He called upon reserves of strength and tightened his bleeding fingers around the cold steel of the sword's handle.

Constantine met his father's cutting glare with one of his own. "I *am* a dragon," he insisted between his ragged breaths.

Henry cocked a brow at him, a sneer twisting his mouth. "Then finish him, boy."

Constantine looked back at Geoffrey, who lay defeated on the ground. The soldier was beaten. He'd fallen beneath Constantine's sword, which was no small feat for a child who'd seen only ten winters. To "finish" him would be a disgrace to all Constantine believed being a knight meant.

Raising his chin a notch, Constantine met his father's frigid glare defiantly. "I will not, Father."

Henry went red with rage. "You dare defy me, boy?"

Constantine puffed out his chest, ready to face his father's wrath. "I will not kill him."

When his father pulled free his sword from the scabbard at his hip, Constantine held fast to his resolve. The long polished blade winked in the moonlight as Henry leveled the tip of the sword at Constantine's throat. Outwardly, he struggled to appear unfazed. Inwardly, however, he was terrified.

Rene Lyons

"Kill him or I'll kill you," Henry vowed. "Better you die now at my hand than grow into the weak man you promise to be."

Though his heart thundered with morbid anticipation of death, Constantine raised his chin higher to give his sire better access to his throat. "Do it then," he taunted with false bravado.

Geoffrey scrambled from the floor and placed himself between father and son. "Nay, my lord," he cried. "Do not!"

Henry's angry gaze shot to Geoffrey. "You dare to presume to tell me what to do?"

Geoffrey, instantly contrite, bowed his head. "Nay, my lord, but he is your son."

Constantine nearly laughed at that. Geoffrey, he knew, was new to Draegon Castle. Geoffrey had yet to learn there was no paternal bond between him and his father.

"All the more reason to end his worthless life now and be done with him."

Try as he might, Constantine couldn't stop the tears that slipped from his eyes. He wanted to slap away the evidence of his weakness but he didn't dare move for fear his father would push the blade in.

"Pathetic," Henry sneered. "That's what you are." He took the sword from Constantine's throat and put it to Geoffrey's. The young man's eyes bulged in horror. "I will not abide insolence from any man who serves me."

Without hesitation or hint of remorse, Henry rammed the blade in Geoffrey's throat. The soldier let out a sick, choked sound. His hands flew to his neck as blood bubbled in his mouth. He fingered the blade sticking in his neck, horrified as he rapidly bled to death.

Henry pulled the sword free and Geoffrey slumped to the ground. Constantine gagged at the sight of the soldier's blood

38

seeping out over the lists. When he looked back at his father, it was to see Henry bending to wipe the blood from his blade with Geoffrey's shirt before he rose and sheathed the sword.

"That's what I expect of you, boy. Anything less and I swear on God you'll be next."

With the regal bearing of a king, Henry marched back to the keep as if he hadn't just taken an innocent young life. Constantine, however, remained frozen to the spot for a long while, staring at Geoffrey until the last of his blood spilled out.

He looked to the imposing crenellated square keep, which rose in the center of the large bailey. A disgusted shiver wracked him. Four more months and he'd be gone from here. He'd go off to Greaves Castle to serve under Ulric Chambers. Constantine prayed he'd finally find a sense of home and belonging there.

Leaning down, Constantine closed the soldier's eyes and said a quick prayer over his body. When he regained his feet he looked to the sky. A crescent moon cast its faint pale glow upon him. Even with the horror of death lying at his feet, a sense of destiny came over Constantine.

Or was it prophecy that crawled over him?

Something whispered to him that the night was where his fate lay.

Chapter Five

The clash of steel against steel rang out across Seacrest's courtyard. Out on the lists, Tristan's sword coming at him was enough to jar him out of his thoughts about Lex. Unfortunately, not long enough for him not to lapse right back into them.

Deflecting Tristan's attack, Constantine almost wished Guardian would get the better of him. After last night, he needed some sense knocked into him.

What the hell had he been thinking?

Constantine had taken a foolish risk by being alone with Lex. She was too much of a temptation and he'd barely been able to hold himself in check. It had taken all of his restraint to let her leave, especially since her mind opened to him and he'd heard her every thought.

God's Blood, the things she'd been thinking had almost shattered his resolve. He'd almost pulled her back and put an end to his torture by taking what she offered and being done with it. That would have been a disaster of epic proportions.

Hell, what the fuck did he know about women, and virgins at that? Since everything he touched turned to shit, Constantine was damn sure if he continued to dabble in this madness when it came to her, he'd ruin her.

Constantine averted Tristan's next attack. He managed to jump to the side and meet Tristan's blade with his own. It had been a long time since he and Tristan had crossed swords. Though Guardian was an incredible fighter, he lacked the merciless edge Constantine possessed. It gave him the upper hand in battle and had him putting Tristan on the defensive.

Constantine was out here tonight to work off his sexual frustration. It rode him mercilessly all day as he drifted in and out of sleep. More than just the ugliness of his past haunted his dreams. Now they were plagued by Lex as well.

Thank God for Tristan, Constantine thought as Tristan pushed him to the limit of what even a vampire's body could handle. It came down to one of two things, either he was going to take this frustration out on a Templar or he was going to take it out on a human. Although he had no preference—hell as far as he was concerned there were plenty of humans who needed killing—he didn't think God would appreciate it if he damaged up one of His children. After all, he was already treading thin ice when it came to the whole redemption thing. He wasn't about to push his luck any further.

Knowing how hard he was fighting, Constantine almost pitied Tristan. Almost. Constantine had neither the time nor the inclination for a sentiment such as guilt. It was bad enough he was sporting a conscience when it came to Lex. He'd not allow himself further weakness by letting guilt in.

The two Templars were stripped to their waists. With the September moon bathing them, Tristan's smooth and unadorned skin was a sharp contrast to the large tattoos covering Constantine's chest and arm.

He bore two warrior-angels. The one over his right pectoral had black wings and wielded a silver sword. On his left was an angel with white wings who brandished a gold sword.

41

Constantine never spoke of why he chose the angels or what they represented. He knew the Templars assumed they symbolized the act of Michael seizing their souls. They were wrong. It was the tattoo on his left upper arm, of a Templar's sword cutting vertically through a heart, representing the loss of his soul.

When Tristan charged and came close to stabbing him through the stomach, Constantine leapt back and slapped the blade to side. He needed to get his head in the battle. Tristan was still pissed enough to do some serious damage to him if he didn't.

Never one to play nice, Constantine knew he came off as an arrogant prick when he swung his sword at Tristan. He caught his fellow Templar across the arm. Blood spurted from the bone-deep wound.

"Yield, Guardian,"

"Don't be such an arrogant arse."

Their blades crossed again in a terrible crash of steel. Constantine pushed Tristan away with a force that would have felled a human. "You can't beat me."

Tristan rolled his eyes, bringing his sword down in a hacking motion that Constantine managed to repel. "Spare me your ego, Constantine. You aren't that good."

"Bullshit."

Constantine *was* that good and they all knew it. He'd been savage in life, he was even more so in death. Where the others still held to some part of their humanity, Constantine had none.

When he'd joined with Guy Sinclair's army he might have been younger then the other men, but he'd already known enough pain and seen enough blood to last lifetimes. It lent him an edge over the men he'd fought, who were older and more experienced.

He'd followed the others when they joined the Templar Order, to remain close to men he'd come to think of as brothers. Tristan, Sebastian, Lucian, and Raphael believed he'd joined the order of warrior monks as a way to thumb his nose at God.

And maybe they were right. Maybe that had been one of his reasons. If that were true, he was now paying for that arrogance and disrespect every night of his existence.

Swinging his sword in a high arc, Constantine caught Tristan's other arm, opening a deep gash across his forearm.

"Yield."

"To you? Never."

Constantine cocked a brow and swung his sword with enough force that he would have sliced Tristan in two if the Templar hadn't leapt back with the speed only a vampire possessed. "Arc you sure about that?"

Tristan countered with a quick stab of his sword. He caught Constantine in the left shoulder. "Positive. Now stop mooning over Lex and fight."

೦೫೮೦

Lex admitted defeat. After all, what choice did she have? She'd chased another ghost away, for God's sake. She felt as if she should be the one saying *"boo"* and going bump in the night instead of the other way around.

What a colossal waste of time tonight was. Lex knew she should have stayed home. It wasn't just her time she was wasting or her night she was ruining, but Raphael's as well.

Because of what Lex had promised herself, after tonight she'd never go on another hunt. She'd leave the poor souls in peace.

As this was her first walk-through of the barn, the only equipment she'd brought was herself. If Raphael had found it odd that she hadn't loaded up the mountain of equipment Allie had stored at the castle, he made no mention of it.

Over the years, Lex realized her senses were better at detecting ghosts than any of Allie's fancy equipment. Sometimes, she was even able to see their faint aura like fine mist that carried the shape of a person. When she was younger, she had dared to touch that mist. The sensation was one she never wanted to experience again. Ever.

One of the creepiest things she ever experienced, it was the first and last time she had done it.

Lex stood in the center of the derelict barn and tracked the faint sensation of a ghost. Though the spirit was still there, it was fading fast.

"I'm going," Lex whispered. She began to back out of the barn. The closer she got to the door, the stronger the spirit became. "I promise I won't come back. You're safe here."

God, she wished someone would promise her that very same thing.

She pushed open the rotted wooden door and shivered at the blast of cold wind that hit her. She looked at the car where Raphael waited patiently for her. Leaning against the car, arms crossed over his wide chest, Rogue looked miserable from the cold.

"What happened, Lex? No spooks tonight?"

"Not tonight." She hated lying, but telling him the truth would raise too many questions she couldn't answer. When she closed the barn door she took care not to splinter the aged wood, Lex shook her head. "Why aren't you waiting in the car with the heat jacked up?"

"I wanted to make sure I was able to hear you if you needed me."

Raphael gave her a dazzling smile. The moonlight loved him. It played off his pale skin and made the blonder streaks in his hair shimmer. The mischievous gleam in his eyes added to his wicked appeal, which he knew how to work to perfection. Not to mention he had a killer combination of an incredibly muscular body and just enough arrogance to make him devastating to a woman's senses.

No wonder women went crazy for him. Raphael was not only gorgeous, but his rakish charm was something a woman only read about in romance novels.

Thank God Lex's affection lay elsewhere. She'd be nothing more than a Rogue-groupie for sure if her heart didn't already belong to Constantine.

"Come on, let's get you home." He unfurled his arms and held out his branded hand to her. "We can always try again another night."

Lex didn't take his offered hand. When she was close enough, Raphael pushed himself off the car and went to throw an arm around her. She skidded around him and hurried in the car. He looked stunned by her obvious avoidance of him.

Raphael slid in the driver's seat and cast her a curious look. "You okay?"

Lex nodded. "Just disappointed."

He flashed her another killer smile. "I'm sure Constantine will cheer you up like he did last night."

Lex's eyes went wide and her jaw dropped. Raphael, with all the tact of a freight train, pointed out that her mouth was hanging open. She snapped it closed.

She shook her head furiously. "I don't... He doesn't... There's nothing between us."

Raphael cocked a brow at her. "Oh. So that wasn't the two of you I caught macking in the den last night?"

Oh Lord.

"It's not what you think."

He snorted. "Either it's exactly what I think or Constantine was trying to find buried treasure down your throat with his tongue."

Oh God.

Lex wanted to slap the cocky grin clean off his face. Didn't he care that she was mortified beyond words? Of course he didn't. This was Raphael after all, and if she'd learned anything about him in the last month, it was that he loved to tease.

"You're ruthless, do you know that?"

"Decidedly so, sweetheart."

Lex rethought her high opinion of him. No wonder the other Templars all took turns trying to beat him bloody on the lists. If she were able to wield a sword she'd be next in line.

"You're evil."

He gave her a careless shrug. "What's the big deal? I caught you making out. If you ask me, it's about time you two got down to business."

Lex buried her face in her hands. "Oh God, can you *please* stop talking?"

Mercifully, Raphael noticed her embarrassment. "Lex, darling, it was only a kiss."

As far as Lex was concerned, there was nothing *"just"* about the kiss. Maybe to Raphael, and even Constantine, it wasn't a big deal. But to her, it was. It was a giant deal, actually. The biggest deal thus far in her boring life.

46

Despite the fact that she knew she was blushing clear to her hairline, Lex unburied her face. "You're right. It was only a kiss. Can we go home now, please?"

Raphael made no motion to turn the car on. Instead, he sat and stared at her for a long time. Lex wanted to poke him right in the eyes.

Oh Lord, she was getting more and more like Allie every day!

When next he spoke, Lex thought she was going to burst into flames of mortification and die right there. "That was your first kiss, wasn't it?"

Did he have to sound astonished?

Lex wanted to say no, especially to him, who'd had sex with practically every woman who crossed his path. Yet the way he was looking at her told her he already knew the truth. She hated those heightened vampire senses sometimes. With Constantine constantly trying to poke into her mind, it was an effort for Lex to guard her thoughts. God only knew how many times she'd been lax in the effort. She didn't dare think on how many of her thoughts made it into Constantine's mind.

"Yes it was. Now *please*, Raphael, can we not talk about this anymore?"

Begging didn't seem to be working on him. "We all know you're a virgin, but to have never kissed a man...? Damn, woman. Constantine is one lucky son-of-a-bitch."

In his own "Raphael" way, he'd handed her a huge complement. Okay, maybe he wasn't a jerk after all. Still, he was embarrassing her horribly and staring at her as if she had sprouted a second head. Poking him in the eyes was looking more appealing every second he continued to gape at her.

A thought struck her, causing her stomach to twist with dread. "Does Constantine know you saw us?"

Even though she asked that, she knew the answer. Of course Constantine knew. None of them moved without the others knowing—or as Raphael liked to say, *"when one farts, we all fart".* Leave it to Raphael to say it with such eloquence. Rogue certainly had a way with words.

Their connection with each other was strong, except when it came to Lucian. For some reason none of them were able to locate him with their senses. Even Constantine couldn't detect the lost Templar, who had gone missing a month ago. He'd vanished as if into thin air. The only trace of him had been his car, left in The Gate's parking lot. For the Templars, the loss of the Knight was the equivalent of the loss of their souls

"Of course he knows." He winked at her. "And from what I felt coming off him, he was seriously enjoying you."

Lex, never more embarrassed in her entire life, wanted to crawl into the glove box and stay there until they got back to Seacrest.

Doing her best to put aside her mortification and act like the grown woman she was, Lex glared at him. Though from the look of him, it didn't faze him in the least. "Are you going to torture me the entire way home?"

Raphael started the car. First he turned on the heat. Then he flipped on the radio. "Voodoo" by Godsmack broke the silence. His smile was mischievous. "Of course I am."

When he reached out to ruffle her hair, Lex tried to duck away. Unfortunately she was too slow. The second his hand made contact with her he let out a loud hiss and drew back sharply.

"What the fuck...?"

Lex cringed. "Don't go getting all freaked out, okay? It's nothing."

"*Nothing?*" He repeated in disbelief. "You call that *nothing?* Shit, Lex, it felt like I touched the sun."

She began to wring her hands. "It's not a big deal. I was going to tell Allie but I didn't want to worry her."

"Allie doesn't know?"

She shook her head. "Please, Raphael, don't tell my sister."

"Lex..."

"I'll tell her. I swear, just not tonight. *Please.*"

He looked at her long and hard. She thought he was going to deny her plea. Which was why when he agreed to keep quiet—for tonight, anyway—she forgot herself and threw her arms around in a tight hug. Caught off guard when energy surged through him, he hissed again and pulled away from her.

She jumped back. "Sorry," she murmured.

Raphael shook his head at her. "Goddamn, but you pack a mean punch with that." He gave her a curious look before a slow, and incredibly wicked, smile spread across his face. "Bet Dragon got a kick out of that energy last night, huh?"

Leave it to Raphael to put aside the seriousness of a situation and turn it into something sexual.

God help her, it was the longest car ride of her life.

Chapter Six

The night of the Bloodmoon was near.

Julian of Harwick sensed the power growing all around him as he stood out on the battlements of the castle and surveyed the land. *His land.* As it had been for a millennia, long before the time of the Order of the Rose and the Templars. Those had been good times, when renegades were able to cut a bloody path without the worry of retribution from the two factions of righteous vampires.

Righteous vampires. The very concept was absurd. He longed to bring back those days, and he would, as soon as he took in the blood of the Daystar. And unlike the others who'd come before him and failed, he'd not find himself at the wrong end of a Templar's sword.

Julian threw his arms wide, reveling in the sensation of energy that rolled over him. The power of the Daystar grew as time ticked ever closer to Samhain. The Bloodmoon came once every quarter century and he'd not allow another one to pass him by. Too many had already come and gone without him gaining the power of the Daystar. Now was his time. Now was his chance, and he'd not have anything stand in his way to obtain it.

The last time the Bloodmoon sat in the night sky marked the birth of a Hallowed. Come Samhain, when it would be upon them once more, it would mark her death.

Stephan of Penwick had failed to find the last Hallowed. She'd died the night a new Hallowed had been born, and this time, Julian would not miss his chance to seize the power she harbored within her body.

He longed for a time when there would be no more hiding in the shadows. By harvesting the Hallowed's blood he'd take in the power of the Daystar, which would give him the ability to walk in the light. Released from the prison of the night, he'd be virtually unstoppable. He'd usher in a reign of vampires that would put an end to the dominance of humans. Creatures of both the day and the night would bow to his majesty. He'd sit upon a throne of blood as a living god.

All he had to do was get to the Hallowed and the power would be his for the taking.

Almost giddy with anticipation, Julian thought of those who'd failed. They'd paved the way for him. Stephan of Penwick had done most of the work when it came to finding the Daystar. In his relentless pursuit of revenge against his brother, he'd used the Daystar as a bargaining tool to amass a small number of followers to aid him in his vengeance. Julian had been among them.

He'd been recruited back in the time of Queen Elizabeth I, which had been a good time for a man such as himself. An ostentatious time, it was filled with pleasure-loving people, and had been all too easy to seduce such eager women. Oh, and how he'd played them. He'd worked his charm and incited their desires right up to that precious moment just before dawn when he took their blood and left their bodies for his valet to dispose of.

Daniel of Harwick, who'd been another of Stephan's recruits, had foolishly rushed in after Stephan had revealed the name of the woman he believed possessed the power of the Daystar. Julian knew better than to follow his lead. He'd hung back and watched Daniel fail after he'd wrongly assumed Allison Parker was the Daystar.

That crazy bitch was merely the link.

What a bloody fool Daniel had been. He thought to abduct a Templar's female and get away with the offense. True, Julian despised the Templars, but even he wasn't fool enough to cross them unless absolutely necessary. After all, those self-righteous bastards were known to fell entire armies of renegades. For Daniel to believe he could best them where countless others failed had been suicide.

In taking Allison, Daniel had come too close to sparking a war between the Templars and the renegades. All that had prevented war was that Daniel hadn't been the one who held Lucian of Penwick. The Templars had believed Daniel took both Allison and the Templar known as the Knight. Once Sebastian of Rydon had killed that fool Daniel, the Templars were too busy looking for their lost member to declare open war on the renegade population.

With the knowledge Julian acquired over the centuries, coupled with what he'd learned through Stephan, he'd managed to fit the remaining pieces of the puzzle together and locate the Daystar. Now, with the picture complete, he was ready to strike once the opportune moment arrived.

Lowering his arms, Julian turned away from his land and stalked back into the keep. As he made his way out of the chamber and down the long corridor, he reveled in the elation at being back here after the long centuries he'd spent playing minion to Stephan. This was where he belonged, and it was here he'd set up his kingdom of vampires once he possessed the Daystar's power.

When he reached the hall, Julian strode to the hearth and pulled free the missive from the pocket of his slacks. Reading it one last time, he crumpled it in his fist before tossing in he flames. Such a damning piece of evidence was too dangerous to risk being left lying around for greedy eyes to chance upon.

He watched the flames lick at the white paper, charring and curling the edges. A cool smile played upon his lips as he contemplated the future. From the first time since he'd learned of the Daystar, Julian had been maneuvering all the pieces into place in order to take the power as his own. As he stared into the fire and watched the paper burn, he knew his patience and perseverance had paid off.

Only once the flames reduced the note to ash did Julian cross the hall and make his way out into the courtyard.

Julian stepped out into the crisp night. He longed for the days gone by. He ached for the time he'd been borne to. Much of the world had changed around him over the ages and yet he had remained the same. He'd watched the world go by, most nights feeling time drag over him as he craved more power and wealth.

Julian dragged in a breath, filling his dead lungs with air just to know what it was to breathe again. He looked at the crescent moon and bared his fangs in a vicious sneer. The moonlight on him made his skin crawl. He was eager for the time when he'd no longer be a prisoner of the dark.

He caught sight of the motley crew of vampires training on the lists. Unfortunately, they were the only renegades who'd stayed on with him after Daniel's plan failed. Julian's only hope, if he planned to succeed, was to use them as a buffer between him and whoever thought to stand between him and the Daystar.

The hunger came upon him in the form of a painful contraction of his gut and an instant dryness of his mouth. Too lazy to go off and hunt for his own food, Julian called to one of the vampires who watched the melee taking place in the lists.

The vampire, turned much too young, rushed toward him. Julian liked how the boy hurried to do his bidding. It reinforced his sense of power over these pathetic creatures. It also made his anticipation grow for the time when he held the entire world in the palms of his hands.

"I hunger."

There wasn't any need to say more. The boy, whose name Julian didn't care to remember, would know what he meant.

"Aye, my lord."

The boy sheathed his sword and gave Julian a quick bow before he raced across the courtyard toward the gatehouse. The rising of the ancient iron gate echoed across the courtyard. The boy, with his Scandinavian good looks, never found it a trial to procure female company. It was the reason Julian sent him to find him a victim to feed from.

After the boy was gone, the gate slammed back down, sectioning off the modern world from the castle, which seemed frozen in time. For a moment, Julian wished his lover were here. He realized his feelings for her came from being kindred spirits. Her appetite for destruction rivaled his own. Unfortunately, he'd have to end her once his plan came to fruition. He'd not share his power with anyone, not even with her. Of course, he'd lied to her. Made her believe she'd be his queen as he reigned over the world. If she believed otherwise, one word from her could destroy all he'd worked for.

Needing to escape the feel of the night on him, Julian returned inside the keep. Given his mood, he was eager for some sport. He'd play with his victim before he fed from and killed her. He'd wrest screams from the girl, and hopefully, she'd survive long enough to keep him amused for many nights to come.

Chapter Seven

Miraculously, Lex found the perfect way to buy Raphael's silence. She bribed him with the box set of season three of *Buffy the Vampire Slayer*. Go figure, a seven-hundred-year-old vampire had the hots for a tiny blond who kicked vamp butt. Who would have thought it? Certainly not her.

My life has defiantly taken a turn for the bizarre.

Once Lex had Raphael's promise to keep her secret, she'd wrongly assumed she'd have a few days before she'd be forced to drop this information bomb on everyone. Unfortunately, that wasn't meant to be.

She woke a mere two days later feeling like ninety miles of bad road. The source of what she felt centered on the rash-like spot on her stomach. Sweaty and nauseous, not to mention the pounding headache, Lex struggled to get out of bed. By the time she crawled to the bathroom she noticed the skin on her stomach was bleeding from where she'd gouged it in her sleep.

If that wasn't a sign it was time to do something about the situation, Lex didn't know what was.

Which was why she had risked leaving the safety of Seacrest Castle and was now driving down Route 371 on her way to Edessa, the sleepy town some twenty minutes away from Seacrest.

Though Lex was far from materialistic, even she had to admit driving was a dream in the silver BMW 645 Ci the Templars had gifted her with. Despite the cold, Lex had the driver's window down. The crisp air was heaven on her heated body. Though she adored summer, even she appreciated the beauty of autumn in the Adirondacks. The sun shone in the clear sky. The air was rich with the aromas of earth and wood burning in the chimneys of the few houses she passed as she sped down the road.

The leaves were only now beginning to turn from summer's vibrant green to autumn's brilliant yellows, oranges and reds. It made for a beautiful feast of color. The stillness in this rural area of the world seemed almost otherworldly. As the power within her built, Lex became more in touch with her surroundings. She *felt* nature all around her.

It should have been a perfect day, one that reminded her of a time when she, Allie and Christian were kids. Instead, her brother was dead, her sister a vampire, and she was changing.

She left Seacrest with the intention of going to see Dr. Stuart, but after thinking better of it, Lex decided not to. Dr. Stuart, was an old friend of the family. She wasn't up for the myriad of questions he'd force her to answer. She just wanted to get something to ease the itch and the burn then get back to Seacrest. It was bad enough she'd already have to face a virtual firing squad in the form of one irate sister and four furious Templars. Dealing with Dr. Stuart was the last thing she needed to add to her growing list of problems.

The hell she knew she was going to catch from the Templars made Lex run cold with fear. She cringed at the thought of those four enormous and intimidating males handing her ass to her for going to town alone. She wasn't at the point yet where she was unmoved by their bluster as Allie was. Actually, her sister gave as good as she got. No—Lex was far from that point.

As much as Lex might wish she were as...ballsy...as her sister, the truth was, she didn't posses even half of Allie's courage. Lex ran when Allie would stand firm and fight. Lex shied away from the world whereas Allie took it by the horns and wrestled it to the ground. Her sister was the ideal companion for a man as fierce as a Templar vampire. No wonder Constantine held himself back from Lex. She was no match for such a man. She wished to God she were, but, honestly, she didn't believe she possessed the strength to walk in their world.

Didn't she? She didn't know anymore. God, Lex was so confused about where she belonged and who she was.

Driving into Edessa, the epitome of what one thought of when they imagined a small town, she wondered if she even belonged here anymore. The stores were quaint and most were still family owned and operated. People said hello to one another when they passed on the sidewalk. Cars stopped and let pedestrians cross the street, no matter if they were in the crosswalk or not. Parking meters still cost ten cents. It didn't get any more "small town" than this. It was as far removed from the world of the Templars as it could get. And yet, the two worlds ran parallel with each other.

By day Wayne County was small town and peaceful. By night creatures straight out of a nightmare crawled from the shadows to take over this rural area of the world.

After the bustle of Fort Lauderdale, Lex found she loved the laidback mountain life. She felt a connection to the earth here. It was as if time forgot this part of the world. Somehow, as life went on around it, Damascus remained a hidden realm of tranquility. Not even the nocturnal population that gravitated toward this area had destroyed that.

The first four blocks of Main Street were quiet, tree-lined streets. The huge turn-of-the-century Victorians added to the feel of old-world charm. Before the overpass, which marked the end of the residential area and the beginning of the ten blocks of stores, was Days Bakery. Allie used to bring her and Christian there almost every Sunday morning to get donuts still warm from the oven. She missed that morning tradition. If she ever had children of her own, she planned to revive it.

Lex parked her car in front of the pharmacy and dropped a dime in the meter. As soon as she stepped inside she had to take a moment to adjust her eyes to the dim and dusty interior.

Mr. Abbot, as always, stood behind the counter. Today he was busy filing away prescription forms in an old cardboard box. It wasn't the most modern of filing systems but it seemed to work for him.

When he looked up and saw her, he greeted her with a huge smile. "Hello, Lexine. How nice to see you." His rough voice rose over the fifties tunes playing on the small radio he kept on the counter. The thing had been in the same spot for as long as she could remember.

"Hi, Mr. Abbot." Lex went to the counter. Her heart in her throat, she was terrified she'd lose her nerve to ask him about her stomach.

"How's your sister? Haven't seen her around for some time."

Nathan Abbot was one of the few people in these parts who didn't think Allie was crazy. "She's been busy," was the evasive reply Lex gave anyone who asked about Allie. "Can I ask a favor of you?"

He set aside his box, his bushy gray brows furrowing with concerned. "Of course, Lexine. Is everything alright?"

Lex stepped to the counter. "I need you to look at something for me and tell me what you think I should put on it."

"If it's something serious..."

"Oh no, it's not," she lied. Hesitating for a moment, Lex lifted her shirt to reveal the raw skin. "See? It's just a rash."

Mr. Abbot came around the counter to get a better look at her stomach. He reached into the pocket on his blue and white-checkered button-down and pulled out a pair of thick glasses. Perching them on his nose, he got down on one knee and gave the area a long look. He made a sympathetic face and tsked when he saw the damage her scratching had done.

"This looks bad, Lexine. You should go see a doctor for it."

"I'd rather not."

Abbott stood and dropped his glasses back in his pocket. He heaved out a heavy sigh. "It doesn't look infected, but you did scratch it something awful. I can give you a salve for it, but I'd feel better if you went to go see a doctor. I know Dr. Stuart is in today. Why don't I give him a call and see if he can take a look at it."

"No. Really, it's not necessary," Lex assured him, shaking her head. "Besides, I don't have the time. I have to get home."

Mr. Abbot let out another long, drawn out sigh and regarded her with a look that reminded her of one a displeased grandfather might level at a mischievous grandchild.

"Fine. I'll give you something, but," he added sternly, "you have to promise me you'll let Dr. Stuart have a look at it if it gets any worse. Do you understand me, Lexine?"

She nodded vigorously and almost sagged in relief to be going home with something to ease the infernal itch and burn. "I will. I Promise."

He went back around the counter and fished around through a shelf teaming with tubes of ointments and various bottles of medications. A few fell as he searched for the one he wanted. As he did that, Mr. Abbott shook his head as if in bafflement. "I'll never understand you young people and your fascination with tattoos."

In that moment Lex wouldn't have been more surprised had Mr. Abbot sprouted wings and flown away.

"Tattoos?" Lex choked out. Her hand settled over what she had believed to have only been a rash, but now realized was so much more.

He peered her at with a frown. "Yes, tattoos. That one you got there looks to have a nasty irritation on it.

Whether it was his shocking observation or the energy that picked that exact moment to surge through her, Lex couldn't be sure. All she knew was one moment she was about to take the tube of ointment from Mr. Abbot and the next she hit the floor in a faint.

CƆ℘

Once Lex was back on her feet and had enough orange juice in her to fill a lake, Mr. Abbot finally let her leave. She walked out of the pharmacy in a state of shock.

Tattoo?

What the hell was she doing with a tattoo on her stomach? After she was in her car, Lex lifted her shirt. The wind was knocked out of her when she saw the faint mark under the torn skin, which looked like an S with a small dot above it and another below it. Surprisingly, it was rather pretty—plain, but pretty. Unfortunately Lex had absolutely no idea what it was doing on her stomach.

As much as she'd grown used to being surrounded by the supernatural, that didn't stop her from being freaked by this. She didn't mind when weird things went on *around* her. What she didn't like was that they were now happening *to* her.

As she raced back to Seacrest, Lex dreaded what awaited her back at the castle. She wasn't looking forward to facing a bunch of furious vampires. With her nerves at a breaking point, it aggravated the itch on her stomach. Steering down the narrow road, she forced herself not to tear into her skin in a vain attempt to ease the itch.

Instead, she kept her trembling hand gripped on the wheel as wave after wave of fear rolled over her. A million thoughts shot through her mind, each of which was worse than the last. She couldn't think of a single explanation for the mark that didn't involve her being forced to endure a lot of pain.

"What in the fuck were you thinking, woman?" Lex groaned when Constantine's voice thundered in her head.

"I can explain..."

Lex was ever grateful the sun hadn't set, since the daylight would offer her a short reprieve from Constantine's fury.

"The sun won't burn in the sky forever."

Or not.

Lex was fairly positive that as soon she stepped foot inside the keep Constantine was going to kill her. And not the vampire kind of dead where you still walked and talked. Oh no. He was going to kill her the *dead* kind of dead.

After she turned onto Stone Lane, Lex slowed the car as she drove over the unpaved road. Her stomach flipped as she waited for Constantine to chew her out some more. When nothing else was forthcoming, she assumed he was too pissed to speak to her without wanting to wring her neck.

Not that she could blame him. She'd taken a foolish risk by leaving the castle alone. Renegades were known to have human henchmen. As the sole human among the Templars, it left her the most vulnerable.

As long as she was outside of the castle, she'd been a walking bulls-eye.

Lex's car was equipped with a device that automatically opened the gate. Once she drove under the imposing portcullis, it slammed closed behind her. Funny, how she wasn't reassured of her safety as she usually was when the gate closed behind her.

Though Seacrest appeared to be a medieval fortress, it was equipped with the latest home security system. Cameras watched her every move as she parked her car behind Lucian's silver Maserati Spyder. Unused since the night he'd gone missing, the car had been returned to the castle by Sebastian and Raphael. They'd found it abandoned in The Gate's parking lot the night after Lucian disappeared. The car was a sad reminder that one member of her new odd family was lost and alone out there.

Lex hadn't even reached the door when it was pulled open by a *very* angry Anne, who wore a scowl that would make any Templar proud.

"I don't even want to know how you managed to get past me."

Lex flinched at Anne's bellow. "I'm sorry I snuck past you like that but I had to go out and it couldn't wait."

"Like hell it couldn't."

"Will you please get out of my head, Constantine?"

"No."

"What in the world was so important that you would risk your life by leaving the castle?"

Anne was on her heels as Lex crossed the hall to the kitchen. "I wasn't feeling well so I went to see Mr. Abbot."

"The pharmacist?" Anne's shout echoed in the mammoth kitchen. "Why not Dr. Stuart?"

Anne paled and pushed Lex down on one of the kitchen chairs. When she slapped a hand to her forehead, Lex pulled her head away. "I don't have a fever. I have a—rash. Damn! I left the ointment Mr. Abbott gave me in the car."

Lex stood.

"Leave the keep and I'll nail your feet to the floor."

She sat with a sigh. *"You'll do no such thing."*

"Try me."

Anne stepped back with a look of concern puckering her already wrinkled brow. "A rash? What kind of rash?"

"I'd like to explain it once, if you don't mind. So I'll just wait to tell everyone all at once."

"I do mind."

"Please, Constantine, cut me some slack, will you? I feel horrible."

As if on cue, Lex's stomach rolled and a wave of nausea hit her. She squeezed her eyes shut and fought the need to claw at the itch. She needed the medicine before she did even more damage to her stomach.

"I'll be right back." To Constantine, *"Come near me with a hammer and nails and I'll throw a cross at you."*

When she stood, the torn skin pulled and she flinched. Anne, with her hawk eyes, didn't miss it, no matter how subtle it was.

"Do you want me to get it for you?"

Lex shook her head. "No, it's okay. I'll get it."

What she failed to add was, she needed to feel the sun on her once more before it set. The compulsion to take in as much of the light as possible rode her constantly. It woke her early in the morning even after nights when she'd taken to her bed at dawn. The lack of sleep never bothered her as much as missing the sun did.

When she left the kitchen and walked back into the hall, her pace quickened. The fire in the hearth broke the dark and sent long shadows dancing across the walls as the flames flickered and hissed. The dim light seemed to heighten Lex's agitation and made the itch worse. Glancing at the heavy black drapes covering the leaded-glass windows, she wanted to rip them down and have the sunlight brighten the hall. She wanted the sun to chase away the shadows and bring life to this place that knew only darkness and death.

Given the lack of sunlight, Lex wondered why Constantine wasn't already in her face.

"Conserving energy."

"Leave me alone," Lex retorted as she left the hall and went back out into the cool, late afternoon air.

The sun bathed her in its fading light and offered her a bit of comfort. Lex's breath caught when her entire being infused with energy.

She shook off the sensation as she hurried to her car. Ointment in hand, she returned to the keep. She glanced around the hall, at how dark and still the cavernous area was. She still found it odd that an identical fortress stood in

Northern England. *That* Seacrest was the real deal. It had witnessed the passing of a thousand years. The thought served to remind her that the Templars had existed nearly as long.

And they'd go on long after she was dust. Allie too, now that she was a vampire as well.

Anne came into the hall but Lex ignored her. She took the stairs two at a time, the effort making her feel even sicker than she had before. Once shut away in her bedroom, she pulled off her shirt and padded over to the long oval standup mirror set in a corner of the room. Her jaw dropped when she got a good look at the mark. Much to her horror, the S had already grown darker.

"This is *so* not good."

Lex poked at it. She expected it to feel different, yet despite the rawness, it was as much a part of her flesh as an old tattoo. Tentatively, she trailed her fingers over it. The salt of her fingers burned the cuts made by her constant scratching.

Her hand fell away as a tear slipped from her eye. Lex wiped it away with the thought that from this moment on her life was going to change drastically. Again. This time she wasn't going to be a bystander as the paranormal happened around her. She was now more than just an outsider peering into the world she'd always found fascinating. Instead, she was wrapped up in it and it scared the hell out of her.

As if on cue, the voices began to whisper to her. The jumble of women's voices echoed in her head. As always, Lex couldn't discern one from the other as they blended together in one loud din.

Flattening her palm over her stomach, Lex doubled over as a wave of nausea hit her. She slammed her eyes closed and screamed in her head for the voices to leave her alone.

Blessedly, this time they did. She sank to her knees and wept with relief even though she knew they'd be back.

Chapter Eight

Three doors down, a furious Constantine paced in his chamber. He wanted to kill her. Well, mayhap not kill her—but at the very least, he wanted to give Lex a good shake.

The shaking would serve twofold. One, he wanted to put sense into her head after her stunt this afternoon. It would also soothe his temper to shake her until her damn teeth rattled. How could she have been so bloody reckless? Didn't the fool woman know what would have happened had a renegade's human henchman gotten to her? Allie—aye, Allie, Constantine told himself—would have been devastated.

As far as he was concerned, Lex couldn't come up with a good enough excuse to explain why she'd taken such a risk. She knew damn well the ramifications if renegades had managed to get hold of her. They would show her no mercy in their use of her to get to the Templars. And once she'd exhausted her use to them, they'd drain her dry. Such a happening had haunted Constantine from the moment he'd woken to the realization Lex wasn't at Seacrest until the minute the gate closed once she'd returned

For scaring him the way she had, Constantine was going to show her why he'd earned the name Dragon.

Of the two sisters, Lex was supposed to be the rational one. Her actions today proved Lex could be just as impetuous as her sister. This, Constantine would *not* tolerate. He was not going to watch the life drain out of another Parker woman. He'd been there, done that and he'd make damn sure Lex didn't suffer the same fate. He hadn't wanted to turn Allie, yet he'd been faced with no other choice. It was either turn her or watch her bleed out from the gash across her neck. He found it ironic that he'd saved her life by killing her.

Even now, Constantine still tasted Allie's blood on his tongue. Her memories haunted him. They invaded his mind, mixing with his own now that they shared a blood-bond. They had both lived shitty lives, and now, both sets of memories rarely gave him a moment's peace.

At the sudden barrage of emotions slamming into him, Constantine sucked in an empty breath. It took him a moment to discern they were coming from Lex. So strong was the impact of her fear, he had to grab hold of the mantle to steady himself.

Now what in the hell would cause Lex to feel such terror? He tried to get inside of her mind but, as always, it was closed to him. He realized the terror was coming to him on its own accord.

"Lex."

She didn't answer. He wasn't going to wait and repeat the effort to reach her mentally. Constantine sensed something was going on in her head that she couldn't control and he couldn't penetrate.

His anger pushed aside by concern, Constantine strode from his room with confidence that he wouldn't fry. Tristan kept the castle as devoid of sunlight as was possible without sealing off the windows. He'd have gone that far but feared drawing even more unneeded attention to himself and Seacrest.

When Constantine reached Lex's room he barged in without a thought to any danger that might lie on the other side of the door. He caught a glimpse of Lex in her bra before the fading rays of sunlight hit him.

Constantine roared and threw his arms over his head. He stumbled back as pain exploded in his body, which instantly began to burn. He slammed his eyes closed and staggered out of the room. In his haste he stumbled and fell into the corridor. His head cracked into the wall, the pain wasn't half as bad as the sunlight scorching him.

Gasping in horror, Lex pressed herself against the door and slammed it shut. She raced to the windows and yanked the curtains closed. Though they didn't completely shut out the sun, at least they afforded some protection from the deadly rays. Scared at what condition she'd find Constantine in, Lex licked her lips and took a deep, fortifying breath before inching open the door. Daring to open it far enough to squeeze herself out, she nearly wept with relief to find him intact.

Constantine was lying on the floor. She noticed the blood on the wall around his head. Since he wore only his usual black baggy pants and boots, she gaped at the smoke rising from his tattooed chest.

Lex knelt beside to him, afraid to touch him. Though she couldn't see any damage, that didn't mean there wasn't any. He was *smoking* for God's sake.

Instead, Lex smoothed a hand over his hair, brushing the messy mass away from his face. He hissed out a ragged breath. She snatched her hand away. He grabbed her wrist and forced her hand to the cool, hard expanse of his chest. His muscles tightened under her palm as her energy flowed into him.

"What in the world were you thinking?" How she managed those words past the lump in her throat, Lex didn't know.

Following his gaze, Lex peered down at herself and wanted to die of embarrassment. Of course, of all the times Constantine would come storming into her room, it would have to be right when she was getting undressed. Wearing nothing but jeans and a white, lacy Fredrick's of Hollywood bra, Lex tried to hold on to her dignity.

"I need you to touch me." Constantine's voice was hoarse when he made that command.

Lex remembered he'd needed the same thing of her when Allie's mind had connected with his after the renegade, Daniel, had taken her sister. Her jumbled thoughts had all but torn Constantine's mind apart. He'd needed Lex's touch to soothe him and now he needed the same of her again.

Her hands settled on his chest, gently running them over every inch of it as she marveled at how smooth and hard his body was. Nor did she fail to notice how still he was—as still and cold as a corpse—and though Lex knew she should be repulsed by him, that wasn't the case.

"Why did you come busting into my room like that? Didn't you think I might have the curtains open?"

"Apparently not."

Under her loving caress, his skin began to heat. "Couldn't you wait a bit longer to scream at me face to face?"

He leaned up and rested his weight on his elbows. His pain reflected in the depths of his eyes. "Leave them," he commanded when she went to take her hands from him.

"I don't want to hurt you."

The expression on his face told her how absurd that statement was. "Think your hands can hurt me worse than the sun?"

She didn't think anything could hurt him as severely as the sun. She didn't think anything could hurt him at all. He just came across as being larger than life and indestructible.

"Are you going to tell me what made you barge into my room like that?"

His nostrils flared in indignation and he managed to raise his chin a notch. "I felt your fear."

Her brows shot up in surprise. "You risked being charbroiled because you sensed I was afraid?" She shook her head in disbelief. "I'm flattered. Truly. But that was a stupid thing to do."

His cocked brow told her she was about to get an earful. "As stupid as you leaving this goddamn castle alone?"

"That's different. I *had* to leave." His eyes narrowed on her like a predator. The pinch on her brain made her all too aware that Constantine was trying—and failing—to push into her mind. "Give it up, Constantine. You're not getting in there tonight."

Well fuck, her mind wasn't the only part of her body Constantine wanted to get inside of tonight. Both were closed to him, and that just pissed him off to no end.

He sniffed at the air, his gaze raking over her bra-clad breasts. He settled his gaze on her naval. "I know it had to do with that damn mark, so don't even think to lie to me, woman."

She wouldn't dare. Not with him looking like he wanted to tear her to pieces with his bare hands. "Yes it did."

In one swift motion Constantine had them both on their feet, though the movement was a hellish experience in pain. Fuck it all, but the sun *hurt*. "The others *will* be told. Tonight."

If Lex dared try to argue with him he was sure his anger would return. No doubt he'd give her the good shake she deserved.

"I'd already planned on it." She gestured to her stomach, though that wasn't where his eyes went. How could they when her breasts were hidden behind the flimsiest piece of lace he'd ever seen?

And why in the bloody hell did she have to possess such perfect breasts?

He would have continued thinking that as his eyes lingered over her body, but the foul scent of medicine suddenly replaced the sweet smell of honeysuckle. Reluctantly, Constantine moved his eyes to her stomach. He realized she'd covered the raw skin with awful smelling ointment.

"Do I even want to know why you went to a pharmacist and not a doctor?"

Not that he thought a doctor would help. Whatever the cause of the mark and the energy was, it was paranormal.

Lex shrugged with such forced indifference that Constantine nearly burst into genuine laughter for the first time in God only knew how long.

"I knew Dr. Stuart would have called Allie before I got home." Her fingers began to dance absently over his skin. *She* might not realize what she was doing, but Constantine was all too aware of it. "It's bad enough Raphael already threatened to tell Allie. The last thing I wanted was a doctor to beat me to it."

Raphael? As in the Raphael he was going to have to beat half to death?

His eyes narrowed and his fists ached to make contact with Raphael's pretty-boy face. "Raphael knows?"

Her hands fell away from him. The warmth was instantly gone. She chewed her bottom lip and nodded. "He found out the other night when he took me on a ghost hunt."

The same ghost hunt Constantine had made a point to avoid going on since he was still trying to keep his distance from her—something he now realized was impossible.

His upper lip curled back in a sneer. "And the prick kept quiet about it? I'm going to make death by fire seem pleasant by the time I'm done with him."

"I swore him to secrecy."

Constantine couldn't stop the sneer that twisted his lips. "What'd you promise him?"

Lex looked away guiltily. He repeated his question. She looked back at him and Constantine knew if he weren't careful, he'd get lost in the blue of her eyes. "Buffy. The season three box set."

"Bloody hell."

Lex looked back at him, her eyes pleading. "Please don't be mad at him. I swore I'd tell Allie in a few days. He gave me until the end of the week to do it or else he would."

That didn't placate Constantine in the least. True he was being a hypocrite, but that was neither here nor there. As far as he was concerned, what was good for him was *not* good for everyone. Especially where Lex was concerned. "You shouldn't have left the castle."

"I know, and I'm sorry. But in my defense, if you were in my skin, you would have done the same thing."

Before he thought better of it, Constantine clamped a hand on her arm and dragged her down the hall. He ignored her startled gasp and the small protest she gave at being manhandled. The thundering of her heart filled his ears as he kicked his chamber door closed. He released her, locked the door. When he looked back at her, the impact of her emotions was driving him mad with need.

"What are you doing?" She crossed her arms over her chest to hide herself from him.

"I want a better look at that thing on your stomach."

"You stay away from me, Constantine." Lex put her hands up and backed away until she bumped into the bed. She glanced over her shoulder and took in his rumpled black bedding. She looked back at him, her cheeks bright red with an adorable blush. "This is too awkward. Let me go put a shirt on."

Her donning a shirt was the last thing Constantine wanted. Not when his thoughts had been consumed with getting her *out* of her clothes for weeks.

He came at her purposefully, loving the way her breasts rose and fell with her frantic breathing. "I don't think so, elf."

When he put his hands on her shoulders and shoved her backwards, Lex went without a struggle. She fell with a gasp. This was right where Constantine wanted her since the night he first saw her.

Constantine's hand pressed down on her stomach. "You don't know what this is?"

She shook her head. "If I knew, do you think I would have risked leaving Seacrest to try and find out?" By his expression, it was plain Constantine did not appreciate the sarcasm in her tone. "What's wrong with me?" She whispered.

"Not a bloody thing." He growled. "You're so fucking perfect."

All the air left Lex's lungs at the vehemence in Constantine tone. He moved back up her body and she placed her hands on the sides of his face. His scar scraped against her palm and Lex wished to God she were able to take the pain of the memory from Constantine.

"If you think I'm perfect, why do you do everything you can to avoid me?"

They way his silver gaze bore into her gave Lex a good idea of what molten lava would feel like poured over her. "I'm sure as shit not avoiding you now."

No, he wasn't. He was paying *very* close attention to her. "Well, you have been and I didn't like it."

He brought his face down close enough for their lips to almost touch. Her head spun at the wonderful aroma of spice she'd only ever smelled on Constantine. His hair fell forward, making a curtain that closed out the world.

"Do you want me to kiss you again, Lex?"

She could say no and try to salvage some small shred of her pride, but Constantine would know it for the lie is was. Besides, refusing was the last thing she wanted. "You know I do."

He brushed his cool lips across hers, not quite kissing her, more of a teasing of his mouth. His hard groin pressed into her, showing her the proof of his desire for her. Her body undulated with need as dormant things inside of her flared to life.

"Do you want to know what I want?" he whispered against her lips. Lex nodded, beyond words. "I want to feel your warmth all around me as I take your body and claim it as my own."

Right then, every part of Lex opened for him. Parts of her body she'd hardly been aware of ached to welcome him. For the first time, her sexual desire pushed aside reason and silenced the voices that usually protested intimacy. If she didn't know better, Lex would swear they were silent because she was with Constantine.

"Then do it, Constantine," she goaded softly. "Make love to me."

He let out a hiss. The sight of his fangs excited her even more. "I don't make love, I fuck." He leaned away from her and brought his hand to the junction of her thighs. Lex moaned when he cupped her and pressed his palm against the part of her throbbing for him. "The things I want to do to your body would break you."

"I'm tougher than I look." If Lex gave any thought to those words before they fell from her lips, she would have never had the nerve to say them.

His erection ground into her and showed her exactly how he wanted to take her. "You're not tough enough for me."

What Constantine should have said was, *he* wasn't tough enough for *her.*

When it came to Lex he lost his damn mind. He couldn't control his raging needs around her and that was a dangerous thing. God forbid he lost his shit around her...

The thought didn't even bear thinking.

When the familiar prickling nagged at the nape of his neck, Constantine knew the sun was setting. The others would emerge from their rooms and descend upon Lex like a shitstorm after her stunt today. Upon his bed with both of them shirtless was the last place they needed to find her.

"Get up," Constantine demanded, climbing off her. The loss of her touch left him cold once again. It cemented the knowledge of the danger she faced once the power grew strong enough to reach every renegade within a hundred mile radius of her. "The sun is setting."

Lex sat up and ran her hands through her thick hair. He watched, transfixed, as the black cloud fell around her incredible face. "I know. I can feel it." She tilted her head at him curiously. "Do you feel the loss of the sun or the arrival of the moon?"

"The moon." He looked at her intently. "I feel the moon."

Lex stood and Constantine had to look away. She was too tempting in nothing but jeans and bra. He wondered if her panties matched the flimsy piece of material covering her breasts. He could easily tear it off with his teeth and take her quick, before the others intruded in on them.

Constantine shook his head. He'd not treat Lex like some whore who was worth nothing more than a quick fuck and a meal.

"I feel the sun going away." She sighed and walked toward him. He tensed when she touched him. As he knew it would, Lex's innocence and energy crashed into him.

"You have to go, Lex. Now."

She took her hand from him. "I'll go, Constantine," she whispered, her husky voice causing him to grind his teeth as a wave of longing washed over him. "But this is the last time I'll run from you. The night will come when I'll fight for you."

His Lex—yes, *his*—marched from the chamber with the grace of a queen. Her vow echoed in his head long after he heard her go to her room. He focused his hearing on her and listened as she grabbed a shirt out of her drawer, slipped it on and fell onto her bed.

The sound of her muffled cries made him feel more like a monster than anything else had in over seven hundred years.

Chapter Nine

Draegon Castle:

November 19, 1296

Standing before Aislin, who reclined on her chair like a queen on a throne, Constantine drew himself up to his full and impressive height. At eleven, he was nearly as tall as his sire. He also surpassed most of his father's squires when it came to his skill with a sword. In time, if he continued to drive himself with the same ruthlessness he already did, he knew he'd be able to best even the finest of his father's men.

And then he'd become better still.

He'd become as strong and powerful as a dragon and cut down entire armies with a single swipe of his sword. It was all he trained for. All he had come to live for. To become the man his parents believed he'd never grow to be.

With hands clasped in front of him, Constantine stared his mother in the eye. He ignored the sting of the cuts on the top of his hands since they were a small price to pay for his effort to become a master swordsman. He tried not to be blinded by her beauty, like every other man who chanced to look upon her. The beauty of her face concealed the ugliness of her soul and he'd best remember that or she'd continue to break his heart with her cruelty.

Constantine knew men envied the lord of Draegon for his luck at securing himself a comely young wife. She bore him a son, which added to her appeal. If those same men heard the same whispers Constantine had of his mother's infidelity, he wondered if they'd still begrudge Henry his wife. Or the lord's good fortune at having a son to carry on his name. Unfortunately, Constantine knew his mother's heart was as cold as a slab of stone. Her soul was black as the devil's. And he knew he was a miserable disappointment to her as a son.

He saw no love reflected in her eyes as she raked her gaze over him. "On the morrow we'll be well rid of you."

Constantine puffed out his chest with a pride he didn't feel and fought back his fear. "Lord Ulric comes for me?"

He hated that his voice was still that of a youth, having not yet broken into the deeper pitch of a man. His body was growing , and yet he was still but a boy. Trapped between the two, Constantine had no place where he belonged.

Her lips twisted in her usual cruel smile. "Oh no, Constantine." Her tone was arctic and she spat out his name as if it were poison on her tongue. "A knight as powerful as Lord Ulric would never lower himself to come to collect one such as you. You go to him."

A knight as cruel, and as brutal, was what she should have said. Those were more apt descriptions of Ulric Chambers—or so Constantine had learned.

Tales of Ulric Chamber's viciousness had reached him. The men all spoke of the Lord of Greaves Castle's callousness. Constantine knew the lord's ways was one of the reasons why his parents agreed to give the man their only son as squire. From what Constantine had overheard, his parents believed Ulric would shape Constantine into the warrior they wanted him to be but often voiced their doubts of him becoming.

The bag of gold Ulric paid them was merely a bonus.

One afternoon, while taking a short break from the lists, Constantine heard the older men talking. The two knights had gone on about how Ulric had bought him for a bag of gold and how, given Chambers' reputation, he had a perverse reason for doing so. Hearing that had chilled him clear down to the marrow of his bones. Yet not until they went into gruesome detail of what might await him at Greaves did he lose what little food he'd eaten. So awful were such things they spoke of that Constantine had shamed himself right there at the knights' feet.

"I would ask you a question."

He almost called her "mother", but thought better of it. Best he'd start now at putting them out of his mind—and his heart.

Though he knew better, he could not leave Draegon Castle without knowing the answer to the one question that burned within him for years.

"Ask," Aislin bit out, accepting a goblet of spiced wine from a young male servant.

The servants at the castle were divided to a certain degree, Constantine had noticed years ago. The young male servants fluttered around his mother while, more often than not, the women could be found occupying his father's lap.

It took Constantine a moment to find his voice once he was given leave to ask his question. "Why do you hate me?"

He watched as his mother took a long, leisurely drought of her wine. When she moved the beaten gold goblet away from her mouth, she licked a stray drop from her bottom lip. She regarded him with open disdain. "Because you breathe."

He nearly buckled under the weight of his mother's hatred.

"I see."

Though he'd said that, the truth was, Constantine didn't see. A mother was supposed to love her child. He knew this because he'd secretly watched the servants with their children. They laughed, they embraced and they loved. He'd known none of those things, nor did he ever hope to.

"I've hated you since before you took your first breath." Her voice was sharp. It cut him deeper than any blade could.

So now he knew. Her answer left nothing more to say. All he was left to do was wipe away his tears. Constantine leveled a cold glare at his mother. The abhorrence in his eyes rivaled the coldness in hers. He realized that he had one last thing to say to Aislin Draegon.

"Goodbye, mother."

With a dignity he never knew he possessed, Constantine turned and stalked from his mother's receiving chamber. She said nothing to him as he walked out, though he did hear her call for more wine. When he turned to shut the door, he saw her caress the face of her servant. Her mouth curled into a beautiful smile as she pulled his face down to hers. Just before he could witness her infidelity, Constantine squeezed his eyes closed, unable to look upon her even one more moment.

On the morrow he'd leave Draegon Castle. Though he knew he would be exchanging one hell for another, he also knew he'd never willingly return here. And if he did, he would do it with an army at his back.

When Constantine reached his room, he sank down in the corner to wait out the last night he would ever spend here. His fear robbed him of the ability to sleep, so he was left to dwell on all the horrible imaginings his active mind could think up. He drew his legs up, and hugged them with arms only now beginning to show the first signs of his well-earned muscle. He rested his chin on his knees and let the tears of his broken heart flow freely. After all, there was no one here to witness his shame.

It was his eleventh birthday.

Chapter Ten

Over the years, fate had shown Constantine most of the horrors and wonders that would come to be. From the birth of nations to the two World Wars, he'd seen nearly all of the major events play out in vivid—and agonizing—detail. More often than not his visions were ones he wished he could un-see.

Fate had also shown him glimpses of the destinies of his fellow Templars—all but his own, of course. But then, he didn't need to see his to know where he was going once his existence came to an end. Yet of all the things Fate had shown him, why had the bitch kept the fact that Lex was the Daystar from him?

He'd seen the mark Lex carried on her stomach once before. It had been on a piece of parchment Kenny Buckman had found in his senile grandmother's attic. The junkie had been up there looking for shit to steal to feed his heroin habit. Years before, renegades had killed Paul Buckman when they'd stolen the scroll the piece of parchment had been torn from. Unfortunately, the Templars were never able to track down the scroll. Like all things associated with the Daystar, it frustratingly faded away into the unknown.

The implication of the mark, coupled with the power that radiated from Lex, added up to one hell of an ugly situation. Or as Constantine liked to put it, it was a giant cosmic *"fuck you"*.

Fate had given him a lot of those over the centuries. So much so, he was raw from them all.

Given the degree of energy raging in her, it was safe to assume it would only be a matter of time before the power radiated out to anyone with a set of fangs and a penchant for the dark. That's when shit was going to get really ugly, really fast.

Normally, Constantine liked nothing more than a good fight. Hell, he thrived on violence. Back in his day men fought hand-to-hand and sword-to-sword. One had to look his opponent in the eye before he killed him, which was something his violent nature had always relished. As far as Constantine was concerned, if he took a life, the life deserved taking. That way of thinking, coupled with his lack of conscience, was what allowed him to kill without remorse.

The medieval age had been a good time for a man like him to live. Bloody, dirty and dangerous, Constantine had been the perfect product of his day. He'd always thrived on the thrill of battle, of the not knowing if he'd live long enough to see the end of the fight or if someone was finally going to best him and send him to Hell. More often than not he'd tempted fate and had come damn close to meeting Lucifer long before the French killed him by fire.

Once he'd died and made his oath to God, all that had kept him from breaking it was the chance that his fellow Templars would be sent to Hell with him. Until Lex. Because of her, for the first time in his seven hundred years, Constantine wasn't so eager to tempt fate and tease death.

Constantine couldn't comprehend why Lex cared for him. Hell, no one liked him, even the Templars couldn't stomach him most of the time. On a good day he was an ornery asshole. When the hunger rode him—well, that's when things turned downright vicious. Yet Lex seemed to enjoy being around him, and God help him, he liked her being around as well.

With Lex housing the power of the Daystar, it put her in the center of a dangerous situation. Once renegades found out what she was—and he harbored no false hope that they wouldn't—they'd stop at nothing to gain possession of her. It would come down to a fight to preserve Lex's life and if they failed her, not only would vampires gain a power that would make them virtually indestructible, they'd acquire it by draining Lex dry. For her, there would be no coming back, and that was something Constantine wasn't about to let happen.

Constantine ran his hands down his bare chest. He still felt Lex's touch on him. Everything about her drove him mad with need. Grunting with frustration, his body raged for what he knew he could never have. This was a dangerous game he played when it came to her.

The proof of that came a moment later when the stab of hunger twisted his gut and ran his mouth dry. He'd have to feed again before he became a danger to himself and everyone around him. The more he allowed himself to indulge in Lex the more the hunger gnawed at him and the more frequently he was forced to feed. If he kept going down this road, it would lead to only one place. Though he was already fairly certain he was going to Hell, it wasn't someplace he was in any hurry to get to.

Which was why he took his time in donning a shirt and putting a series of heavy silver chains around his neck. He pushed various metal rings on his fingers, one of which bore a claw that he'd honed to a razor-sharp point.

Before he quit his room, Constantine grabbed his sword, something that was rarely out of his reach since the day the

Grand Master bestowed it upon him—save for his years in Chinon.

On the day of his arrest, Constantine had almost lost four fingers—including his thumb—before the French soldiers were able to wrest the sword from him. He'd put up one hell of a fight before one bastard snuck up behind him and nailed him across the back of the head with the hilt of a sword. He'd been knocked cold. The next thing he knew, he was bound and being carted off to Chinon Castle.

When he woke after his rebirth as a vampire it was to find his sword laying a few feet from him. He'd lain there for a long time, adjusting to the agony of his body and the realization of what he had been damned as. He'd looked long and hard at the raw brand on his right hand. It was a stark reminder of what he once was and what he had become. He'd gripped his sword in his branded hand as he dragged his burnt body across the cold night sand.

Once Constantine had taken his sword in hand, he'd made damn sure he was never parted from it again.

CRSO

Over the last hour Lex had endured a mix of being yelled at and lectured for leaving the castle alone and for keeping what was happening to her a secret. When they'd seen the mark on her stomach, the collective silence was worse than the screaming had been.

Now, her head was pounding. Allie, Sebastian and Tristan were still handing her ass to her and it looked as if they weren't about to calm any time soon.

Perched on the sofa, hands clasped in her lap, Lex zoned out as she stared into the flames dancing in the hearth. All around her, they raged on. Raphael, however, remained silent as he sat at the table looking like warmed over shit. He'd caught hell for his part in the deception.

Leaning against the mantle, arms crossed and gaze scanning the other occupants of the hall—all save for her—Constantine blocked most of the hearth. Because of that, it was unavoidable for Lex to look at him. With every word said, his brows drew together more and more until he wore a scowl that made her wish she were anywhere but in the hall.

Lex guessed he didn't like them lighting into her either. The only difference was, Lex kept silent and let them go on. Constantine didn't appear to be content to do the same. As a matter of fact, he looked about ready to explode and do them all some serious harm.

When Tristan turned his attention to Constantine and pinned him with a furious glare, Lex cringed. She could almost imagine the ticking of the time bomb that was Constantine's temper.

"And you. How the hell could you keep this from us?"

Lex's jaw dropped when she heard Tristan yell. Tristan *never* yelled. She'd even begun to doubt he possessed the ability to raise his voice. Obviously she'd been wrong. Tristan could bounce it right off the walls.

She looked at Constantine for his reaction. Given his expression, he wasn't taking it well at all. She looked back at Tristan, who cocked a brow, a silent dare for Constantine to come back with something.

Constantine pushed away from the mantle. He stepped up to Tristan. The two formidable Templars were nose to nose. "Slow your roll, Tris, and watch who the hell you're yelling at." There was no missing the warning in his tone and the murderous look in his eyes. "I owe you no explanations for my actions."

Lex was about to jump up from the couch and try to calm Constantine before the situation erupted into a full-blown war. Allie motioning to her to stay where she was stilled her. Sebastian grabbed for Allie but she shook him off and squeezed herself between Constantine and Tristan. Surprisingly, the men parted, although they continued to give each other the most ferocious glares.

"C," Allie said softly. "You have to realize that because this was kept from us, you put us all in danger. But most of all, it was Lex's safety in jeopardy."

An expression passed across Constantine's face that Lex couldn't quite place. Was it hurt? Disappointment? "Is that what you think, red?" His tone was low and laced with acid. "That I couldn't protect her?"

No one dared counter that he couldn't—wouldn't—do everything to ensure her safety.

"No doubt you could, Dragon," Sebastian interjected. "But that doesn't make it right for you to have kept this from us and you know it."

"The decision was Lex's to make." Constantine leveled them all a glare. "And before you all keep ripping into her, remember, we all know a goddamn thing or two about secrets."

"One has nothing to do with the other."

Constantine paid Tristan no mind. He folded his arms over his chest and shook his head in disgust. "Fucking hypocrites. The lot of you."

"I've just about had it with your bloody attitude, Constantine," Tristan warned.

Obviously Constantine wasn't going to budge on his stance. By the hard gleam in his eyes, Lex suspected they could argue this matter for centuries and he would hold to his convictions. As much as it flattered her that he'd stand by her, she hated being the cause of this tension.

"Please don't blame Constantine. I forced him to keep quiet," Lex interrupted, hoping to defuse a situation rapidly nearing combustion.

Her admission of guilt worked to break the tension. Lex almost crumbled under the weight of their incredulous stares. When Sebastian let out a laugh, Allie gave him a good slap to the arm. He quieted instantly. Raphael shook his head in bemusement. He still looked like he was going to be sick. Tristan gave her a look that told her he wasn't amused by her declaration.

"Lex, honey, do you have any idea how serious this is?"

Lex shot to her feet when Allie posed that question to her. Though generally slow to anger, the question, coupled with the condescending way it was voiced, had her livid. Fueling her anger was the fact that everyone seemed to be in the know about what was going on with her except *her*.

"You're joking, right?" Lex's glare was so cold, she was sure it rivaled even one of Constantine's. "I don't think you realize what it's been like for me to have this thing—whatever it is— inside of me. I wake every morning feeling worse than the day before. There are some days when I can barely drag myself out of bed, yet at the same time I have this compulsion to be out in the sun. Sometimes I feel this energy trying to bust right out of my skin. I hear voices in my head. Yes, voices. And sometimes, they get so loud it hurts my brain. Oh, and let's not forget this mysterious tattoo that magically appeared on *my* body." Her gaze shot to each and every one of them. "So yes, I think I have some idea about how serious this all is."

Once she was finished her tirade did she realize she'd inched her way closer to Constantine. Sometime during her rant he'd also moved toward her. When Allie walked over to them, Constantine put a protective arm around her, which made Lex feel oddly comforted.

"Back off, C. She's my sister."

Lex was stunned when he didn't pull away from her. He left it to her to disentangle herself from his arm, which she thought was just about the most supportive, and possessive, thing she'd ever known a man to do.

Allie went to take her hand but dropped it quick and bared her fangs in a hiss. She'd obviously not been expecting to get hit with the energy surging through Lex. Given she was an emotional mess, it seemed to make the energy grow to a feverish height.

"*Jesus Christ,* Lex. You got some serious mojo going on in there." Allie shook her hand as if it'd been burned.

Lex sighed and sank back on the sofa. Allie sat next to her. Sebastian hovered near his mate while Constantine came to stand behind the sofa. His hands settled on Lex's shoulders, which surprised her. He was treating her like they were mated.

"Whatever this is, it hurts my bones sometimes." A slight quiver passed over Lex as her hand went to the mark on her stomach. A short while earlier everyone had been poking at it and examining it like some weird science project gone wrong. "There are times it scares me so bad it makes me wonder if I'm dying."

Allie grabbed her hands. She saw the way her sister fought back the need to drop them as energy, once again shot through her. Lex's eyes glistened with tears as she stared back into Allie's silver gaze. She felt like a walking disease.

"Of course you're not dying!"

Lex looked over Allie's head to Sebastian and Tristan. "Then what's wrong with me?"

"There's nothing wrong with you." Allie's soft, soothing tone didn't fool her for a second.

When Lex stood, Allie did too. Unconsciously, Lex moved over to Constantine as he came around from behind the sofa. He threw his arm back around her and she nearly wept with relief when he didn't even flinch as her power surged into him.

"Either you tell her, or I will," he warned them all.

"We have to tell her." That agreement came from Raphael. He looked a bit less green around the gills.

"This is getting ridiculous," Lex exclaimed. "Will *someone* tell me *something*?"

When Allie came to stand before her, Constantine tightened his hold. Lex stiffened, knowing whatever it was Allie was about to say to her wasn't going to be good. Visions of all sorts of horrible, slow deaths came to her mind. Diseases. Suffering. Hospitals. *Oh God.*

"Lex, sweetie," Allie took a deep breath as if her lungs needed the air. They didn't. She was either stalling or fortifying herself. Maybe even both. And then she spoke again and Lex's world crashed down around her. "That's the mark of the Daystar."

Chapter Eleven

So now she knew. At least she wasn't dying. Although, being a vessel of supernatural power ran a close second on Lex's shit-o-meter.

This all seemed impossible and yet it explained so much— like the mysterious mark on her stomach for one. It also explained her odd connection with the sun. She wasn't sure how the voices fit into things, though she wasn't positive they connected to this as well. She figured there was a lot that came part and parcel with being some supernatural being. Time would tell just how much of herself was going to change now that she knew she was a creature that could give vampires nearly unstoppable power.

Suddenly, the walls of the hall closed in on her. Lex pulled away from Constantine, needing to put some space between herself and everyone else. Much to her surprise he let her go. She stepped back until she bumped into the hearth. Stepping aside so as not to catch fire, she dragged in a harsh breath and stared at the faces around her.

Every one of them, save for Constantine, wore expressions of sympathy. Constantine's was unreadable.

Lex pinned him with a pointed look. "How long have you known?"

If he would have shrugged or grunted or did anything else very "Constantine-like", Lex would have lost the fragile hold she had on her emotions. Thankfully he did none of those things, and put aside his sarcasm. Lex didn't know if that was a good thing or not.

"The moment I saw the mark."

"But you suspected even before that, didn't you?" His silence was a betrayal and all the answer she needed. "I see."

The cold of Lex's voice brought Constantine back to a time when he was a boy and he'd said those same two words to his mother the day before he left Draegon Castle.

When Lex turned away from him, Constantine wanted to spin her back around and demand she wipe the cold look from her face. Instead he left her to stand stock still as she stared at the fire. In that instant, something changed in her. Something otherworldly overtook her—something far out of the Templar's league.

Constantine noted he wasn't the only one who watched as Lex wrapped her arms around herself. Violent tremors wracked her. From where he stood, he knew he was the only one who saw the tears glistening in her eyes. When one of those tears escaped to slip down her ashen cheek, it hurt his goddamn heart.

As much as he wanted to take her in his arms and hold her and assure her all would be well, Constantine knew nothing of comforting someone. He had known such little kindness and tenderness in his own time that he knew he'd just muck it all up if he tried.

As quickly as her tears came they were gone. Constantine sensed she'd wrapped a wall of dignity around herself. She discreetly wiped the tear from her cheek and took a deep, fortifying breath. When she turned and faced them all, Constantine was moved by her grace and pride.

Her profound gaze raked over them. "What happens now?"

Allie hurried over to her sister. She went to take Lex in her arms but hesitated. Lex moved away at Allie's faltering. Allie sighed and walked back to Sebastian, who wrapped an arm around her waist and drew her close to his side.

"Now we do everything we can to keep you safe until we can figure this whole thing out," Allie announced. Her determination to protect her sister rolled over Constantine like a weight pressing down on him.

"This is some deep Druid shit." Everyone's attention focused on Raphael when he made that announcement. "I can go to the Order and see what they have to say about it. Hell, maybe I can even have Briana get hold of the First."

No one protested Raphael's suggestion, not even Constantine, who was none too fond of the Order of the Rose.

Raphael was supposed to have met with Briana Kerr a month ago to discuss the Daystar, but the meeting fell through. As far as Constantine had been concerned it was for the best since involving the Order might have stirred up a shitstorm of trouble. Besides, none of them wanted to be indebted to the Order of the Rose. Although, with this turn of events, the logical road to take would, unfortunately, lead directly to the First.

Tristan's nod caught Constantine's attention. "You think you can get an audience with her?"

Raphael shrugged, "I don't see why not. One mention of the Daystar and the First will come out of hiding."

The First rarely left her fortress, which was believed to be hidden somewhere in Wiltshire, England. Yet Raphael knew for this she would. Or at least she'd better. He hated admitting it, but they needed the Druid's help. And though it irked the shit

95

out of him, the truth was, for Lex, he'd step aside and accept the help of Lucifer himself if needs be. She was like a sister to them all and he'd be damned twice over if he sat back and did nothing while this whole thing played out around him.

Besides, Lex was good for Constantine. The surly bastard may think he could hide it from them, but it was obvious he cared for her. And Lex, well, she wore her feelings for Constantine on her sleeve. Though he couldn't comprehend that she'd never even kissed a man before Constantine, it somehow seemed right that she'd only known him. To Raphael's way of thinking, Fate was whispering to them all that the two of them were meant to be.

Oh Lord, he thought, he was beginning to wax poetic. He'd better stop that shit right now or else Constantine was going to hear his thoughts and give him hell for them. The last thing he needed was for Dragon to have more reasons to taunt him.

"You don't have to do this, Raphael," Lex offered.

Raphael knew his pathetic attempt at a reassuring smile wasn't fooling anyone. "She's bound to learn about you sooner or later. Might as well make it sooner rather than later and get on her good side."

"Can you go tonight?"

Raphael nodded to Sebastian. "I just have one stop to make and then I'll head over to Kerr's shack."

The "shack" Raphael referred to was, in fact, a massive fortress disguised as a luxurious estate where the Order gathered. Owned by Briana Kerr, whom they knew came third in the hierarchy of the Order.

The stop he had to make was at Shakers, a local strip club. For the last three months he made sure to go there and check in on Cyn every night she worked. Why he felt such a connection to the human woman, he had no idea.

Unlike the rest of his brethren, Raphael didn't steer clear of humans. Hell, he didn't avoid much of anyone, save for renegades. He was, as Sebastian liked to say, a friendly fucker, who mingled with nearly everyone. His easy-going manner gave the other Templars fits, but since Raphael possessed a wicked sense of humor, he got off on annoying his brothers-in-arms about it and they finally began to leave him alone about his social choices. He just couldn't see spending hundreds of years, or more, in isolation as Tristan had, or in a perpetual state of anger like Constantine.

Of all the humans he'd come across over the last seven hundred years, it was Cyn he returned to night after night. Cyn who was the one woman he didn't allow himself to take advantage of and use to sate his sexual and blood needs. She was—different. Special. He liked being around her. She made him feel alive.

Eager to get to Shakers and then on to Briana's estate, Raphael stood and moved to leave. He stilled when Lex strode over to him. "Thank you for doing this."

It seemed even in the short time since Lex entered their world, she knew the severity of involving the Order. Allie must have filled her in on the details they knew about those vicious bitches.

"Anything for you, boo." He meant that with everything he was. "Don't worry, Lex. You're not alone in this."

Once Raphael had left, Lex looked to Allie. "Are we done here? I'd like to go to my room."

Allie shook her head. "Of course, sweetheart." Her small smile was meant to be reassuring. It fell very short of that. "Don't worry, we'll work through this. I promise."

"I hope so, sis."

As Lex left the hall all she wanted to do was crawl in bed and put this hellish day behind her. Fighting back tears, she clawed at the mark in a vain attempt to ease the merciless itch. Only once she'd made herself bleed did she stop and don a white tee and pink pajama bottoms. She dropped onto her bed and let loose her tears.

When she heard heavy footfalls coming down the hall, she bit back her cries and dried her face. She'd not have the others see her emotionally broken.

At the knock at her door, Lex expected it to be Allie. She dragged herself up and bid her sister to enter. Much to Lex's surprise it was Constantine who strode into her room.

For a moment he stood frozen in the center of her room and peered around at the pink haven she'd made herself. The look on his face almost made her laugh. In his black cargo pants and black tee reading *Sarcasm: It beats killing people* he looked out of place in such a feminine lair.

Then he pinned her with his intense stare. He shut the door and crossed the room and without word or warning, pulled her to him and kissed her hard enough to leave Lex breathless and dazed.

As if she weighed nothing, Constantine lifted her. Lex wrapped her arms around his neck and held on tight. He laid her on the bed before he kicked off his shoes. He sat and pulled her across his lap. Lex settled into him, comforted by the feel of his arms around her. When he shifted, she sighed, thinking he was going to deposit her on the bed and leave.

He did set her back on her bed, but to Lex's surprise he didn't leave. Instead, he turned off the light and climbed in bed with her. He forced her to lie down before he stretched out next to her. After he drew the covers up over them, he tucked her in.

Lex nearly wept when he hugged her close and kissed her forehead.

"Thank you, Constantine. I didn't want to be alone."

He grunted in answer. "Go to sleep."

"Will you stay all night?"

He hugged her even closer. "I'll stay as long as I can."

With her emotions thrown into chaos and Constantine's gruffly offered comfort, Lex couldn't hold back her tears any longer. She released them as Constantine held her silently, taking in her fear with the strength of ages she wished she had.

Raphael was right.

She was not alone.

Chapter Twelve

What a beautiful time of day.

And if Lex were being honest with herself it was a sad one as well. She stood in the courtyard with the early autumn sun fading in the sky. Night was coming, and with it the death of another day.

Now that she knew what she was, she better understood her connection to the sun and the elements.

After less than twenty-four hours, she was far from coming to terms with this newfound knowledge. Nevertheless, she understood she had no choice but to accept it and not wallow in self-pity. She couldn't afford to sit around bemoaning fate. Not with renegades all around them gunning for the power she possessed.

Hours earlier, Lex woke to an empty bed and the sensation of the walls closing in on her. Sometime before dawn, Constantine had been forced to leave her. She vaguely recalled his whisper of a kiss before he slipped away to retreat into the dark. That was where he was now, trapped in the shadows even as she turned her face to the sun to take in the last of its warming rays.

Their existences were at such odds. He was a creature of the dark and she was of the light. And yet, somehow, she couldn't imagine loving anyone else. Someone normal. Someone human. The very idea seemed absurd since she had the distinct feeling that fate, or God, had a hand in their finding each other.

Seasonably cold today, the air held a chill that failed to affect her. The power thundering through her body warmed her from the inside out. This was the same warmth she was able to pass into Constantine whenever they touched. She was able to sense his relief as it seeped into him and offered him a reprieve from the torment of constant cold.

Under the loving caress of the sun, Lex threw her arms wide and a flood of voices sounded loudly in her head. She still didn't know who they were, but somehow, now that she knew about the Daystar, she listened a bit harder to hear what they were saying. Unfortunately, the voices all blended together, as they always did, in a loud din of indistinguishable noise.

Breathing in the cool air, for one moment Lex was one with everything around her. She was part of the grass and dirt beneath her feet, the stone of the massive keep, the flowers and plants in the garden. Even with the birds in the sky and the clouds they soared beneath.

But most especially, she was connected to the sun. It wove its way through her, merging with everything she was. Even her heart beat in time to the pulsating rays.

When the voices began to quiet, their noise was replaced by the soft hum of energy. The surge of power pulsating within her traveled from the tips of her fingers clear down to her toes. It ran through her in a hot wave that brought her so close to something she couldn't see that she swore if she reached out, she'd be able to touch whatever it was just out of her range of sight.

A wonderful sense of calm settled within her. It lifted away the worry and fear and most of all, the loneliness of being the sole bit of life in the world of the dead. Try as she did to hold the moment, it shattered like glass all around her, slamming her back into the ordinary world.

The sudden loss of nature left Lex shaken. She lowered her arms and looked around the courtyard. She realized night had settled in around her a moment before the keep's doors were thrown open and Tristan stepped from the entrance.

Catching sight of her, he came toward her. "What are you doing out here, Lex?"

"Just enjoying the last bit of daylight.

He nodded in silent understanding as he came to stand beside her. "How are you doing?"

"How should I be doing?"

There was no trace of emotion in the tall, blond Templar's eyes. In the month that she'd known him, there were times when Lex wondered what secrets lay hidden behind his cool façade.

"I think you should be confused and scared, and even angry, if you want to know the truth." He raised a brow as his gaze bore into her. "I know that's how I would feel if I were in your situation."

"I'm all of those things and more, Tris. Believe me. I'm just hiding it well." Then Lex cast a curious glance at him. "Did you feel those things when you were damned?"

He was silent and thoughtful for so long it looked as if Tristan wasn't going to answer her. Then he surprised her by breaking the silence. "My death was horrific. After Michael damned me, I woke in a field near Seacrest. My body was nearly burnt to ash and an agonizing hunger tore at my insides. It took me a fraction of a second to realize I was a vampire." He looked directly into her eyes and in his steely gaze Lex saw the pain of his past. "No, I wasn't scared, Lex. I was terrified."

Lex found it difficult to imagine Tristan terrified. He came off as a powerhouse of strength and resolve, which was what made his confession that much more profound. His honesty comforted her, made her feel normal for feeling the things she did.

"Yes, terrified sums up how I feel."

He placed a heavy hand on her shoulder. He cringed but at least he didn't pull away. That helped to make Lex feel less like a leper. "I know, Lex. We're going to do everything to keep you safe until we figure out what to do."

"You can't hide me here forever."

Tristan cocked a brow and laughed bitterly. "You don't think so? We have forever."

"Well I don't." She looked to the towering wall surrounding the courtyard. Suddenly, that wall turned Seacrest from home to prison in the span of one heartbeat to the next. "Hidden away behind a wall is no way to live."

When Lex looked back to Tristan, she realized he was staring at the walls with the same sorrow as she had. "No, Lex, it's not."

Lex blew out a sigh and slapped her hands at her side. Tristan looked back at her. "So, what do we do now, Tris?"

"We do nothing until Raphael gets back."

When her jaw dropped open, Lex had to remember to snap it back closed. "Raphael hasn't come back from Briana Kerr's place yet?"

"Rogue called late last night and told me he ran into some trouble leaving Shakers. A member of the Order of the Rose happened to be in the area to feed, followed the scent of renegades and lent him a hand. By the time he got to Kerr's estate, it was nearly dawn." An expression Lex couldn't quite read passed over Tristan's face. "He made contact with the First."

Lex's heart leapt into her throat as hope flared to life. Not merely hope, she realized, but fear as well as at least a million other emotions to go with it. "What did she say?"

"He didn't want to tell me what she said over the phone." Tristan must have seen her disappointment. "He's on his way back to Seacrest now. So, it seems we'll know soon enough."

"I think the not knowing what comes next might be the death of me."

Tristan laughed, his fangs showing. Lex wasn't at all put off by the sight of them. "Well, whatever the future holds, we'll all be here to protect you. Especially Constantine."

It pulled at her heart that they would all add the burden of her to their nights. "It's not fair to him, Tristan. It's not fair to any of you to take me on as an added responsibility. I mean, my God..." she waved her hand through to air, indicating the chapel, "...you guys have enough to worry about without the added burden of me."

"What's in there," he pointed to the chapel, "is my responsibility alone, and you are no burden. Besides, Constantine needs you, though let's keep that between us."

"I have a feeling he would disagree with you."

Tristan snorted. "Yes well, he's an ornery bastard who doesn't know what's good for him." Then he turned serious again. "But he does care for you, Lex. He's just too damn stubborn to admit it."

Lex looked away shyly. "He's admitted it. In his own way, of course."

"Of course." He tilted his head to the side and regarded her thoughtfully. "You fancy him, don't you?"

She looked back at him, her cheeks pinkening. "You know I do. Everyone knows I do. It's embarrassing."

"Don't be silly," he scoffed. "We're all glad someone took the time to see the man he is."

"He's incredible."

The simple statement led Tristan to realize how right Lex was for Constantine. He knew in that moment how wrong he'd been about Lex being too innocent. If anything, her innocence just might be what Constantine needed to finally put his past to rest. At least that's what he was hoping. As much as Constantine was a pain in the ass and a miserable prick, Tristan loved him, just as did the other Templars. They were all part of the same family, the same blood, their oath binding them for the rest of time. When one hurt, they all hurt, and Constantine's pain affected them all.

Constantine and Lex had a long and difficult road ahead of them. Tristan hoped, with everything he was, that once they reached the end of it, there would be happiness waiting for them.

When the time came for the Templars to once again stand before Michael and be judged, at least Sebastian, and hopefully Constantine as well, would face their judgment with peace and love in their hearts. For Tristan, that was enough to get him through whatever fate awaited them after their time here was at an end.

"Come on, we'd better get you back to the keep."

As they walked back, Tristan noticed Lex trembling. She may be putting on a brave face, but she wasn't exaggerating when she admitted she was terrified. And how could he blame her? From one moment to the next, Lex's entire world had turned upside down for the third time. The first being her brother, Christian's, death, the second being Allie's rebirth as a vampire, and now this. She bore the burden with a grace he was proud of.

Before he stepped into the keep, Tristan couldn't resist one last look at the chapel. Constantine's premonition nagged at him. Yes—his fight was coming soon.

CRSO

When the vision came to him, the pain of it sliced through Constantine's mind like a million blades. He grabbed for the wall, slapping his hand against the stone to steady himself, but the agony was too much. He fell to his knees, instinct kept his other hand curled around the hilt of his sword.

The visions, despite what Tristan called them, were no gift. They were a goddamn curse—as if being damned as a vampire wasn't bad enough. It hadn't been long after he was thrown back into the world as a vampire that he'd realized he'd possessed the ability to read people's thoughts. Stronger minds were closed to him, but weaker minds were an open book.

The visions manifested soon after he'd been damned. The first vision had come at him like needles stabbing him in his eyes and a sword cutting clean through his brain. The rest that followed were nearly as bad. So much so that even after all this time, he still wasn't used to the pain of them. If he could, he'd shove this fucking gift straight up Fate's ass and tell the fickle bitch to go to hell.

He'd just reached the hall when it hit him. With no warning, the vision came, bringing with it the usual agony. Bracing himself against the wall, Constantine slammed his eyes shut and gritted his fangs as fragmented images tumbled through his mind.

He saw Lex standing on the stone balcony of an ancient castle. Vaguely familiar, it was as if the keep was pulled from the recesses of his mind. The sun shone on her, bathing her in its radiance. A light wind whispered all around her, lifting the glossy black strands of her hair. She wore a long white robe, which made her seem as if she'd stepped from a page in history. She stared out intensely over a land he knew all too well.

That image was replaced by one of complete darkness. The despair Constantine sensed in the blackness was the same as what he'd experienced in Chinon. The sound of metal scraping against stone echoed in his head. As much as he tried he couldn't lock to what lurked in the dark, be it man or woman— human or something else. When a faint glow of light came from the darkness, the silhouette of a man passed in it. Constantine knew he was seeing Lucian.

Though Constantine knew the routine well enough by now—he was merely an observer, never a participant in the visions—he tried to use this mental connection to reach out to Lucian. All it worked to do was cause him more pain. When the two images of Lex and Lucian overlapped, his hand uncurled from the hilt of his sword. He slapped his hand to his head as his body convulsed from pain.

Relief came when Tristan and Lex entered the keep. The connection was severed and Constantine was released from the hold of the vision. He raked his gaze over Seacrest's hall as he fought to get his bearings now that the vision had ended. He sought out Lex, who was the anchor of his control. He used the sight of her to help fight against the agony that continued to rip through his head.

"Constantine!"

Oh good God, Lex, please don't touch me.

The words were trapped in his mind. He hurt too much to speak them or send them to Lex as she ran to him. Her concern spilled into him and made the already riotous storm in him rage harder still. For the first time since she entered his existence, Constantine couldn't gain comfort from her.

When she went to put her hands on him, he slammed his back against the wall and pushed her away with a hiss. He couldn't handle the impact of her energy. Not then, when it would add to his pain.

Thank God Tristan knew he couldn't handle being touched. He caught Lex and pulled her away before her hands settled on him. "No, Lex, don't touch him yet."

She looked over her shoulder at Tristan, which put her throat on dangerous display. Constantine groaned and closed his eyes as he fought the bloodlust that rose in the wake of the vision.

After seven centuries Constantine thought he'd be used to this shit by now. He wasn't. He never wanted the damn visions or the telepathy and couldn't understand why Fate had stuck him with them. He chalked it up to another major cosmic "fuck you".

"What did you see?" Tristan asked, setting Lex aside. She hovered close to Constantine, careful not to touch him as Tristan helped him stand.

Constantine opened his eyes. "Not enough," he bitched, even though he was infinitely glad the vision was over. "I saw Lucian."

He purposely kept the fact that the vision had centered around Lex to himself. He didn't need to add to her worry about the future by telling her he'd seen her in this vision. No doubt she'd chalk it up to something bad, and until he was able to understand it better, he'd not add to her fears of the future until he knew what the hell it meant.

"Where is he?"

"I don't fucking know," he gritted out at Tristan.

Tristan helped him settle in one of the chairs near the hearth. Lex was right there by his side. She brought him his sword, which she leaned against the chair. She made sure it was in his reach before offering him a small, reassuring smile.

"Thank you."

His tone was gruff as emotions he couldn't understand heightened the bloodlust that always came after a vision. Tristan came to stand before him and drew Constantine's attention from Lex.

"Do you know here Luc is?"

Constantine stiffened with frustration. Since helplessness was anathema to him, it caused his fury to come to the forefront. "If I did, do you think I'd still be sitting here?"

"So what did you see?"

"Like I said, not enough." Heedless of the pain it caused, Constantine shot out of the chair. His frustration at not being able to get a lock on Lucian rode him hard. "He's in the dark, Tristan. He's in the fucking dark and I can't get to him."

Tristan went to put a hand on his shoulder but Constantine stepped out of his reach. He grabbed his sword and shoved it roughly in the baldric strapped to his back.

"Go easy, Constantine. It's not your fault we haven't found Lucian."

"Yes it is." Furious, he turned on Lex. He snarled even though he knew he had no right to focus his anger on her.

She backed away from him. "What's wrong with you?"

He took hold of her upper arms and bit back a roar when her power surged through him. "You. You're what's the matter." He tossed her toward Tristan, who placed her behind him, putting himself between her and Constantine.

"You'd better get a hold on yourself, Dragon."

"Keep her the fuck away from me."

His helplessness was killing him all over again. All he saw was Lucian alone in the dark. As long as Lex continued to consume his thoughts, he'd never find Lucian, and that was something he couldn't let happen.

When he went to leave, Tristan clamped a hand on his arm. Constantine let out a growl and pushed him away. Jesus Christ, if he didn't get away Constantine was afraid he'd hurt Lex.

"Dragon," Tristan called his name in an unspoken warning.

"Fuck off, Guardian." Constantine snapped.

Lex's thoughts invaded his mind as he stomped up the stairs. He slammed the heel of his hand against his forehead again and again in a vain attempt to knock her voice out of his head. Of course, it wouldn't be that easy for him. As he stomped down the long corridor toward his chamber her thoughts continued to haunt him.

"Get the fuck out of my head," he ground out as he pushed open the door.

Once in his room, he smashed his fist into the stone wall out of sheer frustration. Blood exploded from his knuckles when the skin opened. A few bones shattered as well. The pain was good. It helped him gain a small measure of control over himself.

Needing to get as far from Lex as possible, Constantine grabbed his trench. He had to get someplace where he couldn't smell honeysuckle and where her emotions and thoughts couldn't play havoc on his sanity. He needed to regain his indifference, which had helped him get through the last seven hundred years.

And he needed blood.

Constantine pulled on the trench as stomped back down into the hall. He didn't see Tristan or Lex. The faint sound of her weeping made him cringe. How the hell was it possible that the sound of Lex's cries hurt his heart worse than Michael's blade had? He stormed out of the hall and made his way to his car with the intent of driving Lex out of his mind.

As he sped out of the courtyard like a bat out of hell, Lex's soft cries followed him all the way to The Gate. In all of his life and his death, Constantine had never felt more like a monster than he did then.

Chapter Thirteen

By the time Raphael returned to Seacrest Castle, he couldn't be more grateful to be home. After spending the day with Briana Kerr, he was glad to be back in the fold of the Templars. Though in all honesty, Raphael owed Briana big time. Because of her he wasn't roasting in Hell right now.

Six on one had been odds he wouldn't have been able to fight his way out of, which was why when Briana arrived on the scene, he was grateful for her help at defeating the renegades who'd ambushed him at Shakers.

He'd been about to leave the club when he noticed two humans giving him the hairy eyeball. Calling them on their shit, he realized too late that renegades had used them as patsies to get him outside alone. Once in the parking lot, six renegades greeted him—all eager to beat him to death in order to gain information on the Daystar.

The pricks had been doing a damn good job of it when Briana had showed up like a beautiful angel of death. The two of them took out the renegades before going to her estate, perched atop a mountain that overlooked the Delaware River.

Though Kerr had been a pleasant host, reserved, yet pleasant in her own way, it was good to be away from a stronghold belonging to a member of the Order of the Rose.

Although, he had to admit, his perception of them was now drastically altered after his long conversation with the First.

It seemed the Order had pulled a fast one on them all. The First wasn't the bloodthirsty bitch the nocturnal world believed her to be. She had actually been—nice. Raphael hadn't sensed any threat coming from her. True, he'd communicated with her via phone. Nevertheless, he'd sensed no hostility. Normally it would have eaten at him that he was indebted to the Order after one of their numbers had helped him out with the renegades last night. Yet after talking with the First, it left him less resentful to owe them anything.

Raphael couldn't believe the things the First had told him about the Daystar. She laid it all out and told it to him straight. Good God almighty, all hell was going to break loose once he relayed the information back to the family. Allie wasn't going to take what he had to say about her sister's fate well at all. Not that he could blame her. He hadn't handled it well himself. Truth was, he liked Lex. She was a good kid and she didn't deserve to have to face what was coming.

As soon as he stepped into the hall, Raphael sensed the tension. Lex was perched on a chair near the hearth having a good cry. Tristan sat solemnly on the sofa with his back to the entrance. He cast a long and desperate look at Raphael from over his shoulder. Tristan was begging him for help in soothing Lex's tears.

Raphael just *knew* Constantine was the cause of those tears. Damn, but he wanted to beat the shit right out of Dragon for making Lex cry. "What did Asshole do now?" Raphael demanded as he crossed the hall.

"Nothing," Lex whispered brokenly.

"The usual," Tristan grunted.

Raphael thought it was admirable that Lex was trying to stick up for Constantine. Her effort was wasted, however, since they'd all known the pissy bastard for over seven hundred years. Suffice it to say, if Lex was crying, there was no doubt it was over something Constantine had done.

As much as Raphael wanted to offer Lex some small comfort, he didn't dare touch her. The air around her was already charged with the Daystar's power. The last thing he wanted was to be burned by it.

"He had a vision, was his typical pleasant self and then stormed out of here a half an hour ago," Tristan explained.

Tristan was pissed, not that Raphael blamed him for his anger. They were all getting sick and tired of Constantine's constant attitude lately. It went far beyond his normal ornery self and entered a whole new realm of nasty, which was damn near driving the rest of them mad.

They all knew it was his frustration that had Constantine acting like more of a prick than usual. His attitude grated on all of their nerves, especially since they were all worn with worry over Lucian.

When he failed to detect Sebastian and Allie, Raphael frowned. "Where are the lovebirds?"

"They had to go feed." Tristan glanced at Lex, who grimaced in distaste at his announcement. "They should be back anon."

Raphael sat on the other chair opposite Lex. He knew Allie wouldn't stay gone long. He directed a cutting glare at Tristan, avoiding Lex's curious, and teary, stare.

Raphael dreaded having to relate the information he'd learned from the First.

"How was it at Kerr's?"

Lex looked at Tristan when he voiced that question. "Not what I was expecting."

When he said nothing more, Lex wiped her tears away and looked back at him. "What did the First say? Does she know how to fix me?"

"You're not broken," Tristan declared in a low growl.

Raphael ran his hands through his hair and blew out a heavy, breathless sigh. "I'd rather wait for everyone to get back before I go into it."

"And I'd rather you treat me like an adult and tell me what she said right now."

Raphael was taken aback by Lex's sudden temper, although he understood it. Still, he didn't want to have to tell her what he'd learned without Allie here.

"Lex..."

She cut him off with a raise of her hand. "Start talking, Raphael, or I swear to God..."

Admitting defeat, Raphael leaned forward and looked desperately at Tristan for help. Tristan didn't seem inclined to come to his defense. "Look, I'm going to be blunt here since there's no way to sugarcoat this. From what the First told me, you're not *the* Daystar. According to Druid lore, you're what's called a Hallowed. It's the sacred vessel that holds the power of the Daystar."

"You're kidding, right?"

He shook his head and shifted in the chair. He wished Allie were here. He knew Lex would want her sister with her when she learned what it was the First had said. "You were born under something the First referred to as a Bloodmoon. It marks the birth of a Hallowed."

Raphael found it unnerving how calmly Lex sat there. He sensed nothing from her, not fear, not anger, not even curiosity. Her emotions were hidden behind the mask of calm she wore.

Tristan glanced at him inquiringly. "Why haven't they tried to make contact with her?"

"They didn't have to." He looked back at Tristan. "They've been watching her since the day she was born."

That last bit he directed at Lex. Her expression was eerily unreadable. "This is all just so unbelievable."

"I know, boo, and I wish I could take it all away. We all do."

Tristan was quick to nod in agreement. "You're part of us now and we'll get through this together, Lex."

"Thanks, guys." Her smile was small and forced as her fear radiated from her.

"Did the First say what's to be done to keep renegades from discovering Lex's power?"

Raphael shifted again. If he were capable of it, he'd be sweating with dread. As it was, his insides twisted at what other news he had to share. "Yes and no."

Tristan cocked an inquisitive brow when he said no more. "Stop being so cryptic and just say what needs to be said."

With a heavy heart, Raphael steeled himself for what needed to be said. "Come Halloween, the power of the Daystar is going to reach its full strength."

In the span of one heartbeat to the next, he watched helplessly as an array of emotions played out across Lex's face as the implication of his statement sank in.

She brought her hands to the mark of the Daystar, slid her eyes closed and took a deep breath. When she opened them and pinned him with her intense stare, all of her fear, hopelessness, and anger came at him in a rush.

"And then what happens?"

Raphael swallowed down the lump of dread in his throat. "There's a chance you could be transformed into pure energy."

Lex went numb. For just one blessed moment her mind quieted and her body ceased to feel. A second later fear, cold and crippling, ripped through her and robbed her of breath. Tristan was on his feet and by her side when she choked on a breath. He touched her and hissed, yanking his hand from her as if he'd been burned.

Once he was recovered from the effect of the raging energy, he stopped shaking the pain out of his hand and turned to Raphael. "How do we stop this?"

"There's a ritual the First can perform, but there's no guarantee it will prevent the—event—from occurring."

The tremors that wracked her body were painful. Unshed tears filled her eyes as she put up a valiant fight to hold them back. Right now she needed to be strong. Raphael joined Tristan at her side, careful not to touch her. The way he made a point to hover close—but not too close—had her feeling like she had a disease.

"It's going to be all right."

Tristan tried to reassure her but she wasn't buying his optimistic outlook. "No, Tristan. You're wrong. It's not going to be all right." Without realizing what she was doing, she fisted her hand in her shirt and twisted it as if that alone would pull the power out of her. "I want this out of me. Oh God, please, take this out of me."

"Easy, Lex," Raphael said to her, taking her shaking hands in his. He barely flinched when the intense heat of her flowed into him. "The First can stop it, sweetheart. We just have to get you to England."

117

"England!" She hadn't meant to yell but couldn't stop her voice from coming out in a hysterical screech. "You might as well dip me in blood and fling me at a pack of starving renegades."

"The Order has people to travel with you and protect you."

Lex looked to Raphael incredulously. "I have to go alone? Without you?"

"If we could, we would, Lex. You know that." The regret in Tristan's voice stabbed at her.

Defeated, Lex dragged in a deep, painful breath and struggled to hold herself together. She didn't want to go to England without the Templars. If the worst happened and she either died or ended up a creature of pure energy like Raphael said, she didn't want to meet such a fate alone. These beings, though damned, were her family now. The thought of going off to face her fate without them left her feeling more alone than ever she had.

"I'm sorry, but I can't." She choked back a scared sob. "I can't do this alone."

"You have to be strong now, Lex. You have to find the strength to make it through this."

Couldn't Tristan see she wasn't strong? Allie was the strength. She was the one who had held them together through the years. "I don't want to leave."

"If you don't go, the power *will* overtake you. There will be nothing to hold it back. If you go to England and the First performs the rite, there is a good chance the power will be neutralized."

In other words, Raphael was telling her if she stayed here, come Halloween—her birthday—she'd be as good as dead. At least if she tried to make it to England and the First performed this ritual, she'd have a fighting chance at survival.

When put like that, did she have a choice?

At that moment the double doors of the entry banged open. A gust of cold air swept into the hall. Constantine came storming in, a scowl on his face and a curse on his lips

"You're not going to bloody England alone."

Tristan and Raphael jumped to their feet. They looked toward the doorway, which Constantine filled looking damn near fit to kill. Lex wiped her eyes, lest he see her tears. She tried to stop her body from trembling as he stomped over to her but it was a losing battle. She folded her hands in her lap and made a conscious effort to keep them from shaking. Bad enough she knew Constantine would sense her fear, he didn't have to *see* it as well.

"I thought you had to feed."

"Mind your business," Constantine shot back at Tristan as he came into the hall and slammed the doors closed behind him.

"You *are* my business, Dragon." Tristan matched Constantine's fierce frown with one of his own.

Constantine came to stand in front of Tristan. "Leave off, Guardian. I'm only warning you once."

Lex pressed herself into the chair; terrified at the hostility coming off Constantine and the way Tristan wasn't about to back down. The two looked like they were about to draw swords and start hacking off body parts.

When Tristan sniffed at Constantine, Lex had only a second to wonder why when he let out a vicious growl that had her slipping from the chair and inching toward the stairs. Raphael caught her, hissed, but didn't let go of her hand. Instead, he pressed her to his side.

"What have you done, Constantine?" Tristan demanded.

Constantine seemed unfazed by Tristan's temper. "Get off your bloody moral high-horse, Tris. I know your past."

Tristan narrowed his eyes menacingly on Constantine. "I'll let that one slide. But it's your last freebie. Keep shooting your mouth off and you won't like what comes of it."

"You threatening me?"

"You bet your arse I am."

"Tris," Raphael called, letting go of her hand. Lex continued to inch toward the stairs. All she wanted was to get to her room and to think in peace. "I think we have bigger problems here than whatever it was Constantine did while he was out." Then he looked at Constantine. "And you better watch your mouth when talking to Tristan. You of all people know bloody well what he sacrifices for us every goddamn night."

"Constantine?" Three sets of furious silver eyes locked on her. "I know you didn't hurt anyone tonight."

Lex wasn't sure how she knew that to be true, she just knew it was, even if Tristan and Raphael doubted him. Constantine moved away from Tristan, who stepped aside with a whispered warning that Lex failed to hear but Constantine cut with a nasty glare.

Constantine pointedly ignored Raphael as he came toward her. "No. I didn't."

He offered no further explanation, not that Lex needed any. She had faith in him, even though she knew he didn't have it in himself.

Raphael went to join Tristan near the hearth. Lex wanted to touch Constantine bad enough that she had to fist her hands at her side to keep from doing so. "Did you hear what Raphael said?"

"I heard."

She looked away, ashamed at her weakness of spirit. "I'm scared."

He grabbed her chin and forced her to look back at him. "I know."

In that moment, Lex needed Constantine more than she needed air to breathe. Scared and feeling alone, she wanted— no, she needed—his strength to help hold her together.

God forgive her for feeling the way she did for him, but Lex wanted to take all of Constantine into her. She wanted all of the good and all of the bad, everything that shaped him into who he was. Her need to draw Constantine into her and cleanse him of his pain and give him peace was a burning need within her.

And as she stood before him, fighting to hold herself back from him, Lex realized something she'd only suspected until now. She loved him.

When she saw Constantine stiffen, Lex knew her mind was open and he had been able her hear her thoughts. His lips parted, giving her a hint at his fangs. It looked as if he were going to say something, but words failed to be forthcoming.

He backed away, shaking his head. *"No."*

Lex wanted to die of humiliation. *"You heard that, didn't you?"*

"Lex..." His voice, no more than the rumble of distant thunder in her mind, trailed off.

Lex swallowed hard. "I...I need to go up to my room."

"Lexine."

"Leave me alone, Tristan. Please."

As if the devil himself chased her, Lex ran from the hall. She had to get to her room where she could hide and let the shame eat away at her until it pushed aside her fear of what was to come. She'd crawl into bed and let sleep claim her, putting an end to this hellish day

And then she'd wake tomorrow. One day closer to facing her destiny. One day closer to her death—or worse.

CR§O

She loved him.

Constantine had heard Lex think it as vividly as if the thought had been his own. She loved him. Or so she thought. Constantine had heard what Raphael told her. It had left her an emotional mess, which would explain her incredible belief of love for him.

Constantine turned around slowly, saying nothing. He glanced at the stairs before he turned to Tristan and Raphael. Tristan took one look at his face and shot him a bewildered look. "What the hell is wrong now?"

"Wrong? Nothing."

Over the centuries Constantine had know many forms of rage and suffered unimaginable pain. What he'd never had was a moment of perfect happiness. Although now was not one of those times, it came damn close. Right then was as close as he'd ever dared to dream.

Smiling, Constantine cocked a brow at Tristan. Just when he was about to answer Tristan, Raphael let out a loud whistle of surprise. "Holy shit. Is that a smile, C?"

"Shut the hell up, Rogue," Constantine snapped, the smile gone as fast as it had come.

When Constantine looked toward the stairs again, he inhaled, taking in the sweet scent of honeysuckle. "I'm going with her to England. The First is going to work her shit and this is all going to be over." The finality in his tone brooked no argument from Tristan and Raphael. "She's mine and I protect what's mine."

With one sentence, Constantine had claimed Lex more powerfully than any bonding ritual could.

Tristan stepped up to him and clapped Constantine on the shoulder. "Then that's it, Dragon. You go and you bring her back to us. Do you understand me? Don't let her slip away."

"Like I said, I protect what's mine." Constantine turned and crossed the hall to the stairs. As he followed the scent of honeysuckle to Lex's chamber, he spoke to God.

"You gave her to me and I mean to keep her, so You better not take her from me."

Chapter Fourteen

At the sharp knock at her door, Lex didn't even bother to get up. Her muffled "come in" was said into her pillow. She assumed it was Allie coming in to give her the usual "older sister spiel", which was why, when the door opened and no Allie was forthcoming, Lex sat up to see who it was.

Her heart slammed against her ribcage at the sight of Constantine filling the doorway. As much as her mortification reached epic heights while he stood silently staring at her, she was glad he'd followed her. It meant he cared. Didn't it? Or was she just reading more into his recent behavior than was healthy? Whichever it was, Lex was still glad he was here.

"What are you doing here? Come to point and laugh at the silly girl who just made an ass out of herself with her wayward thoughts?"

He shook his head, his expression, for once, not unreadable. In fact, the shock on Constantine's was almost comical. "You can't mean it."

"Oh Lord, I don't want to talk about this."

"Neither do I."

That surprised the hell out of Lex. She stood cautiously, as if trapped in a room with a wild animal. By the look on Constantine's face, she had the feeling she wasn't too off the mark. One sudden move and she had the distinct impression he'd pounce on her.

Not that she'd have any problem with Constantine doing some pouncing. Given how pissed he looked, she didn't know if it would be the *good* kind of pouncing or the sort that would make her wish she'd locked her door to keep him out.

"If you don't want to make fun of me and you don't want to talk about my little bomb, then what are you doing here?"

Though Lex thought it impossible for him to frown any deeper, Constantine proved her wrong. "I don't bloody know why the fuck I'm here."

Like the demanding, and sometimes annoyingly arrogant, warrior he was, Constantine walked right up to her and yanked her into his arms. When she slammed against him, Lex knew what it meant to be manhandled.

She didn't have a chance to protest—not that she would—before he brought his face close to hers. For a moment she thought Constantine was going to kiss her, but he didn't and a momentary stab of regret pierced her.

"I'm not leaving."

His tone suggested that was a warning and not an announcement. Warning or no, it left Lex was a bit breathless. "I'm glad."

He bared his fangs. This close, Lex saw just how lethal they were. Yet every time he kissed her, never once had he hurt her with them. His control astounded her.

But then, everything about Constantine was tightly controlled rage and power. His body was a work of art, from his tattoos to his scars. They were marks of his life—and his death. The thick cords of muscle that moved under his pale flesh were a testimony to his discipline as a warrior. She couldn't begin to imagine what it had taken to hone his body into the fine weapon it was.

"I can't be around you without wanting to bury myself in you."

That healthy does of honesty ignited a fire in Lex that burned its way through her entire being. "Then stop denying us both. I can't make it any clearer, or easier on you than that."

Pride be damned, Lex laid herself out for his taking. Now— she just hoped he'd take it and stop torturing them both.

"You've no bloody idea what you'll be inviting into your body."

That statement spoke volumes to Lex and it broke her heart. How could Constantine think so lowly of himself? No matter what'd done in his life, or what he'd done after, God loved him enough to give him a second chance. Didn't that mean anything to him? Didn't it mean anything that *she* loved him?

And, oh God, how she loved him.

Lex placed her hands on his cheeks. "Don't I?" She dropped her hands and placed them on his chest. It was high time she gave him back that same raw honesty. "I think it's you who doesn't know me. I'm not the delicate flower you all treat me as. I'm a woman, Constantine, and I know what I want. And what I want is you."

The expression of shock Constantine had worn before was replaced by a beautiful play of emotions as he fought a battle with himself to either leave or take what she so blatantly offered him.

For a moment Lex expected Constantine to leave and a stab of disappointment pierced her. She knew that if he left her, he wouldn't just be leaving her chamber. He'd be leaving *her.*

When his mouth came down on hers, there wasn't a shred of tenderness in his kiss. Instead, it was a brutal, almost punishing, joining of their mouths as he showed her exactly what manner of man he was. Not that Lex needed the reminder. She knew Constantine wasn't a gentle man. She expected things to be a bit—rough—with him. Given who he was, she didn't think otherwise.

Stepping up on her tiptoes, Lex pressed her body against Constantine's as her hands ran over his back. His lips were unyielding, demanding, and when she sighed into his mouth she felt him inhale it. There was something extremely erotic about that. His tongue moved over hers hesitantly and Lex realized he was struggling to be careful with his fangs. When he brought them into play, they added a certain amount of danger to his kiss.

Hoping Constantine wasn't going to bring this to an abrupt end, Lex melted into him. She wanted to touch all of him, know every inch of his body, but there was so much of him she didn't know where to start. His size scared her just a little and she prayed he couldn't sense it since she knew he'd probably stop if he did.

When she trailed her hands down his back and came to settle on his ass, he hissed. She squeezed and he growled. She pulled him closer and he tore his mouth away. That was definitely not the reaction Lex was expecting.

"I shouldn't have come here."

Was he joking? He wasn't going to start that again. He wanted to be here. She wanted him here and she was going to fight to make him realize he was being foolish in resisting what was between them.

He set her aside and went to leave. By a will of its own, her hand settled on his arm. He stopped dead, his gaze fixed on the door. "You can't keep doing this to me, Constantine. You can't keep playing me like this. One second you want me, the next you can't wait to be rid of me. I mean, my God, my pride can only take so much."

Cursing, Constantine turned and pinned her with a glare. "You've no idea of the things I want to do to you."

"No, I don't." She ran her hand through his hair, not an easy task given their height differences. "But I can't make it any clearer that I'm not afraid to find out." Something warned her he still might flee, which was why Lex decided to play dirty. "Besides, they can't be half as nasty as the things I imagine you doing to me."

Right then Lex knew she had him.

The look that darkened Constantine's eyes caused her heart to race. Liquid heat poured through her when he brought his mouth close to her ear and whispered the most wicked things. Heat settled between her legs. In the wake of the warmth came wetness, which brought the ache of emptiness.

"I won't give you a gentle ride."

God, she hoped not. "If I wanted gentle I wouldn't be here with you."

The intensity in the silvery depths of his eyes cut Lex right to her core. "If I stay I'm taking this to the end."

She smiled at the thought of him being the one to show her the wonders of her body. "You'd better."

"You're mine, Lexine" he gritted out between his fangs. "No other man will ever put his hands on you but me." He fisted his hand in her hair and pulled it so she was forced to arch her neck. "Say it. Tell me you're mine."

She tilted her head back so she could meet his searching gaze. "I'm yours, Constantine. Always."

He pushed her away and ripped his shirt off. He closed his eyes when Lex's fingers lingered on the puckered scar over his heart before moving to the two angels tattooed on his pectorals. She'd never had the opportunity to see them up close, so this was the first time she was able to see their incredible details.

As she examined him, Lex felt a stab of shyness when, unbidden, the thought of how many women came before her invaded her mind. How could she hope to compare to the women he had known prior to her? The closest she'd ever come to sex was his kisses. Before that, she'd only ever held a man's hand—and that was years ago. The voices had prevented her from dabbling in the sexual side of life and right now, as she stood on the verge of losing her virginity to a man who'd been around for ages, she was unsure of herself.

She stopped looking at the tattoos and met his steady gaze. "I'm afraid I'm going to disappoint you."

"You couldn't disappoint me, Lex."

The way he said her name gave her chills. "You do realize how little experience I've had in this department, don't you?" He nodded. "So, that means I've no idea what you expect of me."

He ran his hand over her hair while his other wrapped around her waist. He dragged her against him, forcing her to tilt her head back to look up at him. "I expect nothing of you. All I want from you is to enjoy what I'm going to do to your body."

If he weren't holding her, Lex would have crumbled to the floor.

She swallowed past a throat gone dry. "Sounds like a plan," she shot back lightly, even as a rush of emotions and anticipation ran through her.

With a growl, he pulled at her clothes. "I want these off. Now."

Well now, who was she to gainsay such a demand?

129

She watched as Constantine kicked off his boots expectantly. When he removed his pants she dared a glance down and nearly tripped over her own feet as shock slammed into her. Good God, the man was tremendous. She had to remind herself that he wasn't going to tear her apart. After all, she knew the basic mechanics of sex and was fairly certain her body would stretch to accommodate him. Still, the thought of all of *that* in her sent a shiver of expectancy and dread down her spine.

When she realized she was standing there staring at him, Lex moved her gaze to the tattoos decorating his left thigh. Up her gaze went, traveling leisurely up his body. The sight of all that flesh and those hard planes of muscle rendered Lex dumb. She couldn't help but stare in fascination as she took in his powerful body.

At her lack of action, Constantine stepped in and all but tore her shirt from her. The flimsy material of her white bra did nothing to shield her from his greedy gaze. Lex had no sense of shyness. How could she when he seemed to appreciate the sight of her?

With a flick of his fingers, Constantine popped open the button of her jeans. He ran his knuckles along the line of her white panties. His light touch tickled her. When she giggled he smiled and Lex nearly melted. Constantine had such an amazing smile. Too bad he hardly used it. That was something Lex hoped to remedy.

When he tickled her again, Lex gave him a shot to the arm. "Stop that. I'm really ticklish."

He cocked a brow. "The first lesson of war is never to let your opponent know your weakness."

"So, we're at war, are we?"

Constantine's smile lacked emotion. Lex mimicked his cocked brow. "There is a fine line between love and war, didn't you know that?"

All playfulness fled her. "But we both know you don't love me."

In answer, Constantine grunted and went to push down her jeans. Honestly, she hadn't expected him to declare his love for her. Why she was crushed that he hadn't was beyond her.

Since she'd already removed her shoes, she held on to Constantine's shoulders and stepped out of the jeans. He kicked them aside as if they were most offensive things in the world. When he pushed her backward, onto the bed, and climbed on top of her, Lex loved how her energy had given warmth back to his body. As her hands moved up his back, she reveled in his warm flesh. When she reached his hair, she buried her hands in it and brought his mouth to hers for a kiss.

With the ease of a man who knew exactly how to strip a woman of her clothing, Constantine opened her bra. Lex sucked in a breath when he cupped her bare breasts. His fingers moved over her nipples, hardening them. She arched into his touch, wanting all of him—everything he had to give. And then she wanted more. Looking up into his face, Lex marveled at the intensity of his expression. This wasn't a casual joining of two people. By the look of him this was so much more. This was Constantine accepting not just her body, but her love as well.

Constantine met her steady gaze, his eyes burning with fire he struggled to hold back. "I won't hurt you."

She smiled just before she released a small gasp when he gently rolled her nipple between his fingers. "I know."

"We're going to do this nice and slow. I'm going to work your body until I make you mine in every way."

Well now, if that wasn't a promise of pleasure Lex didn't know what was. "I don't know what to do."

"Relax, elf. Just let yourself feel what I'm doing to you."

Lex did exactly that. As Constantine lowered his head to her and trailed kisses from her neck to her breasts, she squeezed her eyes closed and enjoyed the feel of his lips and tongue on her.

The flick of his tongue over her nipple had Lex sucking in a sharp breath. She grabbed fistfuls of his hair and moaned as his mouth played over breasts.

"Oh God..."

"Not God. Say it," he demanded roughly as he continued his assault on her breasts. *"Say my name."*

She hadn't even been aware she'd put that in Constantine's mind until he answered her. Oh Lord, the things he was doing to her with his mouth had her letting go of his hair only to fist her hands in the sheets. She pulled on them as he laved her flesh.

"Constantine," she whispered.

Somehow Lex managed to get Constantine's name past her lips as his mouth left her breast and worked down her stomach. She tensed when he worked her panties off. Tensed even more when his hand moved to the junction of her thighs. Lex ground out a throaty moan and arched her back when his fingers stroked her intimately. Funny how she felt comfortable with his face being so close to part of her body she herself barely acknowledged.

Everything about being with Constantine felt right, the silence of the voices in her head was proof of that. This—what she was sharing with him—was meant to be. She realized this, even if Constantine didn't.

When his tongue touched her, Lex couldn't stop her squeal of shock. The play of his fingers and tongue had her panting and moaning as she writhed on bed. In answer, Constantine let out a *very* masculine grunt of satisfaction.

Constantine thought he was going to die all over again at the taste of her. Lex was molten honey on his tongue. After knowing nothing but blood for hundreds of years, he savored her, taking his time as he drank her in.

The higher she arched off the bed, the more he realized how close he was to spilling himself even before he slid his body into hers.

Her power thundered through him, electrifying him. Warming him. Giving Constantine's body the remembrance of life—even if just for a short while. It made his entire being burn for her and moved him that much closer to losing control.

Tearing his mouth away from her, Constantine moved up Lex's body. As he went, he teased her flesh with his mouth, loving the way she pressed into his touch. When he covered her, he stared down into her flushed face. Never had he seen a woman look as beautiful as Lex did just then. With her lips parted, eyes hooded and cheeks flushed, he put the sight to memory—knowing he would need it to help get him through the centuries.

When Lex took hold of him by wrapping her arms around his neck, Constantine lowered his head and kissed her for all he was worth. He needed to keep her just like this—soft and compliant—in order to make the loss of her virginity go as smoothly and as painlessly as possible.

"Are you ready, elf?" he asked when he released her mouth.

She nodded and he positioned himself against the opening of her body. Constantine grabbed her leg and lifted it to his hips, his fingers biting into her thigh as he held it right where he wanted it. The wet heat of her guided him in. Her body stretched around him as the rest of her stiffened at his assault.

Constantine hissed and dropped his forehead down on Lex's, dragging in hard, rasping breaths purely on instinct. He closed his eyes; unable to look at the raw passion etched on Lex's face without losing what small hold he had on his control. Instead, all he could do was grit his teeth and push gently into her, taking care to not cause her too much pain.

He ground his teeth together and forced himself not to push fully into her warmth, as his body ached to do. It took all of his restraint to keep himself from driving hard into her and taking what she willingly offered.

Her gasp as he drove into her tore through him. "Oh God, Lex, I'm so fucking sorry."

He reached the barrier of her virginity as her pain rolled over him. He knew he had no right to be the man to take her innocence. He was sin incarnate and she was everything beautiful and pure. His past came back to him as she whimpered beneath him. He remembered, with a clarity that blinded him to all else, lying facedown on a bed making much the same sounds as his body was invaded.

He couldn't do this to Lex. He couldn't take her purity from her. Before he moved further into her and broke through the thin veil that marked her as untouched, Constantine began to inch out. Lex, however, had other ideas. She slapped her hands on his ass and used what strength she possessed to hold him inside of her.

"No, Constantine, please don't stop."

"I have to, Lex."

She lifted her hips, forcing him in even deeper. The tip of him pushed against her virginity. She cried out at the pain her movement caused. "Make me yours."

Feeling her urgency, Constantine pressed forward. In that moment, nothing mattered but the two of them. Not the past, or the future. All of his memories faded under the glow of her love and the offering of her body. As he strained to refrain from driving into her warmth, Constantine knew he was as close to loving anyone as he'd ever come.

Thank you for her.

How could he not thank God for the gift he was about to receive? Her innocence chased away his sins when he felt the resistance of her virginity. Gritting his teeth, he gave a hard thrust forward. Her virginity broke and he slid into her to his hilt. Her cry echoed through the chamber, flooding his mind as he fought not to feel like a fucking monster.

Jesus Christ, nothing had ever felt as good as being inside of Lex. Nothing cleansed him of his past like her love. And nothing had ever brought him this close to Heaven as the look on Lex's face.

As soon as he was deep inside of her, he stopped. Giving her body time to adjust to him was one of the hardest things he'd ever done. With her tightness squeezing him and her wet heat surrounding him, his body screamed to pump into that warmth.

"Are you okay?"

Her smile was beautiful, and hid the pain he knew she had to be in. His amazing woman was trying so hard to be brave for him. "I'm okay."

Lex's racing heart slammed against his chest and her breathing was coming in gasps. He sensed no fear in her as her body began to relax. Her muscles loosened and he inched out of her. She grabbed at him again and tried to hold him in.

"Don't worry, elf. I'm not going anywhere."

He couldn't leave her even if he wanted to. He'd waited lifetimes to be here, in this moment, with her. Constantine just hadn't realized that fact until now.

When he moved, Lex sucked in a sharp breath. It took all of his control not to thrust into her with the force his body craved. He had to test her body first, make sure she was ready to take him as he needed her to. Each time he slid out of her she shivered, and when he thrust forward, Lex moaned. Her energy surged into him, lighting him up from the inside out. It caused his control to snap.

As much as Constantine wanted to be gentle with Lex, he couldn't. Unlike with other women, he had no control with Lex. And that scared him, but even so, he still couldn't stop.

As he drove into her, Lex clung to him, her soft moans filling the room, mixing with his guttural sounds as sensations he'd never felt exploded within him.

"You still with me?"

"Uh huh."

"Am I hurting you?"

"Not any more."

So, Lex was right—she was tougher than he'd thought. "Good. Because I'm going to take you for one hell of a ride."

Constantine teased her with the tip of his cock and his mouth came down on hers In response, Lex arched and moaned, causing his control to slip a little further. The warmth of her pulled deep groans from him as he inched himself back in, prolonging the sensation as much as possible.

He'd never known sex could be like this, something amazing and not just two bodies slapping together. Lex touched him, begged for more of him with every movement of her gorgeous body and every sweet moan torn from her. She made him feel like a man—one who wasn't scarred from a past full of disgrace. He felt...blessed.

Lex didn't merely open her body to him. Her mind was open to him as well. Constantine was getting all of her thoughts and they were driving him to madness. He knew what she was thinking and what she was feeling. A lesser man would be shocked at what she imagined him doing to her.

His woman, it seemed, had an imagination that rivaled his own.

Lex's soft touch as she stroked his back soothed him, keeping away the worst of his memories. It pulled him further away from his past, which brought him closer to her. Pleasure built within him as the burden of past pain faded. The beauty of Lex replaced the ugliness of his living years as he stroked her body. Her breathy sighs replaced the echo of his own screams as her body throbbed around him, squeezing him as she climaxed. It heightened the power inside of her and flowed through him like a warm wave. He'd never thought to feel the like and it humbled him. Bloody hell, did it ever humble him.

He marveled at the play of pleasure on Lex's face. Good God, she was a sight to behold in her ecstasy. With her lips parted, her body arched, and the clear blue of her eyes sparkling with unshed tears, Lex whispered to him brokenly as she soared to heights she'd never been. And not without a certain degree of male satisfaction, he had to admit he loved her reactions.

Unable to hold back any longer, Constantine spilled himself into her. His climax seemed to go on forever as her power pulsated around him, causing him to experience a whole other level of pleasure. It took nearly a thousand years and the gentle touch of one blue-eyed beauty, but he'd finally learned what ecstasy was.

Though moving off of her was the last thing Constantine wanted to do, he knew his weight had to be crushing her. He eased out of Lex, biting back a groan as he did so. He collapsed facedown next to her. She lay beside him on her back, eyes closed, breathing erratic as her energy vibrated throughout the room.

For once, Constantine didn't hold himself back or question his reason when he rolled onto his back and stretched his arm out to Lex. Nor did he stop his smile when she sidled up next to him and rested her head on his shoulder. Constantine stared up at the ceiling, wishing he could hold on to this moment forever.

He wanted to keep *Lex* with him forever.

As Constantine lay with one of the purest souls God ever released into the world, he prayed for Him to keep Lex safe and to forgive him for daring to need the innocence of her to erase the stain of his past. He prayed to God to give him the ability to love her as she deserved to be loved. When he felt Lex's hand come to rest on the scar over his heart, Constantine dared to hope God was listening.

Chapter Fifteen

November 1295

Morning dawned brutally cold despite the fact that the sun shone in the clear winter sky. The day was crisp and clear, the rain having broken after the drenching of the last weeks. Yet despite the pleasant day, Constantine's mood was dark as he rode away from Draegon Castle.

Greaves Castle, though a handful of miles away from Draegon, seemed much further today. Truth was, after all he'd heard about Ulric Chambers, Constantine had the distinct feeling he was riding right into Hell.

Clothed in little more than rags, Constantine shivered beneath his threadbare cloak as they rode across the flat Wiltshire. He gripped the reins of the feeble brown mare, the oldest and sickliest horse in his father's stable, with trembling hands. Constantine wondered if it was from cold or from fear. He gave it some thought, since there was nothing to do but think, and realized it was a mix of both.

Beside him was Sir Walter. The gray-haired knight had always treated Constantine as kindly as he was allowed to, living in Henry Draegon's hall. It wasn't much, but it was enough to help get Constantine through some of the more brutal of nights.

No relief was to be found, as Constantine had hoped leaving Draegon Castle would bring him. Instead, all he felt was a sense of impending doom as he rode closer toward the unknown awaiting him at Greaves Castle.

Ulric Chambers.

The foul man's name echoed in Constantine's mind as he neared Greaves Castle. He found no shame in his fear. Given the whispers he'd heard throughout his father's garrison over the last weeks, Constantine knew he had reason to be afraid.

Most of what he'd heard, Constantine hadn't understood. All he knew was that the man had to be most sinful since some of the soldiers went so far as to cross themselves after saying Chamber's name. Some even spit in the dirt as if to rid themselves of the poison of his name from their tongue.

"You cold, boy?"

Brought out of his somber thoughts by Sir Walter's question, Constantine shook his head curtly. "No, Sir."

He knew there was no need to lie to Sir Walter. The man had already proven his kindness by secretly offering him comfort when no other dared. Still, Constantine could not bring himself to admit weakness. Some lessons he'd learned from his father he'd never forget. Never showing or admitting weakness was one such lesson.

"Here. Put it on, son." Sir Walter removed his heavy woolen cloak and tossed it to him. "I know you're cold."

With hurried hands Constantine wrapped the large cloak around his shivering body, grateful for the warmth it provided. He'd not forget this unselfish gesture.

The old, grizzled knight stared at him for the longest time. Constantine grew uneasy under the intensity of his gaze. Sir Walter narrowed his gaze and shook his head. "It was foul business if you ask me."

"What say you?"

"To sell you to that prick of man is inexcusable."

The knight's anger was apparent and it shocked Constantine. No one dared speak out against Henry Draegon. Ever. To do so was suicide. Obviously Sir Walter cared not, for he shook his head again and spat on the ground.

Constantine had nothing to say to that. He didn't dare voice his agreement, nor could he defend his sire's actions. His father had sold him to a most depraved man, and though Constantine was still unsure what awaited him at Greaves, it couldn't be any worse than what he'd already suffered at Draegon.

"Heed me now, boy." Constantine gave Sir Walter his full attention. "Whatever happens during your time at Greaves remember, you are never to blame yourself. You may wish to be a man full grown, but the truth of it is, you're still but a boy. You're not ready to take on a man yet, but the time will come when you will be strong enough to defeat even the greatest knight. I know this. I see the power in you. When that day comes, you swear it to me that you will do whatever you can to free yourself from Chambers. You get as far away from Greaves as you can and never look back." He heaved out a great sigh, his breath making smoke as it mingled with the frigid air. "What happens at Greaves, you leave it there. Do you understand me, son? You leave that evil behind."

Constantine swallowed past the lump of dread that formed in his throat. "I'll leave it behind."

"Swear it to me, boy."

"I swear."

Walter looked none too relieved to have his oath. "May God be with you, Constantine."

Sir Walter spoke just as they reached the peak of the hill they were climbing. Greaves Castle came into view and Constantine's heart sank. The sinister stone fortress rose up from a courtyard enclosed by an impregnable wall. Something warned Constantine it would keep him in as much as it would keep Chambers' enemies out.

As they passed through the gatehouse, manned by four sentries, Sir Walter's words echoed in his mind. They continued to haunt Constantine for the rest of his days at Greaves Castle.

Chapter Sixteen

Lex packed a suitcase with meticulous care, carefully cramming in all she would need to take with her to England. The plans had been arranged last night. Tristan and Briana Kerr had done it all over the phone while Lex and Constantine had been—otherwise occupied.

Just before dawn, Tristan found them in Lex's chamber and explained the details of the plan to get them both to England. From what he'd said, it was going to be a day of traveling that would begin at dawn end sometime the next morning. Most of Constantine's journey would take place with him sealed in a sunlight-proof crate. The same one, he explained, he'd come to America in. The idea of him traveling in a coffin-like crate didn't sit well with Lex to say the least—even if she did grasp the importance of such a thing.

Kerr was going to be sending human bodyguards to pick Lex up in the morning. From what Tristan said, they were going to be glued to her side from the moment they left the Seacrest until they reached Lowel Castle in Wiltshire.

Once Tristan told them the plan, Constantine had gone with him when he left. With the sun taking over the night sky, he'd needed to retreat to the safety of his own chamber. Lex would have gladly gone with him, but he hadn't asked and she hadn't offered. Besides, there was much she had needed to do today and not much time to get it done. So, with one last hard kiss, he left her. Lex was about ready to go to sleep when Allie came bursting in a moment later.

Allie gave her a fierce hug and a kiss to the forehead before she was forced to race from the room lest she be caught by the rays of the coming dawn. Once alone, Lex climbed into bed, not even bothering to put clothes on. She curled into a tight ball beneath the covers and wept with fear and hopelessness ripped from the depths of her soul.

When she woke sometime in the early afternoon, Lex had a better handle on her emotions. She showered and dressed before going to the kitchen to grab something to eat. Since it was Friday, Anne wasn't home. Today was her weekly trip to town to run errands. Alone, as she usually was during the day, Lex went back to her room to begin packing for their trip. She doubted she'd come back from this journey.

As Lex packed, she was oddly calm. In between her memories of last night and the thorough way Constantine had rid her of her virginity, she came to accept her inevitable death. She could handle death, since she more or less knew what might come after. Heaven. Peace. Seeing Christian. Those were not things to be feared, but anticipated. It was leaving behind Allie, Constantine and the other Templars that had tears running rivulets down her cheeks as she folded her clothes and laid them in the suitcase.

Also, the possibility of being transformed into pure energy wasn't one Lex was looking forward to. She'd rather meet her death than face such a fate. But that was something she couldn't think of now. If she did she'd lose herself to her fear, and she couldn't afford to let happen. There would be time enough in the coming weeks to wallow in fear.

Since they were leaving early in the morning, doing most of the ground travel by day to avoid confrontations with any renegades who might track them, Lex didn't have time to prepare. Knowing this night might be the last one she had with them, Lex wanted to spend as much of it with her family as possible.

With night creeping ever closer, Lex wondered if Constantine was awake yet. If he was, she wished he'd talk to her. She was lonely, and after last night, a bit unsure of herself.

Constantine had been true to his word and given her one hell of a ride. Her body was sore today, making her feel like nine miles of bad road, but it had been well worth it. The things Constantine had done with her and the way he made her feel, Lex had almost been able to imagine what being loved by him would be like. Almost.

Today, the harsh light of reality chased away any fanciful musings. Though she loved him, Lex suffered no delusions about Constantine returning the sentiment. He wasn't the sort of man who could give his heart away. Oh, she knew he liked her well enough. But love? She wasn't going to fool herself into believing Constantine felt the same. To go down that road would leave her devastated in the end. Lex had enough to worry about without adding to it by trying to fight that losing battle.

Lex finished packing and realized there wasn't anything left for her to do until the next morning. After she showered and got ready to go, some last minute items would get packed. Tristan had assured her the Order would provide anything else she might need once she got to England.

The thought of being surrounded by the formidable women of the Order of the Rose terrified her. After all the things the Templars had said about them, Lex wasn't looking forward to spending the coming weeks in the home of Isobel of Lowel, who'd held the castle for more centuries than Lex was comfortable contemplating.

They were to stay at Lowel Castle until Halloween—or Samhain as Tristan referred to it. On that night the First would join them at the castle and perform the ritual that might (and the "might" was stressed a bit too much for Lex's peace of mind) save her from either being transformed into a being of energy or killed.

At the knock at her door, Lex glanced at the window. There was no need to have a repeat incident of a nearly fried vampire. She walked to the door, hoping it was Constantine, but not expecting it to be. After all, he'd been silent in her mind all day. True, he'd probably slept most of the day, but he was known to torment her more often than not by "talking" to her throughout the day while shut away in his chamber.

Lex had the distinct impression he liked having someone to talk to as a means to help get through the long day. It hadn't taken her long after she came to live here to realize Constantine passed much of the days drifting in and out of sleep. When he woke, he'd talk to her, his voice a resounding rumble in her mind, until he fell back to sleep. She liked when he talked to her, or rather, she did most of the talking and Constantine did most of the listening. Lex had the feeling that his nightmares tormented him while he slept, which was why he never stayed asleep for too long. And, she had an even better feeling that her talking to him helped to chase away whatever memories haunted his dreams.

When she pulled open the door and saw it was Constantine, Lex was more than mildly surprised to see him. She was downright shocked.

He looked gorgeous as usual, dressed in black, with one of his signature sarcastic tees on—this one read, *Crazy enough to kill (smart enough to get away with it)*. She wondered if he owned any pants that didn't have chains hanging from them. Not that she minded, since his Goth-god get-ups suited him perfectly.

His hair was damp and messy, the glossy black of it such a sharp contrast to his pale complexion. The way he was staring at her made her ache to throw her arms around him. Instead she settled for a shyly whispered "hello."

Lex was pleasantly shocked when Constantine grabbed her and pulled her into his arms. His chin came to rest on the top of her head. "You're well?"

Constantine's concern touched her. "I'm fine."

Lex sighed and melted into him when he began to stroke her hair. "I was...worried."

Though she hadn't known Constantine for that long, Lex knew it must have taken much for him to admit such to her. Anger, he was good at. The more tender of emotions? Not so much.

"I'm just a little achy. Other than that, I feel fine."

"That's not what I was worried about."

Lex pulled away from him and frowned. "Then what else... Oh." He meant the business about the Daystar. "I'm dealing with it." She turned and moved back to the bed. She didn't realize Constantine followed her until his back pressed against her and his arms came around her. He took hold of her hands, stopping her from lifting the suitcase.

"I've got it."

He stepped away and Lex wanted to drag him right back to where he'd been. He set the suitcase on the floor before giving her his full attention. Lex bristled under the intensity of his stare and looked away. When he placed a finger under her chin and forced her gaze back to his face, she chewed her bottom lip. She hated his blank expression and wished he'd betray a hint of what was going on in his mind.

"After last night I'm surprised you're in one piece."

Oh, he was a cocky one, wasn't he? Although, he was right, Lex grudgingly admitted. "So am I."

"I didn't mean to be so rough with you, but I don't know any other way."

That sounded an awful lot like an apology, or as close to one as Constantine might get. Lex was having none of that since there was nothing to apologize for. He'd been as careful with her as was physically possible. "I told you last night that I was tougher than I look and I meant it."

His black brows drew together in a frown as he sniffed at the air around her. "Then why the fuck do I smell blood on you."

Lex swore she turned about seven shades of red. How could he smell that? She'd taken a shower when she first woke and saw blood smeared on her thighs. She'd been expecting that, since she knew virgins bled. Such a happening was simply a fact of life, especially given how—large—Constantine was. "I hate those vampire senses of yours. Not to mention the telepathy."

Ignoring her declaration, Constantine grabbed her by the arms and dragged her to him. He leaned in close and gave her a good sniff. "Why didn't you tell me I'd hurt you?"

"It was inevitable, Constantine." He gave her a furious glare, as if she had deliberately withheld some bit of vital information from him. When he didn't grasp her meaning, Lex let out a dramatic sigh. "I was a virgin and virgins bleed the first time. Didn't you know that?"

Now how the fuck would he have known that? He knew nothing of virgins other than to avoid them at all costs. So no, he'd not realized *all* virgins bled. He wouldn't have touched her if he'd known that.

His insides twisted sickly knowing he'd hurt her. He might be a mean son of-bitch, but when it came to Lex things were— different. *He* was different. "Was there much blood?"

"No. Not much at all."

Constantine knew her lie for what it was. Lex couldn't lie worth a damn. One of these days he'd have to tell her of that fact—but not yet. For now, he liked being able to tell her bullshit from the truth.

As much as he tried not to imagine it, he was nearly put low by the vision of her virgin's blood. It made him remember those nights when his own legs had been smeared with blood and his cries muffled in his hands as he fought to be strong—as he fought to be a dragon.

Lex's chamber dissolved around him and Constantine was back at Greaves Castle. Once again, he was a scared boy cowering in the corner. His body broken and his soul destroyed, in those desperate moments after he'd suffered the worst of atrocities.

Though centuries separated then and now, Constantine still smelled Chambers' rank breath. That bastard's clammy touch was still on him. If he could he'd go back in time and kill the bastard all over again.

"Constantine?"

The memory vanished when his gaze settled on Lex. She reached out and ran her hands over his bare arms. Her energy shot through him, warming him. "I'm fine, Lex."

Fine. Hell, Constantine hadn't been fine since he was old enough to realize his own parents couldn't stomach him. Yet,

Lex seemed to like him. She even claimed to love him, and as hard as it was for *him* to believe such a thing, he knew *she* believed it.

If he were being honest with himself, he liked her right back. For once in his existence, Constantine wished he knew how to love.

Last night he'd laid claim to Lex and Constantine would dare anyone to try to take her from him—even God.

When she went up on her tiptoes and ran her fingers across his forehead, Constantine had to fight against the need to close his eyes and lean into her gentle touch.

"Are you ever going to tell me what goes on in your head?"

"Trust me, Lex, you don't want my thoughts. Hell, I don't even want them."

Lex trailed her fingers down his scar. Instinctively, Constantine wanted to pull away but didn't. He hated the scar. Hated everything it reminded him of. "I won't demand you tell me about your past." She placed a feather-light kiss on his lips and he could have sworn his heart kicked a single beat. "But I hope the time will come when you trust me enough to confide in me."

Constantine doubted the night would ever come when he shared his shame with her. He couldn't bear for her to know the things he'd lived through—the things he'd been too weak to prevent. She could never know what had gone on within the walls of Greaves Castle. Those were his own dark demons and he'd not have her suffer them as well.

As much as Constantine wanted to believe he kissed Lex to distract him from his memories, the truth was, he kissed her because he couldn't resist the invitation of her lips. When she'd touched her mouth to his tenderly, it had whetted his appetite for more.

The soft sigh she breathed into his mouth when he put his arms around her was music to him. She wrapped her arms around his waist and held him tightly, as if the very last thing she wanted was to ever let him go.

As his body grew hard for her and the scent of Lex's desire filled him, Constantine knew if he didn't stop this he'd slip past the edge of reason and take her again. Her body wouldn't be able to handle him twice in two nights. The lingering scent of blood convinced him of that.

Constantine went to pull away but Lex stopped him by tightening her hold on him. "No," she whispered. "Don't go."

"Lex, we can't do this now. *You* can't."

"Yes we can." She let go of his waist and fisted both hands in his hair. She pulled his head down to hers and kissed him for all she was worth.

Her passion pushed Constantine to his breaking point. He needed her so badly that if Michael himself stepped between them, he'd battle the archangel for this time alone with her.

Needed. Not wanted. He was well past wanting Lex. His need for her transcended anything and everything. She was his and he'd damn well show her what it meant to be his woman.

It was a long while before they joined the others in the hall, and when they finally made it down, Constantine had done exactly as he'd set out to do. He left no doubt in Lex's mind just what it meant to be loved by a dragon.

CRSO

The Hallowed was coming to England.

What an unexpected, and most welcome, turn of events.

To celebrate this news, Julian had retreated to the tower room. The chamber was where he committed his most depraved acts. Here, no sunlight would touch him since he'd long since stoned the arrow-slit windows closed. The protection from the rays of the sun allowed him to continue on with his pleasures long after day broke. Eyeing the naked female, chained and cowering in the corner, he smiled as he contemplated all the ways he'd use her to sate his needs and expend his joy at this fortuitous turn of events.

Toying with his cell phone—dreadful things, phones, even if they did serve their purpose—Julian reclined on the bed. He watched the young woman, frail in her humanity and exquisite in her fear, weeping softly. He'd rather not have to kill her so soon after finding her, but he'd already been rather rough with her and he knew she wouldn't be able to take much more.

And he had much planned for her this night.

With the news that Lexine was coming to Wiltshire, the tension plaguing Julian for the last weeks dissolved. That the girl was leaving the fold of the Templars pleased him greatly, even if he still had many obstacles to overcome to gain possession of her. At least she'd be here, where he'd be a stone's throw away from her at any given time.

Of course, Constantine Draegon would be with her, but one Templar was no match for ten renegades. The infamous, and much feared, Dragon would fall beneath the might of Julian's men and he would drain the Hallowed to her last drop. And then he'd be unstoppable and crush any vampires who dared to try and stand in his way as he brought mankind to heel.

As much as he was loath to admit it, he'd have never gotten this far without the aid of his lover. She'd risked all to deliver to him information over the years.

Never one to take an unnecessary risk, the threat of failure was always a possibility and Julian made sure there were others willing to clean up any mess she might make of things. After all, she did so like to please him and in her haste there were times when she'd come dangerously close to being discovered.

When the girl shifted upon the icy floor, Julian was brought back to the present and his body hardened at the sight of her smooth flesh streaked with blood. He'd already tasted her and wanted more. Wanted all of her until he took all she had to give. And then he'd take more.

He'd take her soul and prevent her from going to God.

Julian reveled in what he'd become. He'd never shied away from the things he'd had to do to in order to survive. He wondered how he'd suffered all the years of his life bowing down in servitude to a God he'd stopped believing in long before he gave himself to the night.

There was a time when Julian was a devoted follower of the Christian God. A monk, he'd lived in a time even before the Templars and he'd worshipped God when most of the world still prayed to sheep and sacrificed humans. By the time he'd reached the age of three and twenty, he'd given up on a God who allowed His children to be slaughtered by the creatures that dwelled in the shadows of the night.

He'd sought out those monsters and begged them to take his life and give him something so much more.

They had. They'd given him eternity.

And now, nine centuries later, Julian stood on the threshold of absolute power. Once he possessed the Daystar's power, he'd take down the powerful Templars and the Order of the Rose. He'd send them to Hell where they belonged and take his place as the leader of the armies of the night.

When Julian moved upon the bed the girl whimpered. How he loved the sound of a human's fear.

He rose from the bed and went to her. The red-haired beauty scrambled across the floor and pressed herself against the damp stone wall. Her blue eyes were filled with dread as he reached out to finger a long, silken lock of her hair. She reminded him of a comely Scottish wench he'd known long ago. The woman's broken prayers, whispered in her thick brogue, put a smile on his lips. His body burned to take her, but he refrained. He wanted to savor this night, for he knew it would be his last with her.

Her long, lean body bore the evidence of his affection for her. His bite marks marred the perfection of her flesh. Purple bruises darkened her thighs where'd he'd held her a bit too roughly as he taken blood from her. The sight of what he'd done to her heightened his need. He was forced to press a hand to his erection as he fought for the control he needed to make it through this night. By the gods, he was close to spilling himself before he was even inside of her.

Given her rapid heartbeat and rasping breaths, the girl knew she was nearing her final hour. He bit back a groan at the spasm of desire that shot through him at the thought of her fear. He licked his lips, remembering the taste of her blood and the feel of it as it slid down his throat.

He stepped to her and wiped a tear from her cheek. Julian brought it to his mouth and licked the salty drop from the tip of his finger, savoring it. She whimpered again and he knew he was lost.

Taking hold of her arm, Julian hauled her up against him. She gasped, too weak to fight him. She wept harder, the sound orgasmic. "That's it, sweetheart. Cry for me."

Like a good girl, she did.

Since the chain attached to the manacle around her ankle was long enough, he didn't have to release her in order to toss her onto the bed. She hit it hard before trying to scramble away. He caught her by the ankles and pulled her down to where he wanted her.

Julian rid himself of his clothes and climbed atop her. He bared his fangs and she let out a piercing cry that fed his sadistic need to hurt her. "I'm going to send you to God. Isn't that what you want? To go home to your Lord?"

The girl shook her head. "I don't want to die."

"None of us do, and yet death comes to take us all."

"Oh God, please don't hurt me anymore."

Julian closed his eyes, his erection painful as she begged for her life. He had to cover her mouth to keep her from saying more. He didn't want to spend himself before he took her. He had to know the feel of her body tightening around him when he came inside of her.

He opened his eyes and took in the exquisite sight of her crying beneath him. "I'm only going to hurt you once more." He leaned down low to whisper in her ear. "Then it will all be over. I'm going to show you your God."

A wrenching cry came from her when Julian removed his hand from her mouth. Her body began to tremble beneath him. He smoothed her glorious mass of red hair away from her face. The sight of her tears was driving him to madness. He'd not be able to last much longer if she continued with her delightful struggles.

He ran a tongue over his fangs and lips, preparing for the pain he was about to cause himself. The agony was always worth it when he played this particular game. It was the ultimate insult to a God Julian no longer had a use for.

"I'm going to show you what happens when Evil prays."

The girl tried to kick out but he easily held her. Her futile fight incited his desire, which was why his cock ached and grew as it pressed against the warm opening of her body.

A smile twisted his lips as he stared down at his victim and Julian began to say the Lord's Prayer.

"Our Father, Who art in Heaven."

The pain came, sharp and intense. He held back a growl as it cut through his mouth and throat.

"Hallowed be Thy name."

Smoke wafted from his mouth as the hallowed words burned his tongue. The back of his throat felt as if molten lava poured down it. His fangs ached as the tissue around them began to bleed.

"Thy kingdom come."

His lips cracked and bled. His palate dripped blood, landing on his tongue to mix with his saliva. It trickled from his mouth and down his chin.

Still, Julian pressed on.

"Thy will be done."

She released a musical scream when the rest of his mouth began to bleed. The blood dripped from his mouth and onto her face and neck. When it dropped into her mouth, she sputtered and tried to spit it out. He smiled, blood filling his mouth at the feel of her struggling for her life beneath him.

"On Earth as it is in Heaven."

The girl scratched and clawed at him, her screams filling his ears sweeter than a chorus of angels. Through a haze of pain he gazed down at the sight of his blood coating her. He groaned and nearly entered her then.

"And forgive us our trespasses."

His tongue and throat were now burnt raw. Blood poured from his mouth. Violent tremors rocked him as agony shot through him. Still, Julian pressed on. He'd finish this. He'd bring this perfect moment to completion.

"As we forgive those who trespass against us."

He thought about forgiveness for a breath of a moment. He'd known it in his life. As a monk he'd lived by all of God's laws. He'd wasted his years abstaining from all of life's pleasures in his twisted belief in a God who preached forgiveness and love and yet remained detached as His children suffered. He had no use for God's forgiveness. He made his own rules now. And made damn sure he enjoyed his death to the fullest. As he was doing this night with his beautiful victim.

"And lead us not into temptation."

Finally the girl stilled in her fight. He sensed her spirit take flight and knew her sanity had slipped. Yet her soul remained. He'd rip it from her and keep it, trapping her with him until he decided to release her to God.

"But deliver us from evil. Amen."

This torturous game was one he loved to play, but one he couldn't do often for obvious reasons. It would take nights before his mouth was completely healed.

There was something satisfying to him about the embodiment of sin praying over the innocent. It was an abomination and he relished the insult to God and his victim's horror as he tortured them.

As he pushed himself into the girl's body, Julian sank his fangs deep into her neck. He took her body and her blood, leaving her soul for last. And once he'd torn it from her, he left her in the tower for his men to dispose of.

With dawn fast approaching, Julian retreated to his solar. There, he ran his hands down his bloody chest. The stolen soul he took within his body thundered with life. It made him wonder what the Hallowed's lifeforce would feel like inside if him—what her power would feel like running through him.

Soon, he'd find out.

Chapter Seventeen

Lowel Castle rose up from behind a massive wall to almost touch the sky. The crenellated keep was everything Seacrest was not. Though every bit the ancient fortress, there was something less hostile about it. And though it could never be called "inviting", the sight of it didn't frighten Lex as she thought it would.

Lex eyed the four armed guards manning the massive gatehouse as the car carrying her passed under the iron gate of the main entrance. She didn't miss that they were strapped with both guns *and* swords.

Sandwiched between two beefy—and human—bodyguards, Lex tuned them out as they droned on and on about Lowel Castle. It was obvious they were proud to serve the women of the Order of the Rose.

As much as she wanted to learn everything she could about the Order and the place she'd be forced to call home for the next month or so, she couldn't handle having it all thrown at her in a hailstorm of words.

Once in the bailey, Lex was disappointed to see that time had reduced the inner buildings to rubble. Sadly, all that remained besides the keep was a small stone circle set in the center of the courtyard. The starkness of the castle made Lex wonder what it must have looked like back in its day—which preceded even William the Conqueror's conquest of England, or so her talkative protectors informed her.

As they drove past the circle, Lex leaned forward and peered around one of the bodyguards, Angus. The brawny Scot took up most of the window, which was why she found herself leaning on his thigh in order to get a good look at the stones. Only when Angus grinned awkwardly did Lex realize she was practically lying across his lap. She sat back, blushing, but at least she'd been able to glimpse the stones. They were beautiful, decorated as they were with strange and mystical symbols.

As a matter of fact, everything about Lowel Castle had a supernatural feel to it. When they drove under the gate, it was as if they'd passed into another realm. The feeling had come and gone, the armed guards standing sentry atop the wall-walk gaining her full attention and driving away the shudder that had passed through her.

Lex wished Constantine were with her instead of following behind in a truck large enough to accommodate the crate he was forced to travel in. The only reprieve he'd had from the confines of the crate was in the plane. Down in the cargo hold, where no sunlight could touch him, Constantine had been able to escape his coffin-like prison.

Away from the watchful eyes of her guards, in the hold was also where Lex and Constantine became the newest members of the mile-high club.

While the others were above, finding mundane ways to pass the time during the long flight, Constantine had made sure not an inch of Lex's body went undiscovered by his hands and mouth. By the time they'd arrived at Heathrow Airport, she had given back to Constantine every bit of bodily worship he'd given to her. And though she began the trip none-too-skilled in the sex department, when they'd reached their destination, Lex could've taught a class on the subject.

When the driver stopped the car before the grand entrance of the keep, Finn, her other bodyguard, had to coax her out of the backseat when she retreated further into the car. "Come, Lexine, there is naught to fear."

Taking his offered hand, Lex stepped from the car. The flood of sunlight felt wonderful. It rejuvenated her lagging spirit and lent her the strength to face the coming night.

She turned and watched the truck come to a stop behind the car. The driver and passenger both jumped down from the cab and went to the back. They slammed open the doors and Lex hurried toward Constantine. Finn's grip stopped her. She scowled at him and went to pull away.

"We must get you inside. Lady Isobel awaits you."

Well, she can just keep on "awaiting".

Angus came to stand by her side. Lex struggled not to be intimidated by these hulking brutes. She wasn't used to standing up for herself or fighting back. With Allie for an older sister she'd never had to until recently. Left to her own devices, Lex leveled what she hoped was one hell of a glare at Finn. "I'd rather stay with Constantine."

"Yes, you would, but you must understand the veil of protection is strongest *within* the walls of the keep."

She was sure it was. That didn't change the fact that she wanted to stay with Constantine. Lex knew she was being ridiculous. After all, she was going to be just a few feet away from him. She'd had a hell of a week and only wanted to be near the one person in this terrifying world who offered her a sense of safety.

Besides, she didn't trust these people and all it would take was one careless mishap—or a timely placed "accident" and

Constantine would burn. Not that Lex assumed she'd be able to stop any such thing from happening, but as long as she was there she had to think they'd be a bit more careful in their handling of him. They couldn't plead an accident with her watchful eye on them.

When Finn tried to drag her into the keep, blabbering on about it being for her own good, Lex dug her heels into the dirt. Angus took hold of her other arm and the both of them forced her to move. The roar that came from with the crate stilled their efforts. They released her arms and Lex couldn't resist giving them one hell of a smug look.

"Like I said, I'll stay out here with Constantine."

"Get the fuck inside the keep, woman. Now."

Constantine's furious shout came muffled from inside the crate. Defeated in her stand to remain with Constantine, Lex cocked a brow and straightened her spin. "Fine. But if they accidentally open your crate and you fry, it can never be said I didn't try to stop it."

She gave the two strapping men about to begin to get the crate out of the truck the hairy eyeball. Not that it did any good. They weren't paying her any mind.

Lex turned to the keep. She didn't want to go in there without Constantine. She was scared and as much as she wanted to make sure his transfer from truck to keep went smoothly, she needed him by her side as she stepped into a world that downright terrified her.

"Will you come now, milady?"

Did she really have a choice?

This time, when Finn extended his hand to her, Lex took it. Angus walked by her side as they approached the keep. She wondered if he wasn't there in case she decided to fight again. Well, she wouldn't. She might not fear Constantine. But she'd sure as hell respect him, especially in front of these creatures. Once she had him alone it would be a different story altogether. She planned on letting him know exactly how much she didn't appreciate his yelling at her.

When the huge steel-banded wooden doors burst open, Lex rethought the fighting thing. Framed in the doorway was a stately old man with steel-gray hair and a weathered face. His mouth, drawn into a thin line, looked as if it had never known a smile. His watery blue eyes raked over her and she had to fight the need to turn and run away.

"Welcome to Lowel Castle, milady." The man's voice was as dry as his wrinkled skin. And if that was his idea of a smile, he really had to work on it a bit more.

"Thank you," Lex greeted as he stepped aside so they could enter. Finn went first, his hand still clasped around hers. With Angus behind her, flight wasn't an option.

As she entered the shadowy lair of Isobel of Lowel, Lex realized how close to the real thing Seacrest was—right down to the arrow-slit windows. Although here, they were sealed closed with stone.

Only the enormous tapestries covering the stone walls broke the austere feel of the hall. Beautiful and elegant, they depicted scenes of medieval life in rich splendor. The scent of damp stone and the oppressive sense of loneliness and death gave Lex the feeling that she was standing inside a tomb.

When Constantine's crate was brought in, Lex wanted to weep with relief. She didn't want to have to face alone what awaited her. The fact of the matter was, Lex was afraid and she needed Constantine by her side.

Unfortunately, her reprieve from fear was short-lived. Before Constantine emerged from the crate, the weathered old man banged the doors closed. Lex gasped when a gorgeous and statuesque blonde emerged from the shadows. She smiled and Lex saw fangs.

"Hello, Lexine. Welcome to Lowel. I'm Isobel." The vampire embraced her. She smelled of flowers. "The power is already strong within you."

The vampire pulled away and Lex fought the urge to shiver as a chill passed through her. Finally, Constantine opened the lid to the crate and stepped out. Lex ran to him, not caring that everyone in the hall watched. He wrapped his arms around her, both protectively and possessively, before he placed a kiss on the top of her head. When he turned her around and moved her to his side, he kept an arm around her shoulders.

"It's good to see you again, Constantine."

Lex's jaw dropped. They *knew* each other? Unbelievable. She'd been under the impression that Constantine couldn't stomach the Order. But then again, he'd been around for seven hundred years. God only knew if something had happened to *cause him* to hate the women of the Order. Such as a love affair gone bad.

The thought of Constantine—her Constantine—with this exquisite creature made her stomach turn. How could Lex possibly compare to such a beautiful woman, who had the wisdom and secrets of the ages reflecting in the depths of her mysterious sliver eyes?

"No it's not."

"I see you haven't changed."

Was that sadness that flashed across Isobel's face? "Nor have you. But that's the way it goes for our kind, does it not?"

"This land is poisoned with the past. I'd hoped being away from it might help you to..."

"Forget?" Lex dropped Constantine's hand and stepped away from him. His fury scared the breath right out of her. "Forgive? That's never going to happen. *Never.*"

Isobel wasn't as put off by Constantine's rage as Lex herself was. That much was obvious when the elegant vampire walked up to him and pressed her palm against his unscarred cheek. "No Constantine, not forget. But forgive? Yes. I'd hoped you'd come to finally forgive yourself."

"Fuck you, Isobel."

Lex gasped when Constantine slapped Isobel's hand away. Four powerfully built humans moved toward him—as if they would be able to take him down. Lex realized Isobel wasn't the only member of the Order in the hall. No, two others were there as well, skulking in the shadows. One had a crossbow aimed at him. The other looked primed to embed her dagger right in Constantine's throat.

With a slight wave of her hand, Isobel ordered them to back off. She merely smiled at Constantine as she moved past the guards. "Come. I'll show you both to your chamber so you can settle in after your long journey."

Lex slipped her hand back in Constantine's as they followed Isobel up the long flight of stone stairs. The corridor seemed to run on forever. The walls were lined with gorgeous oil paintings of women in various times throughout history. The woman all seemed to stare down at them as they passed, their secret smiles hinting at more mysteries than Mona Lisa herself.

When they came to an enormous chamber, done up in rich burgundy and gold, it was like stepping into a dream. A dream she desperately wanted to wake from.

Isobel moved aside so they could enter. Constantine brushed past her without even sparing Isobel a glance. "Your things will be brought up anon."

165

"Thank you for letting us stay in your home."

Whatever was between Constantine and Isobel was none of her affair. Nor did it allow her to be rude to a woman who'd opened her home to them, putting her entire household in jeopardy.

Isobel waved her hand through the air. "Nonsense, Lexine. You're one of us now. You're family." With one last look at Constantine, Isobel turned to leave. "If you need anything, all you need do is ask."

Once she was gone, Constantine slammed the door and let out a curse that had Lex backing away from him. He cut her a look that would have had a lesser woman cowering. "If you don't want to stay here, we'll leave."

He raked a hand through his hair. "You can't leave and I won't leave you."

"I don't want you to have to be somewhere that brings you back to your past."

He grabbed her, lifted her clear off her feet and kissed her long and hard. When he pulled his mouth from hers, Lex was breathless. "This is my problem, elf, not yours."

"Yes, but, I..."

"But nothing. Like I said, this is my problem and I'll deal with it."

He set her back on her feet just as there was a knock at the door. Constantine threw the doors open and yanked their bags from Finn. He tossed them aside as Angus came to fill the doorway. He looked none too pleased at Constantine's attitude—not that Constantine seemed to care. He growled and snapped his teeth at the man, unfazed by his look of disgust. Angus walked away with a shake of his head.

"That wasn't nice."

Constantine cocked a brow at her as he set the bags down. "And when did I ever claim to be nice?"

"Good point."

Constantine *never* claimed to be anything other than what he was. He may be an ornery bastard, but at least he was honest about it. It was one of the reasons she adored him.

After what seemed like an endless trek down a relentless road paved with worry and fear, Lex eyed the huge, curtained bed longingly. She was about ready to drop out of sheer exhaustion.

Taking a good look at the chamber, Lex was impressed. The Order certainly knew how to do it up in style. Hanging from the stone walls were stunning tapestries, which, with the help of the fire burning in the massive hearth, did much to cut the dampness. There was a trunk at the foot of the enormous bed as well as a tall wardrobe to hold their clothes. The mirror above the white oak dresser had rosebuds etched into the glass, which matched the delicate design painted on the furniture.

When she spied a door, Lex peeked in and saw it was a bathroom—complete with toilet and shower. She nearly wept from relief. Though the castle obviously had electricity, until she saw indoor plumbing with her own eyes she didn't dare believe it. Especially since everything about Lowel seemed so—medieval.

"Tired?"

She smiled lazily at Constantine, who had a restless and caged animal look to him. "You might not remember, but that tends to happen to humans. Twenty-four hours of traveling can wipe a person out."

Her sarcasm had him laughing, even as Constantine's goddamn skin crawled at being back at Lowel. "So go to sleep."

He hadn't meant to sound so gruff, although Lex seemed not to notice. Either that or she chose to ignore his grouch. "Come lay with me."

If Constantine got anywhere near her she wouldn't be getting much sleep. Though he'd spent most of the flight devouring her body, he still wanted more. He wondered if he'd ever have his fill of her and then decided there weren't enough lifetimes for him to ever sate his needs when it came to Lex.

The power surged from her to him when her hand closed over his arm. All Constantine could think was, thank God they got her here when they did. No doubt by now, if she was still at Seacrest, renegades would be trying to take down the castle stone by stone to get to her. At Lowel, they had a veil of Druid magic engulfing the castle. It would help to shield her power, keeping renegades from detecting it and knowing she was here.

The magic would also keep Constantine from working his telepathy. Even his Sight would be shut down while they were here. The reprieve from those blinding visions would be a welcomed relief after seven centuries of suffering them. Lex's stomach growled and Constantine frowned. "Why didn't you tell me you were hungry?"

She shrugged, her eyes hooded. "Because I'm too tired to eat."

That wasn't a good enough answer as far as he was concerned. If she was hungry she was going to eat. Tired or not. "Stay here while I go see what there is for you to eat in this godforsaken place."

Her stomach thanked him with another loud growl. "Trust me, I'm not going anywhere in this castle without you glued to my side." She made a disgusted face. "Besides, I feel gross and need a shower."

His body hardened at the thought of hot water dripping down Lex's soapy body. Stressed from the trip, from being locked away within that goddamn crate for the better part of twenty-four hours, Constantine wasn't exactly in complete control of himself. With the bloodlust rising in him and how being at Lowel caused his past to creep up all around him, Constantine needed time away from Lex to regain control.

He gave her a sniff. "You smell fine to me."

Too fine, actually, for his raging body to deal with right then.

Lex went to him and put her arms around him. With a grunt, Constantine's stomach constricted as her power surged through him. Even the force of it couldn't quiet the hunger. "Hurry back. I don't want to be alone here. I'm scared."

He kissed her roughly and then set her away. That she looked to him to be rid of fear astounded him. Usually he was *putting* fear into people, not relieving it. "There's nothing to fear, elf. Go shower. I'll be back before you're done."

Leaving the room, Constantine closed the door. As he stomped down the corridor, he cursed, sensing he wasn't alone.

"I can still recall the night I was told you were among the Templars arrested in France." Isobel stepped from the shadows, as graceful as he'd always remembered her being. And still just as beautiful. "They told me of your damnation shortly after your execution. I wish I had the words to express my regret for the part I played in your life."

He stopped and sneered at Isobel. "I don't blame you, so save your guilt, woman."

"And yet you hate me."

Hate Isobel of Lowel? No, he didn't hate her. Nor did he blame her for what befell him. His fate, his damnation, was a direct result of his own actions. "Leave off, Isobel. I don't need this now. Not from you and not tonight."

He went to walk past her but she stopped him with a hand on his arm. Constantine looked at her hand and remembered the night she'd first touched him. It was the first time he'd ever been touched in kindness.

"You hate that I represent your past. I've always admired the strength it took for you to do what you did that night to free yourself."

"Don't go there, tonight. You won't like what it reaps."

Her hand slipped from his arm. "You need to feed, Constantine."

"No I don't." He pushed passed her and strode toward the stairs.

She ignored his denial. "Let me call one of our..."

He stopped and turned back to her. He let her know right then why he'd earned his black reputation. Grabbing her by the shoulders, he slammed her against the wall. She did nothing to betray her fear—if she was indeed afraid of him. "I said *fuck off.*"

He knew what she offered and the thought of it made his damn skin crawl. As much as Constantine knew he had to feed or else become a danger to himself and to everyone around him—especially Lex—for the first time in his existence he didn't want to give in to the monster trying to claw its way out of him.

"Dragon, please don't do this. You know the needs of your body. If you don't satisfy them, you know what will happen and what we'll be forced to do. I beg you not to let it come to that."

He didn't need Isobel to spell out that if the Order thought him a threat to Lex they'd put him down.

As much as he hated to admit it, Isobel was right. He knew his body, but more importantly, he knew what he'd become if he didn't feed. And yet he couldn't bring himself to do what needed to be done.

Taking his hands from her, Constantine stepped away from Isobel. "I don't want your fucking blood-whores."

"Your loyalty to Lexine is admirable, but foolish." She reached up to put a hand on his face but Constantine jumped back. The last thing he wanted was for her touch him again. "I remember you as the boy you were. You were so full of pain and righteous fury. It was as horrible to see as it was beautiful."

A low, feral growl rose up from deep within him. The threatening sound would have any creature scurrying away in terror. Not Isobel, who stood her ground, her eyes sad as she looked upon him.

"I'm not that boy anymore. I left that pathetic child behind at Greaves. Now move out of my way."

Or Constantine was prepared to move her.

"Constantine, please." She all but chased after him as he strode down the long, stone stairway. "Be reasonable. You need to sate the hunger. Don't make us do something everyone will regret."

For one moment—one brief moment—the ages melted away and it was just himself as a boy and Isobel, once again standing in this same spot as they had so long ago.

"I can't."

Those two simple words shook Isobel right to her core.

Isobel never thought Constantine would have turned into the man he was now. As a child he'd been so full of fear and anger. He'd been a lost soul when she'd been at Greaves and he was even more shattered in spirit when he'd come here seeking her aide.

That night, Isobel had taken him in and offered him a life far from the one he'd known. She'd promised to send him across the world, to start anew and put his past behind him. How she'd hoped he'd leave his shame and fury behind. Much to her sorrow, he hadn't. Instead, all of these centuries, it had continued to build within him, shaping him into the creature standing before her this night. A long time ago, Isobel had taken in a broken boy and hoped to give him the gift of a new life. It had all gone so horribly wrong. Now, she had the chance to gift him one more time. She hoped this one wouldn't end as badly as the other had.

"You can feed from her."

"I said I want no part of your blood-whores, woman."

"Not a donor, Constantine. I speak of Lexine. You can take her blood."

Isobel had never heard a sound as ominous as the one that came from Constantine. The awful sound had the hairs on the back of her neck standing on end.

"What in the bloody hell are you saying?"

"I'm saying you can take Lexine's blood." Not many things frightened Isobel any more, especially since she was usually the thing going bump in the night. But right then, Constantine did. He scared her and she wasn't too proud to admit it. "The Daystar's power can only be transferred on Samhain. And then only when a Bloodmoon sits in the sky."

"You lie," he rasped.

"If I lie and you take Lexine's blood, you will hold the power of the Daystar within you. You will become virtually unstoppable. Think, Constantine. Why would I lie and dare to risk that, especially with a man such as yourself, who regards humans and vampires in such disdain?"

He took a step back and shook his head in disbelief. "No."

Isobel sensed the turmoil in him and stepped away from the wall. She wanted to give Constantine even a brief moment of happiness. She owned him that much for her part in what he'd become. "I know you love her. Please, accept this gift I give you."

This time it was Isobel who walked away. She knew she had to leave Constantine to fight his own mind and emotions. Her part was done. Now it was up to him to make a decision that would impact them all.

Chapter Eighteen

Constantine's roar bounced off the walls of the corridor. Why in the hell had Isobel told him he could take Lex's blood? Didn't she know what it did to him to know this? Jesus Christ, he couldn't do it. No matter what Isobel claimed about the transfer of power only able to occur on the night of a Bloodmoon. He couldn't do that to Lex. He couldn't take her blood like some raving animal. If he did, Constantine knew he'd lose the last shred of decency he possessed.

Frustration overtaking him, Constantine smashed his fist into the wall. Flesh split and bone shattered at the impact. Though the pain helped to level him, the sight of his blood on the wall brought the past back to him in a rush of vivid detail.

No longer the man who'd known war, spilled blood and came back from death after facing an archangel; Constantine was once more the scared boy who'd come here seeking Isobel's aid. Something she'd freely given, just as she'd promised she would do years before.

Alone in the corridor, Constantine held out his hands to no one, mimicking what he'd done that night centuries ago when he'd reached for Isobel and begged for her help. She'd pried the dagger from his bloody hands and brought him to a chamber where he'd been washed and fed and allowed to rest. It was the same chamber he now shared with Lex. Back then, Isobel had given him the promise of a new life.

He'd left the next day for Messina, where he'd met up with Guy Sinclair and his army, all of whom went with the hope of finding something greater in the Holy Land than they had in England. Among those men were Tristan and Sebastian, who had instantly earned Constantine's admiration for their wisdom and prowess. Lucian and Raphael were the first to band together with the two lifelong friends. Once they'd allowed Constantine into their fold, the five of them became an unstoppable force to be reckoned with. Even among such a ferocious army, they'd risen in the ranks to become leaders of men known for their skill and savagery in battle.

Years later, when Tristan wanted to join with the Templar Order, Lucian, the most devout of them, was the first to second the decision. Sebastian, of course, followed as well, since he and Tristan had been as close as brothers since boyhood. What one did, so did the other—without question or hesitation. Their bond was one Constantine envied, and it was one he'd failed to realize he shared with them, until their collective deaths and damnation.

The past fading, Constantine had to look away from the blood splattered on the stone. If he lingered here much longer letting the past haunt him, the bloodlust would grow too great for him to control.

As Constantine stormed down the stairs, he swore his plea for Isobel's help still resonated within the walls. He'd come here, knowing what Isobel was, yet she was all he'd had back then. Besides Sir Walter, she was the only other person who'd ever offered him kindness. That night, when he'd come here broken and bloody, was the last time Constantine had ever begged anything from anyone.

Until now.

Throwing away his pride, Constantine gritted his fangs as he prayed for strength and guidance.

Please God, help me do what's right. Just this once.

CR₰

After her shower, Lex had nothing to do but sit and wait for Constantine to come back. Tired, she lay on the bed and tried not to be afraid, although it was a losing battle. At least with Constantine here she'd have better things to do besides dwell on the thoughts racing through her mind.

The trip had been a long one and it left her strung out emotionally. She was hungry and tired and wished she could call Allie. She needed to hear her sister's voice.

The combination of hunger and fatigue made her cranky. Such a mood was one she rarely found herself in. Jealousy was also a new one for her. Unfortunately, that was one emotion she couldn't fight.

The longer Constantine was gone the more outrageous the scenarios that played out in Lex's mind. She imagined Constantine and Isobel having a passionate reunion after centuries of being apart. She envisioned them stealing kisses in the shadows as he whispered sweet nothings to her.

Lex bit her lip to hold back her laugh. The degree of her fatigue had to be great to have her imagining such a ridiculous thing as Constantine whispering sweet words of love to a woman. The thought was downright preposterous considering the sort of man he was and she felt silly for thinking it. Thank God Constantine couldn't read her mind here. No doubt he'd laugh at her silly thoughts for centuries.

When the door opened, Lex hopped off the bed and ran to Constantine, who carried a tray of fruit, cheese and bread. The moment he set the tray on the round table off in the far corner of the chamber, she saw the knuckles on his right hand were a mess.

Hands on hips, Lex frowned as she took in the damage. "What happened?"

A veil of indifference settled over him. "Nothing."

"Really?" Lex pointed to his hand. "That doesn't look like 'nothing' to me."

Constantine dropped his hand. When he clenched his hands into fists, the skin over his knuckles pulled open. Lex watched as his blood dripped to the floor. She looked back at his face and flinched at the way his gaze bore into her.

"I need to feed."

Getting punched in the gut couldn't possibly hurt as much as his admission did. "Oh." Lex looked back at his knuckles. "And that's why you smashed your hand into what...? A wall?"

Constantine bared his fangs as he turned away from her to look into the flames dancing in the hearth. "Yes."

Lex raised a brow at the way he pushed that word out. She wanted to understand how difficult it was for him. Truly she did. But right then, Lex was too miserable to feel anything other than, well, her own misery. She fell victim to her own private pity-party and gave him a shrug. He missed it, however, since Constantine wasn't looking at her.

"So go feed."

Silence stretched between them for so long, Lex didn't think he was going to answer. She walked over to one of her suitcases and dug out a book. Hopefully she'd be able to lose herself in it as she tried to find the exhaustion that had suddenly fled her.

"The Order has donors."

Lex wanted to vomit. "'Dial-a-donor'. How convenient."

Lex didn't care how bitter she sounded as she carried her book to the bed. She wasn't hungry anymore and didn't give the tray of food a glance as she climbed on the large bed. As she settled back against the pillows, she held the book closed on her lap and stared at Constantine's back.

Right at that moment she hated what he was. Truly hated it with everything *she* was.

The man she loved needed to put his hands and mouth on another woman and take in her blood—her *life*. True it was only to feed, and she tried hard to equate it with her eating a steak, but that wasn't working to make it easier for her to accept. Her heart rebelled at the intimacy of the act and ached for it to be her he took from.

Finally, Constantine turned from the fire. He looked tortured. "Lex..."

She held up her hand, shocked when he stopped in mid sentence. Lex hadn't thought the power of "the hand" would work on Constantine. She had to remember to tell Raphael about this. It would fuel Rogue's evil delight for centuries to come.

"Please, Constantine, don't say anything. I know you need to do this, but right now I'm too strung out emotionally to deal with it. So please, just go do what you have to and I'll get over it once I've gotten some sleep."

Pain, sharp and intense, cut through Constantine as he watched Lex open the book and begin to read. Of all the things Lex could have done, dismissing him was not one he'd imagined. Her cold indifference pained him. He wanted to deny his hunger. He wanted to make her look at him, as she always did, as if he wasn't a monster.

Constantine's pride wouldn't allow him to go to her, which was for the best. The hunger was a raw need pulling his insides apart as Isobel's words haunted him. He growled and turned away from her. He didn't hesitate when he pulled open the door. A second after he left and slammed the door closed he knew the thud that came from within had to be the book being flung across the chamber.

Lex's soft sobs followed Constantine down the corridor. He came to Isobel's chamber and gave her door one hard bang. When it opened, he cut Isobel with a hard glare.

"Call in a fucking donor."

He didn't miss the look of astonishment on Isobel's face before he turned and strode down the corridor, down the stairs and out to the courtyard. He needed to put as much distance between him and Lex as the castle allowed.

Constantine had never been sorry for a damn thing he'd ever done. Yet tonight, with Lex's quiet tears resonating in his head, he was sorry. For once, he was sorry for what he'd been in life and for what he had become in death.

So goddamn sorry he ached with it. Michael should have sent him to Hell. At least then, he'd be the only one to suffer for his deeds.

Chapter Nineteen

Greaves Castle:

Spring 1296

The longer Ulric stared at him the more Constantine panicked. He knew what would come, now that he'd caught Ulric's attention. The thought nearly had him vomiting up his rancid food right then and there.

Ulric's gaze was a thousand insects crawling over his skin. He resisted the urge to scratch the feeling away, though he couldn't stop the shiver of disgust.

Crouched in the corner of the hall, trying to make himself as unnoticeable as possible, Constantine gnawed on a piece of meat that shouldn't even be given to a dog. Rotted it may be, but at least tonight he'd been allowed to eat. God only knew when he'd next be given more than scraps to eat.

The delicious aromas that came from the high table made Constantine's mouth water. Pheasant and venison—their wonderful smells came at him as he tore off a hunk of his unidentifiable rotting meat. His stomach rolled in protest of the foul food as it hit his belly like a stone. He wondered if he'd ever know a feast like the one Ulric laid out for his guest. His heart sank when he thought of such a thing since as the days rolled by, he'd begun to give up hope of one day being free of this life of horrors.

Ulric had laid his finest of everything to impress the beautiful lady gracing his hall. Her name was Isobel of Lowel and, to Constantine's eyes, the lady looked like what he'd always envisioned an angel to be. Blonde, blue-eyed and ethereal, the lady's grace had left him awed from the moment she'd swept into the keep. It made his shame at being reduced to a dog in her presence sting that much more.

Lady Isobel's holding bordered Greaves, yet this was the first time she'd ever come to the castle. In the year since Constantine had been here, he'd heard it whispered that Isobel was a witch. Others claimed she was a creature of the night. A demon. Finally seeing the lady in person, Constantine didn't care if she were all those things and worse. To him, Isobel of Lowel was an enchanting angel sent here to offer him a bit of beauty in his ugly world.

Daring a glance at the Lord's table, Constantine winced when he noticed Ulric still staring at him. Only a depraved bastard such as his lord would watch him instead of the elegant woman in his hall. But then, Ulric's fancy didn't run toward women.

Constantine crouched lower, trying to make himself smaller still, though it was a hard task since he'd gained even more height over the last year. His size did him well on the lists, as did his ever-increasing skill with a sword. Where it didn't help, was keeping him out of Ulric's notice.

With every day that passed, Constantine made certain he fought better than the day before. To become the best warrior he could and fight his way out of this life was all he lived for. Everything he did he made sure it had to do with gaining the skill to break free of Ulric's hold on him.

The things he had suffered at Ulric's hands, almost from the moment he had arrived here, were unspeakable. He'd learned early on what the bag of gold had signified. He'd been bought, body and soul, by the devil.

Isobel followed Ulric's hawk-like gaze to Constantine. Her musical voice rang out, almost bringing tears to Constantine's eyes. "Why is that child in the corner, Ulric?"

"Bah, that's no child. That's my dog."

Ulric's laughter turned Constantine's stomach. It took every bit of strength he had not to give in to the mortification of the callous remark.

Isobel raised a single brow. "Truly?" Her sharp stare bore right through Constantine. He lowered the hunk of greening meat away from his lips and swallowed down the bite in his mouth. "He looks like a boy to me."

Right then, with her odd eyes boring into him, Constantine felt as if she saw clear to his heart—and to his blackest thoughts.

"Come here, child," she commanded.

"Leave him," Ulric ordered around a mouth-full of greasy pheasant.

The man was a filthy piece of foulness, leaving Constantine to wonder why such an elegant creature would lower herself to be in his presence. With his dirty brown hair and beady brown eyes and sadistic ways, no well-born woman dared to enter his lair. On the rare occasions when boys couldn't satisfy his sick lusts, he used whores from around the neighboring villages. And usually, after a night spent here, they didn't return.

If they survived his brutality, that is. Most however, did not. Isobel pulled her gaze from Constantine and leveled a hard, cold look at Ulric. Much to Constantine's shock, his lord leaned back in his chair. He had the look of a chastised youth.

Isobel hadn't even uttered a single word and she'd put him low.

She turned her attention back on him and her expression softened. "Come here to me."

He didn't want to dirty her with his nearness. Yet he found himself throwing his meat to the floor and wiping his hands on his rag of a tunic. The thing was a size too big and had once been white, but was now stained, and so filthy it appeared brown. Since these were his only clothes, it was a rare thing for them to be washed. He did so only when he was allowed to bathe, which was before Ulric called him to his solar—or the torture chamber, as Constantine came to think of it. It was there that Ulric did unspeakable things to him.

Unconsciously, he shook his head, not wanting to think about the nights he was forced to spend with Ulric alone in his solar.

As he treaded over to her, Constantine adjusted his clothing and smoothed down his matted black hair. By the time his feet dragged him to her, Lady Isobel's hand was already outreached toward him. He stopped far enough away from her so that she couldn't reach him. He didn't want her to touch him. He was afraid that if she did, he would shatter into a million pieces at her small kindness.

"What a beautiful boy you are, Constantine Draegon."

How would she know his name? To hear it on her lips made his throat constrict and his chest tighten.

"Come closer to me."

And then it hit him like the cut of a blade to his very soul. Lady Isobel was as depraved as Ulric was. No wonder she had finally come here. She wanted to hurt him and he'd not go quietly. No. Constantine would fight her with everything he was.

He backed away. *No more. Please God, no more.*

183

And not by her, who looked like an angel sent from Heaven.

When she stood, Ulric told her to sit back down and forget the "dog". Isobel ignored her host. Instead, she knelt—*knelt*—before Constantine and took his chin in her icy hand.

"I see you, Constantine." Her voice was low, a mere whisper meant just for him. Glancing around her, Constantine saw Ulric leaned forward in his chair. The nosy bastard strained to hear what the mistress of Lowel Castle said to him. "Oh yes. I see the dragon in you. One day it will give you the strength to escape this life."

She did see. She saw clear to his soul.

As her gaze bore into him, Constantine realized that her eyes glowed with a light all their own. He also saw that fangs peeked out from behind her lips. He knew then all of those whispers he'd heard about her were true. She was a demon, and though Constantine knew he should be afraid of her, he wasn't.

She offered him kindness in a place where he knew only pain. Her touch was gentle. Her eyes looked upon his with tenderness and it tore at his very soul—a soul not worth the dirt this holding sat upon, yet one he would relinquish in a heartbeat if she'd take him from the place.

The real monster in the hall was reclining on his chair like a king on his throne. Ulric fed his gluttony as he struggled to hear what this lovely creature was saying to Constantine. He hoped the fat prick would choke to death on the pheasant filling his mouth.

"There will come a night when you'll need me. I'll be waiting, Constantine."

When she rose and turned back to the table, her deep blue tunic swirled around her legs. She offered Ulric a cool smile in a way that kept her fangs concealed. "So Lord Ulric, tell me about those fine horses of yours."

Constantine glanced up at Ulric and saw the promise of pain in his cruel eyes. Fear, cold and numbing raced through him as he retreated back to his corner. He reclaimed his hunk of meat, but had no stomach to finish it.

The cold of Isobel's touch on his face stayed with him for a long time after. Her voice echoed in his ears long after she'd gone, drowning out his screams as Ulric tortured his body into the night.

Chapter Twenty

Constantine wiped the blood from his face, wishing he could rip the taste of it from his mouth. Sitting on the bottom of the steps, the alcove shielded him from the bitter wind. He felt dirty, and that was a feeling he thought he'd left behind at Greaves.

Obviously he hadn't, since his skin crawled over what he'd done.

He spat on the ground in an effort to cleanse his mouth of the taste of the donor's blood. He needed to wash the taste from his mouth and her touch from his body. Yet, he was loath to return to the keep. He wanted to remain here, lost in his misery and hidden away from the world.

He didn't want to face Lex's disgust of him.

Constantine ran his hands through his hair before dropping his forehead in his palms. Much to his irritation, his knuckles had already healed. He wanted the pain back. Physical pain never failed to rid him of the shit festering within him.

"I'm saying you can take Lexine's blood."

Constantine banged his palms against his head in the vain hope of dispelling Isobel's words from his mind. *Shut up. Just shut the fuck up.*

The plea was screamed inside the recess of his mind, and yet they continued to echo until he wanted to claw at his brain to rip the words from his memory.

The louder Isobel's words resonated, the angrier he became. That anger had caused him to be careless with the donor, who'd offered herself up for him to take with a quiet acceptance that had made him feel even dirtier.

When she'd grabbed at his shoulders and whimpered from pain, Constantine knew he'd hurt her. The girl, however, made no move at trying to fight him off. She'd accepted what he was doing to her. And once he was finished with her, she collapsed to the floor, too weak to stand. Disgusted with himself, and much to his shame, he'd left the girl where she lay and fetched Isobel. He didn't even wait for Isobel to go to the girl before he left the keep.

From the shadows of the alcove he'd watched the donor leave. He'd wanted to apologize for hurting her, but knew such words were beyond him.

Though he was never one to hide from a goddamn thing, Constantine didn't want to leave the dark and the quiet of the alcove. Although with dawn approaching, he was left with no choice but to abandon his refuge.

He walked back to the keep with a heavy feeling in his chest. As soon as he entered the castle he saw Isobel was there, waiting for him no doubt, in the hall.

"Why do you torture yourself, Constantine?"

He didn't even pause as he made his way to the stairs. "Why can't you mind your own goddamn business?"

Isobel rose from the sofa and intercepted him. "Vent your fury if you must, but I had hoped—never mind what I'd hoped. It's no longer important. Go on," she said to him, stepping back. "Go to Lexine. Remain locked in the prison of your memories

187

and never let her close. Never accept the love she obviously feels for you."

She turned away. Why Constantine didn't walk away, he didn't know. Nor did he know why he stopped her cold by barking out her name. She turned around, every bit as ethereal as she was the night he'd first seen her.

"You know of the events that have shaped me, so ask me no more why I torture myself."

Isobel walked back toward him. Constantine didn't pull away when she ran her finger along his scar. "What happened to you was not your fault. You have to know that by now."

With a vicious snarl he turned his head and stepped back. "I should have killed the bastard sooner."

"You were but a boy. You did what you could until you were strong enough to do more. It's time to let it go before the past completely destroys you."

"It's already destroyed me."

Isobel's words followed him as he climbed the stairs. They caused an ache deep within his blackened heart. "Don't throw away the chance at happiness. Embrace it before it's too late. Find peace, Constantine, and put the dragon to sleep."

Happiness.

When he reached their chamber, Constantine was unsure of his next action for the first time in his existence. The sensation didn't sit well with him. He was a warrior, and a warrior never hesitated, not when charging into battle and certainly not when having to face down a woman's displeasure—and hurt. With a grunt of frustration, he pushed open the door and strode in with a confidence he didn't feel.

The scent of honeysuckle assailed him as soon as he stepped into the darkened room. Next, the scent of burning

188

wood came at him. He looked at the hearth and saw a small fire burning there. He assumed Lex had lit it. He stoked it before he took to the bed, hoping it would help chase away the cold ripping through him.

Unbidden, Constantine's gaze shot to the bed. Lex was curled into a tiny ball under the blankets. She was awake, he knew, and yet she did nothing to acknowledge him. He ached to go to her, lay himself next to her, and take away the misery he sensed in her.

But he didn't dare. Not with the donor's touch on him and the taste of her blood lingering in his mouth. With a muttered curse, Constantine stomped to the bathroom adjoining the room. He needed a shower.

When he caught sight of himself in the mirror above the freestanding sink, he snarled at his reflection—at the blood smeared on his face. The sight of it had him wanting to slam his fist into the wall all over again.

Fighting the need to hurt himself, he pulled off his clothes and tossed them to the floor. He then turned on the hot water and stepped in the shower. As he attempted to cleanse himself, he knew there wasn't enough soap in the world to wash away the dirt of his sins.

And still he scrubbed himself furiously, taking in mouthfuls of water and spitting it out. He ran his tongue over his fangs. *Fuck.* The taste of the donor was still there.

Constantine tensed when the door opened. The sweet scent of honeysuckle blended with the aroma of the soap. A moment later he heard the steady beat of Lex's heart over the stream of water. And then Lex's husky voice came at him and he had to close his eyes and slap a hand to the wall to steady himself from the impact of it.

"Constantine?"

"What?"

His harsh tone was filled with self-loathing. He gave up trying to find that sense of clean and threw down the soap. Only Lex's touch could do that—make him feel clean.

"Never mind."

Constantine shoved aside the curtain, heedless of his nudity, to see Lex walking out of the steamy bathroom. "Wait." At his shout, Lex turned back to him. Her sad eyes didn't dip lower than the level of his face. "What do you want?"

She shook her head. "Nothing." She turned to leave again. "I'm sorry I bothered you."

He stepped from the shower and grabbed her arm. He spun her back around to face him. "You're never a bother me, Lex. Never"

Keeping her gaze locked on his face, she blinked as if her eyes stung. He saw they were watery and knew he'd put those tears there. "I'm just wanted to say I'm sorry about before. I had no right to make you feel guilty..."

In a flash of movement, Constantine was out of the shower and standing before her. Her sentence ended with a startled gasp when he gripped her upper arms. Dripping wet and shivering, since Templars felt cold more keenly for their lack of soul, Constantine brought his face close to hers and gave her a good shake. "Don't you dare apologize to me."

"Okay. Fine. No more apologizing. Just don't shake me again."

His hands fell away and he took a step back. He thought the shade of red her cheeks turned when she looked down at him was adorable. Lex snapped her gaze back to his face. Usually making a person uncomfortable fed a sadistic need within him to piss off those closest to him. Not so with Lex, which was why he pulled a towel from the shelf near the shower and tucked it around his waist.

"I didn't mean to hurt you," he replied gruffly as he turned off the water.

Lex followed behind him as he walked back to the bedroom. He went to the hearth and she went to the bed. Her gaze bore into his back as he stoked the dying embers back to life. Her stare moved over every scar left behind after Ulric's punishments. He didn't like her looking at them, and yet he wanted her to see them—to see *him*. A product of his times, Constantine had to let her know that though he was here in this modern age, he'd left his heart and his soul behind in 1310, on the day he'd burned to death in France.

"This isn't an apology, so please refrain from rattling my teeth again." He faced her and saw her fleeting grin. "I didn't mean to blow things out of proportion before. I understand you have to feed and all that. Believe me, I do. Besides, it's not like we have a commitment between us."

"Oh, we have a commitment between us, elf." He advanced on her. Lex's lips parted and a soft gasp escaped her when Constantine tossed aside the towel and pushed her back on the bed. He settled over her, loving the feel of how soft and warm she was beneath him. He ground his erection against her, needing her body to erase the stain of the donor's touch from him. "I'm going to fuck you so hard you'll never doubt you're mine."

With her heat and her energy thundering through him, Constantine leaned off her only far enough to allow him to trail his hand down her body. She squeezed her legs together as if to hold his hand in place, and let out a soft whimper. He dragged his tongue up the side of her neck, her taste taking him over the edge of reason.

"Oh my God, Constantine, you make my body burn."

Every part of him strained against his need for her. All of that passion settled in his cock, making it too damn painful to hold back much longer.

Unable to linger on her neck—he resisted the urge to sink his fangs into her and take her blood. He kissed her deep and hard, growling into her mouth as she clawed at his back. When he pulled his mouth away and stared down at her, he saw she needed him as much as he did her. Oh yes, Lex was his. He'd never allow another man to know her as he did right in this moment. No other man would put that look on her face—a mix of passion and surrender.

He'd hold that look in his mind for the rest of eternity.

"Do I, elf? Do you want to know what else I can do to your body?" Her mouth worked but no sound came out. A vibrating laugh, not one of humor, but of pure male sexual satisfaction, came from him. It was a hell of a thing to know he'd put her in such a passionate state. "I'm going to taste every inch of you before I use every part of me to make you feel good."

Oh God, I hope so.

That thought rang in Lex's mind as she ran her hands along Constantine's back. She loved the way his muscles moved under her palms, even as her heart shattered at the feel of his scars. They crisscrossed his back, evidence of the brutal life he'd been forced to live. If she could, Lex would gladly go back in time and live those years for him and free him of the burden of his memories. But since that was impossible, all she could do was love him as best she could and hope it helped to ease his suffering.

"I love you."

Why the words came from her now, Lex didn't know. She hadn't meant to say them to him. Though she had *thought* them—which he'd heard—she'd never actually said them to him. Once spoken, she was glad she'd said them—even if Constantine did stiffen above her. His expression wasn't comical like Allie joked Sebastian's had been when she'd confessed her feelings to him. No. Not Constantine. He looked as if he'd charged headlong into battle. Her name came from him, more a growl than an actual word, a heartbeat before he took her mouth in a bruising kiss that left little doubt in her mind how much her declaration impacted him. As his mouth worked hers, igniting a flame of desire deep within her, his calloused hands pulled at her clothes. He broke the contact of their mouths to rid her of the offensive items that separated his skin from hers. Once they were both devoid of clothing, Constantine flipped her over so she was lying facedown. His weight settled over her, his body warm from her energy as his arousal pushed against her opening.

"Now we play, elf."

Constantine nipped the nape of her neck and Lex moaned, loving the thrill that shot through her. Of course, he was careful not to break the skin, and she knew he'd never dare, but still, it lent intensity to an already passionate moment.

When he slid into her, Lex whimpered, loving the fullness of him inside of her. Her body stretched to accommodate him, the pressure mixing with the pleasure. As Constantine worked her body, pumping into her with long, steady strokes, Lex began to shatter. The feel of him inside her in this way was more pleasure than she'd ever thought a body could feel. It made her want more.

Lex lifted her hips, allowing Constantine to push deeper into her. He groaned long and low close to her ear. The sound vibrated through her as his body went stiff. He climaxed a moment later, and let out a string of some of the foulest words Lex had ever heard as he spilled himself into her.

She smiled, thinking that was something only Constantine would do.

When she went to get up, Constantine allowed her just enough movement to flip onto her back. He pinned her to the mattress, a devilish gleam lighting his eyes. "You're not going anywhere, elf. I'm nowhere near done with you."

Constantine made good on his promise.

By the time dawn came, Lex was raw and he had fallen into a sated, death-like sleep. It was a good ending to a perfectly hellish day.

CB80

"So, the Dragon survives to face another night."

Madeline smiled coldly at her twin sister, Lenora. "So it would seem."

Lenora slipped her dagger back into her right boot. She shook her head in bafflement. "He makes her happy."

They'd seen Draegon's mood, sensed his hostility, and had come here to end him should he have done anything to endanger the Hallowed. Which was why the assassins were bemused by what they heard going on inside the chamber.

Madeline shrugged. Given his reputation, she didn't trust the Dragon and knew it would only be a matter of time before they had to take him down. "For now."

Lenora's grin was pure evil. "He brings harm to the Hallowed and I *will* end him. Of that there is no doubt."

Lenora's eagerness to take Draegon out was obvious. He was a risk to the Hallowed and for that alone they'd both relish the chance to end him.

Madeline turned from the bedchamber door and walked away lest the Dragon detect their presence. Because of who they were, he'd know how close he came to death.

They were assassins, sworn to protect the Hallowed from all harm. They had stood before the First and bled their oath and it was one they would uphold even if they had to risk their own destruction.

Their sole function from the moment Lexine Parker was born, until the end of all their days, was to watch over and protect her.

And that's what they'd done. They watched over her from the night she'd come into this world. They'd hid in the shadows, taking out any who'd discovered the power she carried. Never once had any vampire gotten close to her, save for the Templars. And even them, the assassins had thought to take out. If the First hadn't stopped them, Madeline and Lenora would have systematically taken them down one by one.

"Come." Madeline, who was younger than Lenora by a handful of minutes, tugged on her sister's arm. "I need to feed."

Lenora walked beside her down the long corridor. The sound of the lovemaking going on within Constantine and Lexine's chamber followed them as they went. "I hate to admit this, but, I'm glad I didn't have to end him tonight. I relish the chance to fight him fist to fist."

"We'll have our time." Madeline motioned toward the chamber. "Right now, it's her time with him."

From the soft whimpers he pulled from Lexine, the sisters realized Constantine Draegon wasn't only good at fighting. It seemed he was good at loving as well.

It was something Madeline had never thought possible. It gave her hope that they might be allowed to let him live once all was said and done. But she doubted it.

The First, with her maternal nature, might want to believe there was good in the legendary Dragon, but Madeline wasn't so quick to let down her guard when it came to him. She knew it would only be a matter of time before they had to end him.

She just hoped the Hallowed wouldn't hate them for it when that night came.

Chapter Twenty-One

Lying on the floor, her head resting on Constantine's thigh, Lex stared into the flames dancing in the hearth and marveled at how far she's come from the life she'd led in Florida. She also couldn't believe how comfortable she'd gotten around the women of the Order of the Rose, something she'd never dreamed would have been possible.

As it turned out, Isobel wasn't the only member of the Order of the Rose to call Lowel Castle home. Over the past week, Lex learned four other female vampires lived here as well. They were an intimidating bunch to be sure.

With her short blonde hair, pale flesh and enigmatic eyes, Daria was stunning. When she walked into a room, she took charge of it without saying a word. The air around her seemed to change, becoming charged with her sexual energy.

Angelica, a beautiful woman with long chestnut hair, a slender body, had an easy smile. She was so nice Lex had to keep reminding herself the woman was a vampire.

Then there were the sisters, Madeline and Lenora. Tiny creatures, not even five feet tall. Lethal, they reminded her of twin shadows moving through the castle. Something about them was downright unnerving. They were dark and mysterious, and they scared the breath right out of Lex.

Surrounded by vampires in an unfamiliar environment, Lex drew even closer to Constantine. Since his telepathy was off, during his waking hours he made sure he was practically glued to her side.

After he'd fed from the donor, he hadn't taken in blood again. Lex knew eventually his hunger would grow too great for him to fight. When that happened, she fully intended on standing aside and letting him take care of his needs—no matter how much it bothered her to watch him go off and share with another woman something they could never have between them.

Since Lex woke in the early afternoon, she always spent the remaining hours of sunlight out in courtyard. Constantine and the Order ceased fighting her on it once they'd realized the sun was something Lex needed in order to make it through the long nights.

To their credit, the Order did their best to make her feel welcome. Lex didn't miss the way they watched Constantine like a hawk. She knew he didn't miss it either. It was as if they waited for him to do something—anything—so they could take him down.

Only Isobel seemed relaxed around Constantine. Though Lex had refused to press Constantine on his past, it was killing her not ask how they knew each other. She was dying to know if they had once been lovers, but she swallowed her curiosity and tried to pretend it didn't eat away at her.

Lex would be glad when this was all over, even as she dreaded the passing days bringing her closer to Samhain. Twenty days separated this night from that night. Twenty days of being locked away in this keep with the threat of impending death weighing Lex down, and thinking about Constantine and Isobel only made it worse.

Not wanting such thoughts to invade the perfect peace of the moment, Lex pushed those ponderings aside. The fire bathed the room in a soft glow of flickering light, lending a certain intimacy that harsh modern lighting never could. Constantine idly ran his fingers through her hair, the slow and steady motion soothing to her. Lex looked up at Constantine's face, amazed by his relaxed expression. This was the first time she'd seen him look completely unguarded.

With the time ticking ever closer to the night that could very well bring her life to a crashing end, Lex decided to voice to some of the questions she had of Constantine's life. She doubted he'd answer them but at least she could say she'd tried.

"Did you always want to be a knight?"

"Always." He didn't take his gaze from the flames when he answered—but at least he'd answered.

Emboldened, Lex tried to keep things going. "I used to want to be a singer."

He tore his gaze from the fire and cocked a brow at her. "Why didn't you pursue that career?"

She laughed, remembering the hours she'd spent singing and dancing in front of the mirror, a brush for a microphone. Sometimes she forced Allie and Christian to be her audience. "Something to do with sounding like a dying frog when I sing kept me from it."

Lex held back her surprise at Constantine's laughter. This was the first time she'd heard the sound—one of genuine humor. "I can see how that would hinder your career."

"Even Allie told me to give it up, and that's saying a lot since she nurtured my every childish whim." She sat up and faced him. He drew in a sharp breath when she ran her hands along his bare arms. The thick cords of muscles tightened at her touch. "I can't imagine how hard you must have trained to learn how to fight the way you do."

Constantine grunted and looked back to the flames. Of course Lex couldn't imagine what he'd had to do to become the man he'd grown into. Most people couldn't, not even the men from his day. He'd pushed himself beyond human endurance in order to be able to fight his way out of the life fate had dropped him in.

When Constantine saw the way Lex was watching him, he slapped a scowl on his face. "Why are you staring at me like that?"

Her smile was wistful as she regarded him. "I'm trying to imagine you as a young boy."

"I was shorter."

"Obviously," she laughed. "What color were your eyes?"

"Blue."

Lex looked surprised. "Really? I imagined them to have been brown." She brushed a chunk of his hair away from his face. It made him feel exposed, which was why he always let it hang over his face in chunky spikes. "Who had blue eyes in your family?"

"My mother."

Lex moved her hand to his scar. Constantine cringed, wanting to pull away as much as he wanted her to never stop touching him. "I'm so sorry your life was so brutal."

No one was more sorry than him.

He moved his head away from her touch and his body went cold. Constantine couldn't take pity on his best day, especially not from Lex. Struggling to keep his anger at bay, which was his usual reaction if he thought someone pitied him,

Constantine shrugged, hoping to downplay the horrors of his life. "What's done is done."

She tilted her head to the side, as if trying to see past the mask of indifference that Constantine had settled over his features. "Is it, Constantine?"

"We all have our crosses to bear."

Lex smiled sadly. "Some of us carry heavier burdens than others."

Of that there was no doubt.

The weight of his life bore down on him, like the weight of the world upon Atlas's shoulders. He knew eventually he'd be crushed by it, if it didn't turn him into a raging madman first. He hoped Lex was someplace far from the ugliness of this nocturnal world when it did.

Constantine stood, barely aware that Lex did as well. She moved to sit on the bed as he began to pace the width of the chamber. His memories were a fist around his heart, squeezing at it, trying to draw blood from a stone. The dead thing, blackened with sin, sat in his chest as a constant reminder of all he'd lost—and all he'd never had.

"The world was different then." He remembered the days when he'd spent long hours on the lists, honing the skills he'd need to survive in his world. "By the age of eleven I'd already thought I'd seen how cruel the world was. And then I went off to squire for a lord who proved I knew nothing of the horrors of life."

As much as Constantine wanted to take back what he'd said—hell, he didn't even know why he'd said anything at all about his past—he felt a small burden lifted from him.

"It was that bad?"

He turned, giving her his back. "Look at my body, Lex. Every mark on me is a testimony to my life."

When Constantine faced her, he was prepared to see pity in her expression—and hate her for it. Instead, he was met by a look of raw love that nearly staggered him.

"It's shaped you into a remarkable man."

"It's made me into a bloody monster."

Lex shook her head. "No, not a monster. Merely a man who has known too little kindness in his life."

He stalked over to her, forcing Lex to crane her neck up to look him in the eye. Constantine knelt before her, remembering the vision of her standing on the balcony overlooking the land as the sun faded around her. She'd looked so beautiful in his vision that even now, the image of her bathed in the light of the sun was one he knew he'd carry with him straight into Hell.

"Until you."

Lex took his hands in hers. Her power flowed into him. Constantine sensed she was fighting to control it. "I don't know if I ever told you this, and I don't know if it's right or not, but I'm glad you're here." She swept her hand through the air. "And I don't mean *here,* at Lowel. I mean I'm glad fate brought us together."

Just like that, everything he'd suffered rushed him. Every moment of pain, every humiliation, every agonizing detail of his death played out in his mind. When his memories were done, Constantine knew only one thing.

"So am I, elf."

When she leaned into him, Constantine wrapped his arms around her. The steady beat of her heart against his chest lent him the illusion of life.

"I want to go home."

Lex's whisper cut through him. "I know. I promise you I'll take you home."

"What if something goes wrong?" Her question was muffled against his chest, her voice vibrating through him.

"It won't.

I'll make damn certain of that.

She leaned away and offered him a weak smile. Her fear for what was to come penetrated the veil of magic and seeped into him. It was poison in his body. "You know, if I become a big ball of energy, Allie's going to eviscerate you."

Constantine flinched. "No shit."

He didn't need the threat of Allie's wrath to inspire him to fight for Lex. He cared too much about her to give her up without one hell of a fight. He'd defy God all over again, his oath be damned, to save her from whatever was to come Halloween night.

For the first time in his life and death, Constantine needed someone. He needed the calm he found only with Lex. He needed her beauty to take away the ugliness of his world. He needed her warmth to chase away the cold and her innocence to wipe clean the stain of his past.

But most of all, he needed her love.

ᏼᏺᏽ

When she was a young girl, Isobel had imagined her life playing out vastly different than it had. For one thing, she'd never imagined being married for three years to a man who'd enjoyed hurting her and who'd nearly killed her countless times.

She'd been the perfect product of her day. A paragon of nobility, Isobel was all things a lady was supposed to be. Obedient, subservient, able to ply her hand at the myriad of menial tasks a gentle lady should. She never showed anger or sorrow. Instead, she presented to the world a serene face, which masked the misery festering in her heart.

And she'd never dared reveal the secrets her mother had passed down to her. The secrets of their Druid ancestry were such that her mother had even withheld from sharing with Isobel's father. Witchcraft. Heresy. Those two words caused the women of her line to harbor their secrets well, lest they be met with a fiery end.

Isobel kept her family's secrets and had been the perfect lady and an ideal wife in a turbulent time in England's history.

Suffering Roland's beatings with grace, Isobel had always believed one day he'd kill her in a fit of rage. Fate proved her right. On the night he'd returned from quelling the Saxon uprisings against William the First, her husband had beaten her so severely he'd knocked her into a sleep that had lasted for days. It was while she'd slept that she knew her time would not come to an end by Roland's hand.

While she'd lay dying, Isobel was given a new life. Eternal life. When she'd woken, reborn of the night, she'd quenched the hunger by feeding from—and killing—Roland.

From that moment on, Isobel know only freedom and luxury, savoring the power that came with her new existence.

She'd been reborn in the year 1070. In all of her time, never once had Isobel known a more tortured soul than Constantine Draegon. His pain, of both body and mind, had moved her to do something she'd never done prior nor since. She'd risked her own existence to aid a human. If she'd known what her decision to send him off with Guy Sinclair would have wrought, she would have left him to Ulric. At least he would have died with his soul intact and God, in His mercy, would have accepted Constantine in Heaven.

When Isobel had learned that Constantine had been arrested in France and was being held at Chinon, she'd done everything within her power—and a bit beyond—to gain his freedom. Unfortunately, Philip of France had been a stubborn bastard and refused to release the infamous Dragon.

She had wanted to be there for his death, a familiar face among a crowd of strangers who'd cheered as the flames delivered them unto death. The sunlight had prevented it. He'd been damned and not a night went by when Isobel didn't feel guilt for having played a role in what Constantine had become.

This was the reason she was the only one of the Order who celebrated their mating. And there was no doubt in Isobel's mind they were mated. Neither Constantine nor Lexine might realize it, but they were as joined together as if they'd performed the blood ritual that would bind them for all time.

Knowing she didn't have all night to linger dwelling on a past that could not be changed, Isobel gave up the privacy of her chamber. She ventured down to the hall, where Madeline and Lenora awaited her. Angelica and Daria had gone to feed. Isobel gave a moment's pause at that. The women could have called in a donor, and though going out to hunt wasn't unlike Angelica, it was something Daria had only recently taken to doing. It sparked an uneasy feeling in Isobel, enough to remember to have one of the twins keep a watch on her.

Though Isobel never wanted to assume a member of the Order would dare betray the First, the truth of the matter was, there were no guarantees to ensure everlasting loyalty. And now was not the time to take chances. Not with Samhain so near.

Nothing could go wrong. If it did, the results would be catastrophic.

Lenora, who'd been honing the blade of one of her daggers, looked at her inquisitively. Madeline, a learned woman, more often than not found with her nose buried in a book, set aside the thick tome she was reading.

"What are we to do about Dragon?"

Isobel understood their enthusiasm to shed Constantine's blood, even if she didn't agree with it. "Nothing. You are to do nothing. The death warrant has been canceled."

As long as the assassins hung back and didn't threaten his existence, Isobel believed peace—fragile though it was—could be maintained and Samhain would come and pass with no blood being shed. Vampire or otherwise.

Madeline was clearly aggravated by this turn of events. "Very well.

Lenora wasn't so quick to comply, however. "One aggressive move and I take him out."

Madeline and Lenora, vicious as they were, were as loyal to the Order as any sister, which was why Isobel nodded in agreement. "Just remember, we can ill afford a war with the Templars."

"We can take them, and well you know it."

"What they lack in number they make up for in power, and well *you* know this. Constantine is not to be taken out. Not now, nor after Samhain. No matter what occurs that night."

Madeline nodded before reclaiming her tome. Lenora grumbled an agreement as she continued to stroke the blade with the sharpening stone.

With that bit of business done, Isobel gave in to the nagging hunger. "I'll be back soon."

Ancient though she was, and well in control of her body's needs, she still craved blood. She could call in a donor, but found the occasional hunt broke the monotony of an existence that had spanned over a thousand years.

She hoped to find Daria in the village, but something nagged at her that she wouldn't.

Chapter Twenty-Two

Julian leveled a hard glare at his lover, who sat perched on the edge of the bed looking demur and positively enchanting. That such evil was wrapped in such an angelic package never failed to amaze, and delight him. "Are you positive? If you're wrong..."

She held up a hand, her manicured pink nails went with the feminine look she worked to its full advantage. "I heard Isobel tell Constantine myself."

Pleased by this news, Julian resumed his pacing of the length of his chamber. His fury knew no bounds. How such a vital piece of information had slipped by him all of these centuries, he didn't know. That the power of the Daystar could only be exchanged on the night of the Bloodmoon was interesting indeed.

It changed nothing, yet everything, at the same time.

He turned a cool smile on his lover, who'd taken a great risk to deliver this information to him. He'd reward her well for it. "Excellent, my love."

Coming to a stop in front of her, Julian admired the way she looked at him with such devotion. It made him giddy to think that the day would come when all of humanity would regard him in much the same manner.

And if they didn't adore him, he'd make damn certain they feared him. Feared him right to marrow of their bones.

Julian stroked her throat, sensing the bloodlust was upon her. "Draegon hasn't taken from her yet, has he?"

She made a purring sound in the back of her throat. The sound excited him. "Her body, yes, but not her blood." Her cat-like eyes slid closed. "A donor was called in for him the first night they arrived. He hasn't fed since."

Julian continued to stroke his lover's throat as he contemplated this situation. A creature such as Constantine Draegon needed to feed more often than other vampires since his fury ran so hot. If he continued to restrict his blood intake, the hunger would eventually drive him mad. The Order would have no choice but to end him. Such a happening boded well for Julian, since it eliminated the complication of Constantine Draegon come Samhain.

"I don't care what needs be done, but keep Draegon from feeding."

She nodded, still making the seductive purring sound. She pleased him well, this one. He'd miss her when she was gone, if for no other reason than he wouldn't have someone to share his bloodlust with.

Her mouth curled into the only type of grin he'd seen cross her angelic face—one of pure menace. "Of course, Julian. Anything for you."

"And all is in readiness?"

She nodded. "I feel certain the Hallowed trusts me enough that I can manage to pry her away from Draegon."

He was less certain of that, but decided to keep that observation to himself. After all, if she failed him, he had another ready and willing to take her out and carry on with the plan.

When Julian pulled away from her and crossed the chamber, his lover's gaze passed over him greedily. His latest victim was bound on the bed. Naked and shivering from cold, it was obvious the poor girl was terrified. Julian idly ran his hand over her head, smiling. He inhaled the aromas of her blood and fear. He was reluctant to share this one with his lover.

Never had Julian encountered a creature who relished the joy of the kill more than his lover. Her life had twisted her into the bloodthirsty vampire here with him tonight. How she managed to hide her true nature from the Order, he didn't know.

From what he knew, the First had found her in the gutter of London, bleeding out from a birth gone horribly wrong. Her master, a wealthy lord who'd got her with child and then cast her out, refused to take her in. His wife forbade him to even call a physician.

The First took her from death and gave her the gift of immortality. The lord and lady, who'd stood aside while she'd nearly bled to death after losing her child, met a tragic end soon after she was turned. Julian had no doubt she'd been the cause of their untimely, and vicious, demise.

"Come here, my love."

She sauntered over to him. He loved the fluid way she moved. Her hunger and desire reached him before she did. Towering over the now whimpering woman upon his bed, his lover laid claim to his mouth, making sure she pierced his bottom lips with her fangs to bring forth his blood.

She broke the kiss and stepped back. She tilted her head to the side and smiled. It never failed to amaze Julian how no one suspected the viciousness hidden beneath her gentle façade. "You will be sharing her with me, won't you darling?"

When asked so sweetly, how could he not? "Of course."

Taking hold of the woman's curls, he thrust her at his lover as if she were nothing more than a rag doll. The girl let out a scream when his lover took hold of her. Ah, what a wondrous sound it was.

His lover cradled her. "Hush now, darling," she soothed.

The woman whimpered. He loved the sound of a mortal's fear. He ached to hear the Hallowed make such a sound as he played with her before draining every last drop of her blood.

Julian couldn't fault himself for his obsession with the Hallowed. He'd been searching for her for centuries. Now that he'd found her, and she was nearly within his grasp, he had to have her. Soon.

The Hallowed would be his. He would take everything she had to give. Her blood sealed the fate of the world.

Chapter Twenty-Three

Greaves Castle:

November 19 1300

Constantine gagged on the stench of his own blood and vomit as he lay face down on the icy stone floor of Ulrich's solar. His entire body shook violently from pain, the cold doing little to numb him against it.

Ulric had been more brutal than usual. At least it was over—for tonight.

Now that Ulric was done with him, he'd already moved on to his other pleasure, which was torturing women. But then, from what Constantine had seen, Ulric liked anyone weaker than him. Women, boys, it mattered not to him.

The petite and comely chambermaid with the blonde curls was new to Greaves Her wide smile and large blue eyes enchanted all the men at Greaves. Yet Constantine knew once Ulric was done with her she wasn't going to be pretty anymore.

Ulric did that to people. He changed them. Robbed them of everything they were. He left them ugly and scarred straight to their souls.

Futile though it was, Constantine tried to move. Pain sliced through his battered body, stilling him. He'd try again once he was able to catch his breath.

His back and thighs were a mess of crisscrossed bloody lash wounds. Blood filled his mouth. His bottom lip was split. His left eye was swollen closed.

And the most private parts of his body...

Tonight the pain overrode his shame. His blood was everywhere. The sticky warmth of it covered him, leaving him weak since he'd lost so much of it. He knew his face was never going to be the same. Ulric had made sure of that when he'd taken the blade to him.

He'd been held down by two of Ulric's most loyal soldiers—men as evil as their lord—while Ulric straddled his chest. He'd used the dagger to taunt him as Constantine fought wildly to throw Ulric off. His fight had been for naught. All he'd accomplished was to tire himself out.

Overpowered, Constantine could do nothing but bite back his screams when Ulric dragged the blade down the left side of his face. The cut began up near his hairline and stopped somewhere near his jaw.

Blood stung his left eye. But at least the eye was still there. Ulric could have just as easily cut it out. He'd be scarred but at least he still had sight. Constantine was grateful for that one small boon.

His anger left him as he lay bleeding. He liked the anger. It cleansed him of the pain. Now, the fury refused to come to the forefront and lend him strength. Instead, Constantine bit down on his already bleeding lip to hold back tears.

He swore the first time Ulric abused him he'd never cry again. He couldn't afford to be weak. Not here. Not when his survival depended on his strength. Yet the thought of pushing himself up off the floor and going on another day brought the sting of tears to his eyes.

He wanted this over, even if it meant his death. He knew that if he managed to fight his way out of Greaves, the memories of what went on here would stay with him for the rest of his days. Each time he saw his own reflection he'd see the evil of Ulric scarred onto his face.

Disfigurement.

It was Ulric's fifteenth birthday gift to him.

When he heard footfalls coming down the corridor, Constantine knew he couldn't be found still lying here. Placing his palm on the blood-slicked floor, he used every bit of strength he had left to push himself up. Once he'd managed to gain his feet, he swayed, the blood loss leaving him dizzy and disoriented.

He looked around the torture chamber, the manacles dangling at the end of the chains set into the wall above the bed making him sick. His eyes fixed on the large stain of blood on the bed.

There were other contraptions in the room, all designed to put a human body through pain. All used to satisfy Ulric's sick sexual gratifications. He'd been forced to suffer each of those torture devices. It caused his hatred for Ulric and his parents to grow over the years.

Ulric was a twisted bastard who preyed on those smaller and weaker than himself. Women. Children. He set his sights on anyone too weak to fight a grown man.

Constantine wasn't going to be weaker than Ulric forever. He was growing stronger every day. He trained relentlessly from dawn until long past dusk, honing his skills with a savage need for vengeance. It kept him on his feet long after his body was ready to give up.

In that moment, the last bit of his humanity and dignity bled out of him. Constantine knew only one thing—the time to leave Greaves was coming fast.

The day was coming when he would wipe the stain of Ulric Chambers from the world.

Chapter Twenty-Four

With arms opened wide and face turned up at the clear sky, Lex stood in the center of the stone circle. The fading sun infused her with its light as she waited for night to come. As much as she regretted the death of the day, with the night came Constantine. After the better part of her afternoon spent out in the courtyard and away from him. Lex missed him.

She'd have stayed with him as he slept, but she'd needed to be outside under the loving caress of the sun's rays. And if there had been any doubt to the necessity of needing the sun, the voices screaming in her head were a loud reminder.

The voices, Lex now knew, were the Hallowed who'd come before her. Or at least the four who had crossed over during their failed rituals to hold them in this plane of existence. This didn't bode well for her, Lex thought as she gazed at the sun. Five had come before her and only one had survived. Those weren't good odds at all, as far as Lex was concerned.

Over the course of the past few nights, Isobel had been a regular font of information. She'd explained what a Hallowed was—simply put—a human vessel that housed the power of the Daystar. The four who hadn't made it through the ritual now existed in another realm, parallel to this one, moving simultaneously through the ages. These were the women who spoke to her, who'd been yelling in her head since she was a little girl. As Samhain neared, Lex felt a deeper connection binding her to the Hallowed—one power divided into separate bodies.

At this point Lex didn't know what would be worse, not making it through and becoming pure energy or having to go much longer waiting for what was to come. Not knowing if she'd live or die was an exercise in torture, the stress of which festered within her. As each day passed she was becoming short tempered and began to retreat into herself, just like she'd done after Christian died. She cut herself off from everyone save Constantine. Her nights were now spent trying to make each moment with him last.

The faint call of a hawk overhead pulled Lex out of her thoughts. She watched the magnificent bird soar across the sky, and in that moment she became one with everything around her.

For a moment—just one incredible moment—Lex was one with the all of the elements. The earth was alive and singing to her, its rich voice blending with the music of the Hallowed.

Lex dropped to her knees and closed her eyes. Words she had never known before now, spoken in a language she'd never heard, rolled as naturally off her tongue as if she'd been born to them.

Her chant was for Danu, the Mother of the Gods, and Druanita, the Queen of the Druids. They were all around her, passing through her, as she prayed to them. Power surged through her. Instinctively, she knew it was that of the goddesses and of the Daystar. It branded Lex right to her soul and made her realize that from this moment on, no matter what occurred come Samhain, there would be no escaping this world of Druids and magic.

When Lex finished the prayers, the voices quieted in her head. For the moment, at least, she was once again alone in her own skin. She rose and looked to the keep. As much as she dreaded returning to it, she needed to be with Constantine. She missed him and hated that she'd had to leave him.

The mark on her stomach burned as she stepped out of the stone circle. Giving the sky one last glance, Lex crossed the courtyard toward the keep. She had one goal in mind, and that was to return to their chamber so she could be with Constantine. The last thing she wanted was to be detained in the hall.

"He hurts."

Lex halted in her tracks when Daria's voice cut through the quiet. "Excuse me?"

Daria Bastille, who Lex had learned was once a courtesan in King Louis the Fifteenth's court, rose regally from a chair set in a darkened corner of the cavernous hall. The silver threading in her white gown shimmered as she sauntered over to Lex.

"Your man. I feel his pain."

Cold dread ran through Lex. "What happened? Who hurt him?"

"He hurts himself, Lexine. He has been since he was a boy."

Lex shook her head, unable to grasp what Daria was saying. "So, Constantine is okay?"

No one was hurting him—that was all that mattered to Lex.

"Dragon is far from 'okay'. But I think it's you who'll save him from himself."

Daria came to stand before her. The rich musk of her perfume filled Lex's senses. The gleam in her silver eyes was hypnotic. There was no mistaking that Daria was a woman who held many—many—secrets within her.

When Daria reached out to her, Lex stared at her hand and wondered whether or not she should take it. Lex didn't know if she dared to go where the vampire would lead her.

Swallowing down her fear, Lex slipped her hand in Daria's. The vampire offered her a cool grin. Her fangs peeked out behind red lips. As if in a trance, Lex allowed Daria to lead her up the stone steps to the second level of the keep. Flickering light from the torches set in iron wall sconces broke the dark. The firelight sent long shadows dancing across the walls as they traversed down the long corridor. For just a moment, Lex had the distinct sensation she wasn't merely traveling through the castle, but through time as well.

When they came to the last chamber, Lex was surprised to see the door open. The last time she'd tried to get in here and snoop around, the door had been locked.

Daria tugged her inside and Lex felt as if she were stepping into a different plane of existence. This chamber seemed frozen in time. From what she could see, there were no modern amenities here. There weren't even doors to close off the massive open balcony.

The only furniture in this medieval chamber was a bed, enclosed in white netting, which billowed from the wind whipping in from the balcony. Everything seemed so otherworldly, as if the very air were charged with an energy that, though just as strong as what burned within her, was something vastly different.

"Can you feel it, lass?" Daria tugged her toward the balcony. "Can you feel the energy all around us?"

"Yes, I feel it." Lex sounded a bit breathless, even to her own ears. "It sings to me."

"It sings to us all, Lexine."

Once out on the balcony, Daria released her hand. Lex moved to the low stone wall and looked out at the night. She sucked in a hard breath when Daria stepped behind her. The vampire pressed herself against Lex's back. Lex wanted to move away yet she remained still, as if under a spell.

"I can feel your heartbeat."

Lex stiffened when Daria wrapped her arms around her waist. When Daria inched up her shirt and pressed the palm of her cool hand over the mark of the Daystar, Lex hissed and tried to push her away.

"The power is great inside of you, Lexine." Daria's voice was an intoxicating whisper in her ear. "Greater than those who came before you. Learn to channel it and you'll hold the world in your hands."

Lex fought against the seductive power of Daria's voice. She shook her head and moved Daria's hand away from her. "I don't want the world. I just want to go home."

As Daria stepped away, a movement caught Lex's attention. She looked to the left and saw Constantine stepping from the shadows at the other end of the balcony.

As much as she wondered what he was doing out here, the sight of Constantine comforted her. He looked as if he'd just risen from sleep, with his messy hair and hooded eyes. He wore only black pants and boots. Lex liked the way the moonlight played off the vivid colors of his tattoos. He really was a handsome man. It amazed Lex he couldn't see his own appeal.

"Give him your energy."

Daria's voice was a seductive purr in her ear. Lex realized how close the vampire was to her when Daria's hands settled on her shoulders.

Lex's breathing was ragged and she watched Constantine's steady approach. His lips were parted, his fangs showing. He said nothing, remaining as silent as a grave when he came to stand before her.

This was a side of Constantine she had never seen. Tonight he was all things wild. He was the night and the shadows. His eyes held the promise of such pleasure she could barely breathe as anticipation gripped her.

Daria used her body to move her forward. "Give him of yourself."

Daria's hypnotic voice guided her, drove her closer to Constantine. His eyes narrowed on her, watching her like a predator would its prey. His sexual need wrapped around her, awakening her own desire and sending a flood of warmth to the juncture of her thighs.

Constantine's hands settled at her hips, the simple touch ignited her. The ache it brought begged for Constantine to fill her.

When Lex released her energy into Constantine, his lip curled into a primal sneer. His fingers bit into her hips as his eyes ignited with silver fire. "Fuck it all..."

His head fell forward and his body stiffened. Lex went to pull the power back but Daria was quick to stop her. "No, Lexine. Let it flow from you to him."

Lex couldn't understand why fear suddenly took hold of her. She slipped away from the moment, needing to find a safe place in her mind. Constantine, however, had other ideas.

He looked at her through the veil of his hair. "Go easy, elf. Relax." He leaned in to her, his cheek brushing against hers. "Trust me."

He didn't need to ask her twice. Lex trusted him as she'd never trusted another person, save her sister and brother. The tension eased out of her and she released even more of her power into him. "I trust you."

His growl reverberated through her, creating a rush of desire to go with the heat and pressure building in the very core of her.

"Leave us."

Constantine's command had Daria moving away from them. Lex was glad to be rid of the vampire's touch.

"Accept the gift, Constantine. This may be your last chance."

With those cryptic words, Daria left them. Lex started to ask what she'd meant, but Constantine's mouth settled over hers and cut off the question.

In the span of one moment to the next, Constantine's demeanor changed. He went from quietly contained to furious abandon. He was all over her, in her head, on her body, and in her soul. Lex was completely consumed by him and she was reveling in every moment of it.

Constantine broke contact with her mouth lifted her. Wrapping her arms around his neck and her legs around his waist Lex held fast as he carried her into the chamber. Once inside, he swept aside the veil of netting around the bed and laid her down. The bed gave under his heavy weight. He settled over her a moment later. Lex held him close enough for him to feel her heart beating against his chest as his mouth once again claimed hers.

That's when the first flash of a vision pierced Lex's mind.

She gasped and her eyes flew open. Constantine lifted off her, bracing his hands on each side of her. His frown was fierce as he stared down at her.

"What's wrong?"

Lex shook her head, beyond words as she struggled to erase the confusing image from her mind. She barely saw

Constantine. Instead, her eyes saw a black-haired boy crouching on the ground against a wall. He was crying. Bleeding. But before she could focus on him, the vision vanished.

"Nothing. I'm fine." He didn't look like he believed her, though she knew without his telepathy working, he couldn't tell if she was lying or not. "Truly, Constantine. I'm fine."

Her lie was a weak one, but one he seemed to accept. He pulled up her robe and tugged off her underwear. When his hand, warm from her energy, touched her between her legs, Lex let out a cry into his mouth. He gently pressed his palm against her. Lex lifted her hips, begging him without words, for more. And he gave. He gave her what her body craved.

When Constantine slipped a finger into her wetness, Lex clawed at his back, ripping at his skin with her nails. Her back arched and a hiss of breath left her as her body strained for more of his touch. With his other hand he tore open his pants and shoved them down. When he couldn't get them off, he broke the contact of their bodies only long enough to rid himself of his clothes.

He came back to her, his fingers playing her body as his mouth licked and nipped a path down to the part of her that needed him most. Using his tongue and fingers, Constantine showed her what it meant to be worshiped by a Templar. He worked magic on her body, bringing her to her first climax. When he took his mouth and hands from her, Lex lay gasping for breath as the last of the tremors subsided.

With a devilish gleam in his eye, Constantine lay back on the bed and dragged her on top of him. Unsure of what he wanted from her, Lex merely sat, taking in the incredible sight of him.

Lex had the basic idea of what to do—after all, she was innocent, not stupid. It frustrated her that she didn't know how to execute all the wicked thoughts running through her mind.

"Tell me what you want me to do."

His hands spanned her waist as he took in the sight of her body greedily. "Ride me."

That sounded simple enough. And it put Lex in complete control, something she found incredibly erotic. Swallowing hard, she pushed herself up and awkwardly tried to settle herself on top of him. All she managed to do was feel foolish when it didn't work out very well. With a grunt, Constantine helped her out by taking hold of his substantial self. With ease, he guided himself into her. Her gasp mingled with his groan as she came down on him. Her body stretched as he filled her.

"That's it, elf. Take all of me."

And she did.

She slid down his shaft until he was seated fully inside of her. The hint of pain mingled with intense pleasure when she carefully moved on him. Constantine was a large man, in every way, and her body was still adjusting to him.

Her movements were slow, tentative, until Lex found her rhythm. She gained some confidence when she dared a peek down at Constantine and saw the expression of raw pleasure on his face. Once she saw that, Lex stopping thinking. Worrying. She just *felt*. The feel of Constantine's hard body sliding in and out of her, stroking her, awakened every nerve in her body.

Needing to touch him, Lex ran her hands along Constantine's chest. She loved the power she had over both of them and used that advantage to tease him with a ruthlessness that matched what he'd done to her the first time they'd made love. She gasped when she lifted herself, coming almost completely off of him, only to come down hard and fast.

By the animalistic growl, Lex knew he enjoyed that as much as she did. So she did it again, and again, until they were both damn near mad with desire. His hands came around her waist and he took control of her movements. Constantine moved her over him, his fingers biting into her as he growled out her name.

Just when Lex thought Constantine was about to reach his peak, he lifted her off him and threw her on the bed. He was on her in an instant, sliding deep into her.

Like a wild animal, he pumped into her, his body straining. When he buried his face in her neck and scraped his fangs over her flesh, she nearly came right off the bed.

"Oh God," she breathed, rubbing her cheek against his hair. She held his head to her as he licked and nipped at her throat.

"You're mine."

He growled that a split second before his fangs tore into her throat.

The pain lasted but a moment. A part of her warned her to stop him, but ecstasy ripped through her as she reached orgasm. The pleasure was strong enough to drive out all thought and fear of consequence as Constantine drank in her blood.

As he pulled on her throat, he held her firmly against him, preventing her from moving. Lex was taken away from the here and now. She squeezed her eyes shut and saw the black-haired blue-eyed boy as clear as if he were standing right in front of her. Living and breathing, and so real she thought she could actually reach out and touch him.

She *did* reach out to him. Her arms stretched toward him but she grasped nothing but air. He stared at her hands with eyes glistening with unshed tears. There was blood everywhere.

Steaming out of the deep gash that ran down the left side of his face.

Constantine...

Lex knew in that instant the boy she saw was Constantine as he'd once been.

A filthy, stained tunic covered his adolescent body. His legs were bare. His pain ran through her, replacing the pleasure of her body with the agony of his. And she took it. Gladly. His burden of pain became her own.

He spun around to face the threat only he saw behind him. He put his hands up to defend himself. Lex screamed when he was thrown facedown on the ground. He curled into a tight ball, his body convulsing as the unseen enemy was beating him.

The vision disappeared and Lex was slammed back to reality with a force that left her momentarily stunned. When the realization of what Constantine had just done dawned on her, Lex went cold with horror.

Summoning every ounce of strength she had, Lex pushed Constantine off of her. His mouth came away from her torn neck a moment before his roar echoed throughout the chamber.

Dread flowed through her as she brought her hand to her throat. It came away bloody.

When Lex dared to look back to Constantine, she saw the blood smeared on his face. She watched her blood drip from his mouth as her world crashed down around her.

Chapter Twenty-Five

Constantine pushed away from Lex with a roar. He fell to the floor as sensations he hadn't felt in centuries came back to him. Through Lex's blood his body came alive. His hand went to his chest, clawing at the scarred skin over his beating heart. Pain sliced through him as his lungs demanded air. He dragged in a hard breath and he slapped his hand to the floor to steady himself. The rush of sudden life tore through him fast and furious.

He licked lips saturated with Lex's blood, the taste of her far sweeter than he imagined. Her blood, warm with life and charged with power, slipped down his throat like liquid fire. He wanted more—enough to maintain the life in his body.

Not since the day he'd died had Constantine come as close to living as he did right then. Death snatched him back, forced out the life as he fought to hold to it.

He closed his eyes and ground out a curse as his heart halted and his lungs kicked out the air they no longer needed. Though her energy continued to wash through him, the sudden life it lent him left all too soon.

With the return of death came the realization of what he'd done.

With a hoarse cry, Constantine stood and stumbled as he grabbed for his pants. He pulled them on, his gaze locked on Lex. She sat on the bed, a hand to her blood-smeared neck. Her eyes, so large, were filled with alarm.

"Lex..."

She shook her head in horror. Her hand fell away from her neck. He saw that, though she was quick to heal from both her power and his, her flesh still bore his bite. He fought the raw need to take more of her even as he saw the tears gathering in her eyes. As they spilled forth, each one that cut a path down her ashen cheeks was a knife in him.

He sank to his knees and dropped his head in his hands. There had been times in his living years when Constantine had prayed for death, but never had he wished it with the degree of conviction with which he did so now. He waited for the devil to come up from his pit and take him. Facing Hell would be easier than facing Lex after what he'd done. But when he lifted his face from the shield of his hands, he saw Satan hadn't granted his wish. Instead he had to stay and reap the consequences of taking Lex's blood.

"Oh God, Constantine. What have you done?"

She leapt off the bed with an agility that surprised him considering she had to be weak from what he'd taken from her. More tears fell from her eyes as Lex pulled down her white robe—bloody hell, he hadn't even taken it off of her, merely pushed it up and took her like a rutting beast. She knelt before him and never, not in seven hundred years, had Constantine felt as filthy as he did then.

He was lost in an emotion he hadn't acknowledged in centuries. *Shame.*

When Lex's warm hands, which should have been cold, came to rest on his cheeks, Constantine had to look away. He couldn't look at her and see her disdain.

She was having none of that. "Constantine, please look at me."

How he managed to meet her tear-filled eyes, he didn't know. Bloody hell, he'd faced torture, death and an archangel. And yet looking Lex in eye was the hardest thing he'd ever done.

It took all of his strength as a warrior to meet her gaze and not break at the sight of her blood smeared on her neck and face. It stained her robe, turned her flesh as white as the material draping her shivering body.

"Damn it to hell, Lex, I'm sorry."

Constantine Draegon, who had never apologized for a damn thing, was on his knees begging Lex for forgiveness. He needed not only forgiveness for taking her blood, but for everything he was. For the things he'd allowed Ulric to do to him. For every indignity he'd endured and every tear he'd sworn he'd never shed.

"It's going to be okay. I won't leave you to go through this alone. I'll be right there with you. I swear it."

Constantine shook his head, unable to hear her past the rush of her blood flowing through him. It was a roar in his ears deafening him to all else. When he realized what Lex was saying, he felt like a filthy piece of shit for what he hadn't told her. She believed he had taken her blood and took in her power as well, forsaking his oath to God and condemning himself to Hell.

She was offering to follow him to Hell.

"Lex." Her name was a prayer falling from his lips, spoken on a tongue still coated with her blood. "You don't understand."

She offered him a watery smile that sliced through him. He never would have believed a dead heart could hurt this much. He wanted to claw it out of his chest to make the pain stop.

"At least you'll get to feel the sun again."

"No, Lex, I won't."

Even after Lex pulled her hands from his cheeks her warmth lingered on his flesh. She sat back on her legs, obviously confused. "I don't understand. You bit me, Constantine. You took my blood."

He stood with a sigh. She rose as well, frowning at him in complete confusion. "The transfer of power can only happen on Samhain on the night of a Bloodmoon."

It took a moment for her to grasp that bit of news. When she did, her jaw worked, as if she needed to give voice to a million questions all at once.

Lex lunged at him, throwing her arms around his neck and hugging him for all she was worth. "So it's okay. We're not going to Hell."

Like the selfish bastard he was, Constantine put his arms around her and held her to him, knowing once this night was over and she knew all, it might be the last time she allowed him to touch her again.

We're not going to Hell.

He'd never known another being as selfless as Lex.

She pulled away from him. Constantine accepted her tender kiss. "That's what Daria meant when she said I should give you of myself, isn't it? Did they just tell you, too? Is that why you knew to be on the balcony? You knew you could drink from me?"

Everything in him wanted to tell her *yes*. He wanted to lie to her, if only to have her continue to love him. God, why did she have to feel so damn good in his arms? Why did he have to *feel* around her at all?

"Yes, Lex, that's what Daria meant."

Her smile was radiant. "I'm glad you can take my blood." That whispered admission was a direct cut to his heart. "And not just because I was jealous of the donor. I *want* to share my life with you."

It would be too easy for Constantine to take her trust. Hell, he'd been a selfish prick since the night he'd escaped from Greaves. He'd lived every day fighting to ensure he'd never be taken advantage of again. He'd constructed a nearly impregnable wall around his heart, protecting him from anything and everything that might work its way to his soul. Yet Lex managed to break down every defense he had.

He'd rather have her hate than to lie to her. "I knew before."

The words came from him almost with a will of their own. She stared at him blankly, her head tilting to the side as she regarded him thoughtfully. "I don't understand."

Constantine broke away from her. Lex followed him when he strode out to the balcony. He stared out at the dark, remembering the night long ago when he came here looking for a way to save his miserable life. He wondered if he knew what fate had awaited him in the Holy Land if he still would have gone.

"Isobel told me I could take your blood the first night we were here."

She moved with such stealth Constantine failed to hear her approach. Her small hand curled over this thick forearm. "*After* you fed from the donor."

"No," he told her flatly. "Isobel told me before."

Rene Lyons

Like any warrior preparing for battle, Constantine steeled himself for Lex's anger. He didn't have to wait long for her reaction. It just wasn't the one Constantine expected.

Constantine saw everything about Lex change. Her hand slid from his arm and a mask of indifference settled over her features. Gone was the innocent lover he'd seen just a bit ago, gone was the passionate woman he'd held in his arms. In her place was someone he barely recognized.

She swallowed hard and touched her neck. The punctures were now healed, though smeared blood remained. A single tear slipped from her eye when she saw the blood on her fingers. She wiped her hand on her robe, for a moment just stared at the bright red mark against the white material.

He wanted her fury. He was prepared for her rage. What he got instead was quiet dignity. "I see."

How the hell could he tell her why he fed from another that night instead of her? Constantine couldn't explain why he'd done what he had without his past coming into play.

He'd been fighting the need to take her from the moment he woke while the sun still burned. Thankfully, Lex had been out in the courtyard, leaving him to face his raging needs alone. When he'd sensed the sun had set and she was returning to the keep, he'd left their chamber in search of a place to gain control of himself without the temptation of Lex driving him closer to madness.

It was why he'd come out here to the balcony. He believed she wouldn't find him here in this abandoned room. But Daria led Lex to him. And the moment he smelled Lex's sweet scent on the night air, he was lost. Unable to resist what Lex so selflessly offered, he'd taken her body and her blood because he was a fucking monster.

"Let me explain."

232

Constantine couldn't believe he'd said that. He'd never explained his actions to anyone. Ever. Not even to Tristan. And yet he wanted to explain. Nay, he needed to tell her why he'd chosen another over her.

He moved closer to Lex and went to touch her but she slapped his hand away with a force that surprised him.

"You don't touch me." Her cool façade broke and the fire of her temper sparked to life. "All this time I believed you took that woman's blood because you *had* to. Because the blood in my veins was poison to you." Without warning, she drew back her hand and smacked him clean across the face. "I trusted you and you lied to me. You won't have a second chance to play me for a fool."

She turned and strode back into the chamber. A moment later the door opened and slammed closed with a bang.

Never in his life or death had he felt as dirty as he did right then.

Not even Ulric had made him feel such shame.

Of all the people who'd come and gone over the ages, no one had ever trusted him. No one had ever loved him. Except for Lex. He'd taken her trust and her love and proved he was no better than the monster everyone believed him to be.

He returned to their chamber with the intention of grabbing a shirt and his sword and getting the hell out of there. Lex's muffled sobs came from behind the closed bathroom door.

Right as he went to grab his sword and slip from the room, Lex emerged from the bathroom. The air became charged, as Lex strode over to him. The hurt in her eyes leveled him.

"I swore I'd never ask you about the details of your past. But I've rethought that oath. I'm asking and I need you to tell me."

That wasn't what she was asking and they both knew it. She was asking for him to explain why he'd hurt her.

He'd never had to talk about his early years at Draegon Castle, and then what went on in the darkest recess of Greaves. The words died on his tongue when he opened his mouth. "I can't," he ground out between teeth clenched hard enough for his fangs to cut his bottom lip.

She regarded him stoically. "You mean you won't."

He sensed how close to hating him she was. The thought sent him into a fury. With a will all its own, his hand shot out and he grabbed her roughly by the arm. His upper lip curled back in a fierce snarl. She stared at him coolly, unmoved by his display of anger.

"Get your hand off of me."

He knew he was hurting her, yet he didn't ease up on his hold. "What the fuck do you want from me, Lexine?" He ground the words out from between his clenched fangs.

"The truth. You do know what that is, don't you Constantine?"

"You want the truth? You want to hear that my father put a bloody sword to my throat and threatened to kill me when I was but ten years old? And that my bitch of a mother told me she hated me before I even took my first breath?" His fingers bit into her arm. "Or do you want to hear how Ulric liked young boys? I spent my fifteenth birthday facedown on a mattress stained with my own blood, sweat and vomit while the fucker destroyed what was left of my soul. You know what I got for it?"

He dragged her in closer. "Constantine, stop."

"This. This is what I got for it." He turned his head so she could get a good look at his scar. "I killed the bastard a year later. I slit his throat and watched him bleed to death. Isobel paid Guy Sinclair to take me on. I went off on Crusade to get out of England before I could be arrested and charged with murder." He shoved her away. "So now you know why I hesitated to throw you on the bed, fuck you and then steal the blood from your veins."

She stumbled back a step, righted herself and wiped the tears from her cheeks. He turned away from her, ready to hate her for her pity. Ready for her disgust. Instead, she gave him her love.

"I'd say I'm sorry for what you've suffered but I know you'll only take it as pity. Instead, all I can tell you is I love you, Constantine."

"How the fuck can you love me?"

Her smile nearly brought him to his knees. "How can I not?"

A growl came from the back of his throat as Constantine pushed past her. She watched him silently as he pulled on a shirt and grabbed his baldric and trench.

"Please don't go."

He clenched his baldric in his fist. It took everything not to fall to his knees and beg her to forgive him.

Instead, he turned and walked out, Lex's sad cries following him out of the keep and into the courtyard.

There, under the pale glow of the moon, Constantine swore he heard Ulric's evil laugh echo on the cold night air. Or was it the devil laughing, waiting none-too patiently for his due?

CR&O

Stunned, Lex couldn't believe Constantine had left. Nor could she believe the things he'd told her. Going over to the door, she flattened her palm against the aged wood. "Come back."

She whispered that to no one as she dropped her forehead against the door. Try as she might, she couldn't will herself to stop crying as the implication of what Constantine said sank into her mind. He'd spent his fifteenth birthday facedown on a mattress in a puddle of his own blood and vomit. Ulric had liked young boys.

Oh God, it can't mean what I think it does. Please tell me I'm wrong.

But Lex knew Constantine had meant it exactly how it came out. No wonder he hated the scar on his cheek. How could he not when it was a constant reminder of his past?

Her heart broke into a thousand pieces as all of her anger drained out of her. Everything fell into place about him now. His anger, his reluctance to take her blood—even the way he made love to her—it all came together in one big, ugly picture of the horrors of his life.

Lex pressed her back against the door, and slid to the floor, unable to stop her tears as she did so. Her soul hurt. For the first time since Christian died she was furious, hurt and miserable all at once. To vent these turbulent emotions, Lex wanted to scream. She wished to God she could go back in time and hurt the bastard who'd tortured Constantine.

The things Constantine must have suffered were unimaginable wrongs that could never be undone. There was nothing Lex could do or say to take away the memories. No amount of time would erase the atrocities from Constantine's mind and his body. All Lex could do was continue to offer him her love, and hope it was enough to give him peace as Constantine moved through a world that had used him and then spit him out.

Why?

Why would someone hurt him like that? What sick monster would do that to a child? No wonder Constantine had lost his faith. How could he not when God stood back and allowed one of His children to be so hurt?

Raw pain ripped through Lex. It robbed her of her breath. It stabbed at her brain and twisted her stomach. Her mouth ran dry and her body went numb with the force of it. She dropped her head in her hands to stifle the violent cries torn from her when she thought of all her proud warrior had been forced to endure alone.

She saw the night he was cut in her mind. Lex saw Constantine, as he once was, a scared boy. Bleeding. Hurting. She saw him as the man he grew to be, a warrior-monk battling the demons of his life as he fought under the relentless sun on a field of sand. The blood red cross on his white tunic a symbol he no longer believed in.

Then there was that dark, and agony, and the echo of screams all around him as the stench of blood and sweat filled the air. *Chinon.* Then came the flames that licked at his flesh, burning him to death. She saw Michael, golden, beautiful and ferocious. She jerked, her back slamming into the door as a horrific stab pierced her chest. She grabbed the front of her shirt, her heart and soul felt as if they were being torn from her.

In a flash of an instant the past was gone. Lex was jarred back to reality by a soft knock on the door. Startled, she jumped up and opened the door, wishing she could be left alone. She needed to think, needed to work through what had just happened. Her heart hurt and all she wanted to do was crawl into bed and cry.

She knew damn well she was losing Constantine to his past and the pain that realization brought was something she needed to deal with—not whatever new problem awaited her on the other side of that door.

Which was why when Lex saw Angelina, she wanted to tell her to go away and slam the door shut. Of course, she'd never do anything so rude. Instead, she made sure no tears wetted her face and asked Angelina what she wanted.

"I hate to bother you, but Isobel asked me to get you. She needs to speak with you."

Lex shook her head. "Now isn't a good time. Can you please tell Isobel...?"

"It's urgent, Lexine."

Isn't it always? In the last month or so, Lex learned swiftly that *everything* was urgent in this world of darkness and shadows. There always seemed to be some sort of catastrophic event about to take place. Honestly, though, right then she couldn't care less if the entire world was about to fall down around them. All that mattered to her was Constantine was in pain and there was nothing she could do to help him through it.

Lex saw the determined gleam in Angelina's eyes. Dragging a hand through her hair to move the tangled mass away from her tear-streaked face, she knew the vampire wouldn't be dismissed. Sighing loud and long, Lex realized this was a battle she couldn't win. Seemed there were a lot of those taking place tonight.

"Let me go get Constantine."

Angelica shook her head frantically. "No. Isobel made it very clear her words are for you alone." Well now, that didn't bode well. Lex's hand flew guiltily to where Constantine had bitten her. Angelina's gaze followed. She also shot Lex's bloody robes a curious look. Damn, she should have changed out of them. "Isobel knows Constantine took blood from you."

Lex went numb with dread. "But she *told* Constantine he could."

Angelina offered a sympathetic look. "Just because Isobel told him he *could* didn't mean he *should*."

Lex began to wring her hands together. "But he didn't mean it. I swear he didn't."

Angelina's smile calmed her somewhat. "All will be well, Lexine. Trust me."

Left with no other choice, Lex numbly followed behind Angelina as she was once again led down the endless corridor. It seemed, as she went, reproach lit the eyes of the women in the oil paintings. The feeling was unnerving.

"Please don't let them hurt him."

Lex assumed Isobel awaited her in the hall, which was why she was surprised—and instantly on guard—when they reached the bottom of the stairs and Lex saw Isobel was not there. "Where are we going?"

Angelina's reassuring smile didn't quite reach her eyes, further setting off alarm bells in Lex's mind. "Isobel wanted privacy. This is such a sensitive matter, after all."

No one else was here besides them. Madeline and Lenora had gone to feed. Daria was off doing God knows whatever it was that one did. Constantine had stormed out of the keep. That left only Angelina, who because of her fear of Constantine, kept her distance from them all. Besides, if Isobel wanted privacy, she could have had Angelina bring her to her private chamber.

Something wasn't right.

And Angelina obviously sensed Lex's apprehension. "Fear not, Lexine. I'm sure Isobel has her reasons for keeping these matters so covert."

That did nothing to quiet the dread screaming at her. As Angelina ushered her across the hall and out of the keep—making for the gate, Lex dug her bare feet into the dirt and tried to pull Angelina to a stop.

"Hurry, Lexine."

"Stop, Angelina. I'm not going anywhere. If Isobel wants me, tell her I'll be waiting for her in the hall."

Angelina's hold on her arm tightened. "Well now, this isn't good at all."

Angelina glared at the sentinels. Lex's jaw dropped at their barely visible nod. She realized their loyalty lay somewhere other than with the Order.

To put it as bluntly as Constantine would, Lex knew she was pretty much fucked.

As much as Lex didn't want to believe a member of the Order would betray the First, when the portcullis began to rise, and she caught sight of the car parked near the gatehouse, there was no denying how dire this situation was.

Lex tried to pull away from her, but Angelina held her fast. "Let go of me."

A slow smile curled the vampire's lips. "I don't think so, Daystar."

Knowing she couldn't outfight a vampire's strength, Lex had only one weapon at her disposal. She could try to harness her power and use it to stun Angelina. Unfortunately, she was caught up in emotions too strong for her to get a handle on it. Left with one resource, Lex let out a scream that broke the perfect quiet of the night.

Angelina twisted her wrist. "Scream again and I'll rip your arm right off."

The threat, combined with the pain of having her wrist nearly broken, brought Lex to her knees. There was enough malice in Angelina's tone to leave no doubt she would make good on the threat.

Lex gritted her teeth against the pain. "Why are you doing this?"

"Preservation of my existence."

Lex found the strength to fight the pain and rise to her feet. If living around the Templars had taught her anything, it was to never go out on your knees. "Then you went about it wrong because I can assure you, Constantine is going to send you right to hell."

Lex saw her own death in Angelina's eyes. The vampire let out a vicious snarl a moment before she punched Lex across the face. Stunned, she flew from Angelina's grasp and landed in the dirt. Just before she slipped into unconsciousness, Lex saw an arrow whiz overhead. Her eyes slid shut as one of the guards atop the gatehouse fell, an arrow protruding from his chest.

Unwilling to admit defeat, Angelina dragged the unconscious Hallowed over to the car as another arrow shot by her. She tossed Lexine into the backseat and slammed the door shut. All she had to do was get safely past the gates. The guards would then drop the portcullis and buy her the few precious moments she needed to get away.

A hail of gunfire exploded over her head as the guards fired at Isobel and Daria, the latter shooting back with her crossbow. Daria was dead on with her aim. Another of the remaining three guards fell.

But when an arrow caught her in her right shoulder, Angelina hissed at the impact. It winded her enough to slow her as she pulled open the driver's door. A second later she was hit again. The second arrow slammed into her back. She might have still tried to get away, but the second fallen guard had been the one raising the portcullis. It slammed closed, marking the end of her futile attempt to escape with the Hallowed.

Angelina admitted defeat.

She'd failed Julian.

Chapter Twenty-Six

Constantine stabbed his sword into the ground and dropped to his knees. Lex's taste was still in his mouth and her blood continued to flow through him. Her power was a living force within him. For that one miracle of a moment after he'd taken in her blood, he'd been alive again. Her power had given him one glorious second of life.

Normally, by now, the effects of taking in blood would have left him cold. Not so with Lex. Her lifeforce continued to thunder in him. When he'd taken her blood into his body, he had felt her soul move through him.

Though Constantine understood why Lex had pushed him about his past, he told her things he'd never wanted her to know. His eyes slid closed as he prayed to God for the strength to go on now that he was certain he'd earned Lex's disgust and hatred. Hell, how could she not look at him and see the ugliness of his past? Lord knew he couldn't look at himself without the evidence staring back at him.

The haunting sight of Lex's heartache came back to him and robbed him of strength. Of all the people who'd suffered him over the years, Lex was the one person he'd never wanted to hurt. And yet, one look into her eyes when he'd told her he'd known he could take her blood had shown him a hurt so deep it cut through him. Shame tore through him, weakening him as he stared at the sky and pleaded with God to give him the courage to face Lex after the things he'd told her.

No more. Those two words came from the empty place inside of Constantine where his soul once resided. He wanted it over. He wanted to be free of the memories of Ulric and his parents. He needed to find peace before his time here was done and he was delivered to Lucifer. Constantine had tasted happiness with Lex and God help him, but he wanted more. He wanted an eternity of it with her.

The subtle ripple in the air came at Constantine a breath of a moment before Lex's scream rang out across the night.

Everything savage in him erupted like a terrible storm. Constantine jumped to his feet and pulled his sword from the ground. Like a man gone mad, he charged around the side of the keep. His sword high, ready to strike just as he'd done countless times running into battle. He had no thought in his mind save for the need to shed the blood of whoever dared pull such a scream from Lex.

As he rounded the keep, the scene that met him was one of chaos. He caught sight of Isobel and Daria. Bullets came at them, stopping short of where they stood. Daria released an arrow from her crossbow. The guard it was meant for managed to jump out of the way.

Near the gatehouse, slumped over the open driver's door of a car, was Angelina. Lex was nowhere to be seen. Yet Constantine sensed her. Her fear rolled over him like a cold wave. He looked to Isobel in askance.

Isobel's expression was bone chilling. "Angelina has Lexine."

Heedless of his own safety, Constantine let out a battle cry and charged toward the car. At that same moment, Angelina regained consciousness and lifted herself from the door. She turned to see him running toward her, and scrambled to get into the car. Not that she would get far since the gate was down. A third arrow stuck her, stopping her vain attempt at escape. Thrown forward from the force of the hit, Angelina fell back over the door before falling to the ground, unconscious.

The chaos going on around her roused Lex. Constantine saw her head pop up in the back window. She looked dazed as she went to bolt from the backseat. She screamed and fell back inside the car when a bullet whizzed past her.

"No!" Isobel shrieked.

"Stay in the bloody car," Constantine roared

Lex nodded once and threw her arms over her head before she slouched down out of his view.

Constantine continued to run toward the car. He had to get her out of there before Angelina woke. God only knew what the desperate bitch would do to Lex if he couldn't reach her in time. He made it a few feet more when the first bullet slammed into his upper left arm. He shook it off and kept running. The second bullet grazed his right cheek and sent him stumbling back. Blood spurted into his eyes. He wiped the blood away as another bullet slammed into his left thigh. The impact felled him but he regained his footing and ran on.

A fourth bullet hit him in the lower stomach, tearing its way out through his back. It left a gaping wound in its wake and was enough to bring him down.

His body was dangerously close to giving out. Though close to going down, Constantine's need to get to Lex overrode everything else. He clawed at the ground, still trying to get to her as he crawled toward the car, dragging his sword with him. He would keep moving until either riddled with enough bullet holes to bleed out, or he burst into dust and went to Hell.

Anything short of those two happenings weren't going to stop him from getting Lex away from Angelina.

When Angelina came awake and gained her feet, he growled as he continued to drag himself over the dirt. An arrow flew over him and hit her as she tried to get to Lex. Daria's triumphant cry resounded across the courtyard when her arrow sliced through Angelina's throat. The traitorous bitch erupted into dust a moment later.

With Angelina destroyed, Isobel berated Daria for killing Angelina. Her secrets had died with her.

In a fit of fury, Daria ran toward the gatehouse. She picked off the last two guards, sending arrows into them with a precision that, if it were any other time, would have impressed Constantine. As it were, he was still dragging himself the last few feet to the car when Lex launched herself from the backseat. She ran to him and dropped down beside him, weeping as she smoothed his bloody hair away from his face.

The bruise on Lex's left cheek infuriated him. "How badly are you hurt?"

"I've been better." Her smile would have felled him had Constantine not already been lying down. "Thank you."

"For what?"

Her gaze passed over him. "For saving me."

He grunted. "Thank Daria, not me."

Lex wiped the blood from his already healed cheek. The rest of him however, was too damaged to mend as quick. He hissed as her energy came into him when she ran her hands over the bullet wounds.

Isobel reached them as Daria moved on to inspect the car. "She must have bribed the guards."

Constantine agreed and went to push himself off the ground. Fuck it all, but his body wouldn't cooperate. He lacked the strength to support his own weight. He didn't fight against Isobel's hold when she lent a hand. Hell, as far as Constantine was concerned, better to be on his feet with help than flat on his back.

"You certainly grew some since you were a boy."

Isobel's humor helped get his mind off the pain and take the edge off of his fury. "I've been working out," Constantine remarked flippantly and looked at Daria as she poked around Angelina's car.

"Bloody hell, I wish she hadn't ended the bitch."

Isobel lifted a brow when Daria let out a string of curses that drifted to them as she slammed her fist on the roof of the car. "I'm sure she feels the same way."

Gaining a bit of strength, Constantine stepped away from Lex and Isobel's hold. Lex went to help him when he swayed, but he righted himself before they could grab for him again. "Any idea who she was working with?"

Isobel glanced at Lex then back to him. She shook her head grimly. "Unfortunately no. If anything, I suspected Daria was the one I had to watch for. Never Angelina."

"Thank you for your trust, Isobel," Daria retorted sarcastically as she returned with cell phone. "Look what the bitch left behind."

Isobel took the cell and flipped it open. She did a quick search through the contacts and recent calls. She snapped it closed with a growl. "Everything has been deleted."

"Fuck it all," Constantine ground out, though he'd expected as much.

Obviously, Angelina had been plotting to kidnap Lex for some time. It was unlikely they'd have been sloppy about it and left evidence of her plans lying around to be found.

"Let's get you back inside, Dragon. We have to get some blood in you before you bleed out."

Looking at Lex, he saw her pale at Daria's callous announcement. Constantine sheathed his sword as the four of them trudged across the courtyard. With Lex's hand firmly in his, her energy lent him the strength he needed to make it back to the keep on his own accord, something his warrior's pride appreciated.

They'd nearly reached the keep when Constantine stiffened. The oddest sensation passed through him, as if death's stale breath blew over him. The damn Druid magic veiling the castle prevented him from zeroing in on it. Instead, the feeling was slight and fleeting. Aggravated to have his senses restricted, he gave up trying to pinpoint it as blinding pain exploded in his head at the wasted effort.

"I want you back inside. Now."

Lex glanced over her shoulder toward the gate. "More renegades?"

Constantine didn't need his senses to know she was scared. "I can't say. The magic prevents me from focusing in on them." The night reached out to him, its icy fingers curling around him. He shivered, for the first time recoiling from the sensation of death. "We just need to get you into the keep."

Isobel was quick to agree with him. "Dragon's right. I can feel something out there as well." Isobel cast a suspicious look around the courtyard. "The gods only know who else Angelina was working with. You do *not* leave the walls of the keep until Samhain. Do you understand, Lex?"

"Trust me, Isobel, after tonight, that's the last thing you have to worry about."

Constantine was impressed with the grace with which Lex seemed to be handling this. Where most people would be a mindless mess after coming so close to danger Lex appeared calm and collected—even though her hand trembled in his.

Isobel gave him a once over, her gaze lingering over the bullet wounds. The loss of blood had weakened Constantine to the point that he was barely able to remain on his feet.

"You need blood, Constantine."

Though a vampire healed fast, this was asking a bit much of the supernatural forces that lent them their immortality. "I'll be fine," he assured Isobel.

She eyed him suspiciously. He knew Isobel was aware of how severe his wounds were, as was Daria. They wisely remained silent as they continued on toward the keep. Only Lex, who lacked the supernatural senses, failed to realize how far from fine Constantine was.

He was dying.

Again.

CRSO

Once they were safely inside the hall, Daria lingered in the open doorway. "I'll clean up the mess." She motioned out to the courtyard, indicating the four dead human guards.

Isobel nodded. "When the twins return, have them search the area for traces of renegades." She turned to him and Lex. "If those bastards were anywhere near here, they will detect it. I'll search through Angelina's chamber and see if there isn't anything to find in there."

Daria went back out into the courtyard, the night swallowing her as she stalked to the gatehouse. That left the three of them there as Constantine slowly bled out onto the floor.

The weight of Lex's stare bore into him as she surveyed the magnitude of his wounds. Before he realized what she was doing, her hands were on him and she was filling him with a small piece of her life. It would do to sustain him until he could get blood into his starved body.

"Come on." Lex grabbed hold of his arm and tried to tug him toward the stairs. He didn't budge. "Don't be stubborn, Constantine. Come upstairs with me."

"No."

"Yes."

He had to slap a hand to the wall to steady himself. "I can't take your blood from you twice in one night. I could end up killing you."

"You're going to fight with me on this? Are you crazy?"

"I won't take the chance with your life," he gritted out.

"You have no choice." She cocked a brow at him defiantly. "Remember, the same stubborn streak that runs in Allie, runs in me as well. I'm not going to lose you, Constantine, not even if I have to force every last drop of my blood down your throat."

Constantine surrendered his fight. The selfish prick that he was, he wasn't ready to let go of this life yet—as it were. He didn't want to give up his time with Lex. He'd miss her smile too much. He'd miss—hell—he'd just miss her. Everything about her. From the light in her eyes right down to the scent of honeysuckle that clung to her sun-kissed flesh. All of it. All of *her*. And though he knew the memory of her would help him get through the tortures awaiting him in Hell, he didn't want memories. He wanted *Lex*. Which was why he allowed her to pull him up the stairs. Isobel released an audible sigh of relief as she helped Lex heft his heavy ass up the stairs and down to their chamber.

By the time they got him on the bed, Constantine was shaking as what little blood left in him bled out.

When Isobel left them, Lex climbed on the bed next to him. "I love you, Constantine."

Her whispered words rolled over him as his eyes slid closed and she leaned over him. He followed the throb of her pulse and sank his fangs deep into her neck. She gasped and gripped onto him as he pulled on her vein.

With Lex's blood came a flood of emotions and power. Whether the emotions were hers or his, Constantine didn't know. All he knew was that love, raw and beautiful, washed through him, chasing away his past. It drove away the ugly images of Greaves, Ulric, and his parents.

That's when he knew, without a shadow of a doubt, there would be no more talk of donors. There would be no more holding back from her. Constantine would no longer resist the love she so freely offered him.

And he would return that love to her tenfold—even if it killed him.

Literally.

CRSO

Sometime during the long day, Constantine was pulled from sleep when the pain of the bullet wounds became too much to ignore. He'd been shot up badly enough that not even Lex's blood had healed him completely. His body was having a hell of a time stitching itself back together and as long as the pain continued, he'd get no more sleep.

Lex lay beside him, curled into him as if this were the best place she could be. He knew otherwise, but who was he to gainsay her when he liked her right where she was? Her breathing was slow and shallow, her tanned flesh drained of color. It pained him that he was the cause of her sickly pallor.

After he'd taken her blood she'd collapsed on him, too weak to do anything more than lay there like a rag doll.

Bloody hell, he'd come damn close to draining her dry.

Constantine still couldn't believe how selflessly she'd given up a vein for him. Like it was nothing. *Well, no. That wasn't exactly true.*

When he'd sunk his fangs into the side of her neck, she'd wrapped her arms around him and clung to him, begging brokenly for him to take all he needed. With her body pressed to his, her scent filling his senses, and her blood slipping down his throat, the life had come back to him in a sudden rush of warmth.

The act was extremely intimate, tender, and it left Constantine shaken from more than the throb of Lex's energy. Her love had moved through him. He'd wanted to hold onto that moment for the rest of eternity.

With her blood came her energy, and as it continued to thrive within him, Constantine's body didn't want to be at rest. He shifted and tightened his hold on Lex as she slept peacefully beside him. Her body was cold for the first time since he'd known her. He'd taken enough of her blood to steal her heat.

His movements woke her and she lifted her head. Her eyes half closed and her teeth chattered. "Are you okay?"

Okay? Hell yes. Better than he'd ever been before, even though his body resembled Swiss cheese. "I'm fine, elf. Go back to sleep."

She didn't lie back down. Instead, Lex sat up with a dramatic sigh. Constantine was starting to think she was as contrary as Allie. She merely hid it behind a genteel facade. Why was she the one person who refused to take "fine" as an answer from him? Everyone else always did. It ended a conversation right quick, which was how Constantine liked it.

"No you're not."

"Yes I am, now go back to sleep."

Her eyes kept closing. And she kept forcing them open. They closed again. Lex continued this fight for about a minute or so before she draped herself over his bare chest. Her cold seeped into his bones. He wrapped his arms around her in an effort to give her back her own warmth. All Constantine succeeded in doing was crushing her. He knew this because she choked on a breath and told him he was breaking her ribs. Disgruntled at having to loosen his hold, Constantine relaxed his arms but didn't let her go. He liked her right where she was. It was where she belonged.

They stayed like that for a long while, so long in fact, given Lex's gentle breathing, Constantine thought she'd fallen back to sleep. Which was why her question startled him.

"I asked if you were okay. I'd appreciate an honest answer."

He smiled. Genuinely smiled. No one could ever accuse Lex of being timid. "I'm alright. Truly."

She grunted. The sound mimicked one he'd made at least a million times. Lex had definitely spent too much time in his company. She leaned up and stared deeply into his eyes. She looked like hell. He felt like hell. What a pair they made.

"I don't believe you, but at least I didn't get your standard 'I'm fine' again." Lex smiled widely.

"What?" he asked, frowning.

She put her hands on his brow, smoothing out the scowl with her fingers. "I wish you'd laugh more instead of always frowning like this."

Yes well, he'd had very little to laugh at in his time. He shrugged. "Aside from Raphael's stupidity, I haven't found many things humorous."

Her hair fell forward when she kissed him, tickling him. Her lips were dry and cool. He wondered if that's what his felt like when he kissed her.

A painful jolt of electricity shot through him. Her power was rejuvenating, growing stronger. As each moment passed, moving them closer to Samhain, the power of the Daystar grew. And she was fast learning how to harness it—if not completely control it. But then again, Constantine imagined controlling it was something she'd never quite master. It raged within her, damn near scorching him if she didn't pull it back whenever they touched.

And it scared him. *Fuck it all*, it terrified him because her power made him feel helpless. He couldn't save her from it. He couldn't do a damn thing to protect her from it.

Lex pulled her lips from his and dragged in a deep breath. She was so weak it was obvious even breathing took effort.

Seeing her now, Constantine no longer saw the innocent women who'd stepped from the church with an eager gleam in her eyes and an aura of innocence burning around her. Now her eyes held the shrewd spark of a woman who knew the touch of a man. In those depths he also saw the all-too familiar gleam of a person who had stared into the night and had the night stare back.

She'd touched the darkness and it had robbed her of her innocence.

"You're so damn beautiful."

She smiled lazily. "So are you."

He grunted. "Men can't be beautiful."

"Oh no?" Her eyes lingered shut when she blinked them. She was damn near falling asleep on top of him. "I don't remember hearing that rule."

"*I'm* not beautiful."

"I wish you could see yourself through my eyes. You'd be amazed at what I see when I look at you."

For a moment Constantine's chest tightened at her words and the way she stared at him. There was awe reflected in her eyes, and just for a moment, he did see. She saw past his scars, past his pain and his rage, to the man hidden away somewhere deep within him.

"I saw you." That came out as a whisper so soft if he hadn't had extraordinary hearing he might not have even heard it.

"I would hope so, since you're looking at me."

She shook her head. "No, that's not what I mean. When you first drank from me, I think your telepathy broke through the magic and kicked in." Her fingers passed over his brow. "I saw you when you were a boy. I saw your blue eyes."

All of Lex's warmth drained from Constantine's body. "What do you mean you saw me?"

"I saw the night you were cut." Her hand shook as she trailed her fingers down the length of his scar. A shiver of dread worked its way up Constantine's spine. "I couldn't see who was hurting you. I only saw you being hurt."

Tears glistened in her eyes. He didn't want her crying. Not for him. He didn't deserve her tears. "That was a long time ago."

And so it was, yet there were nights when Constantine was back in that torture chamber suffering the pain and indignities Ulric forced upon him. Good God, how Constantine wished he'd had the strength to take the bastard out after that first night when Ulric had put his hands on him.

Tears slipped down her pale cheeks. "Not to you."

Constantine wiped them from her face. "Don't cry for me, Lex. Please."

"I wish I could take it all away. I wish I could just make it all go away."

He ran a hand through her hair, loving the way it flowed through his fingers. "You do."

She shook her head. "No, I don't."

"Yes, you do." He assured her. He took her cool, wet cheeks in his hands. His callused palms pressed against the smoothness of her face. "Whenever I'm near you the past doesn't matter."

Lex laid her head in the crook of his shoulder. Her heartbeat thundered against him. He held her close as she trembled. Close enough that she touched his goddamn heart.

"I love you, Constantine."

He wanted to tell her he loved her too, but the words died on his tongue. She seemed to accept his silence with the quiet grace he'd come to treasure about her. He hoped she knew what was in his heart and his mind.

When Lex slipped back into sleep, she stopped shivering. Constantine closed his eyes and prayed. He prayed to God with everything he was, hoping the Lord granted him this one boon— just this once.

"Dear God, please don't take her from me."

Chapter Twenty-Seven

Greaves Castle

February 1302

The dagger slid from Constantine's blood-soaked hands. It landed in the puddle of blood at his feet, which was spreading across the stone floor. He looked at the bed and fought down the urge to wretch. His skin still crawled from Ulric's touch. Tonight was the last time he'd ever allow himself to be bound and used for that bastard's twisted pleasure.

He looked at his bloody hands and knew he was finally free.

With a morbid need to make certain the bastard was dead, Constantine went over to where Ulric's body lay sprawled face-up on the floor. Blood seeped from the gaping wound across his neck. He kicked the body with his bare foot. No movement. He kicked Ulric again. Still nothing. He looked into the bastard's open eyes. With a hoarse cry, he gave his head a kick. The head snapped to the side before settling back into place to stare vacantly at the ceiling.

As far as Constantine was concerned, one death wasn't enough for a man such as Ulric Chambers. It wasn't enough to make him pay for what he'd put him through all these years.

Disgusted, the filth of the last years staining him, Constantine stepped away from Ulric and retrieved the rags he called his clothes from the floor. He pulled them on roughly, covering his bruised and broken body. He cast a sickened look around the room. This was every bit the torture chamber Ulric set it up to be. It was a goddamn room of horrors. Here, Constantine had spent many long and painful nights, suffering abject humiliation until he couldn't suffer it one more moment.

Tonight had been particularly gruesome, causing something in Constantine to snap. All during the ordeal his mind had screamed *no more*. No more pain. No more humiliation. *No more.*

When he'd been unchained, Constantine had managed to slip from the bed and creep over to Ulric's pile of clothes while the disgusting bastard spilled himself onto the floor with his own hand. Grabbing the dagger atop those clothes, Constantine moved stealthily across the chamber. His hand nary shook at all as he came up behind Ulric. The moment Ulric had turned, Constantine's hand had moved with a mind of its own.

Ulric had only a single moment of the realization of his own death before Constantine dragged the blade across his neck.

Ulric's hands flew to his opened throat as he stumbled back. Blood seeped past his fingers, down his bare chest and onto the floor. He couldn't call out for help. He couldn't make any sound other than the sick gurgles that escaped him as his life bled out.

With twisted satisfaction, Constantine backed up until he'd reached a corner of the chamber—the same one he'd spent many a night huddled in naked, bleeding and scared. He stood there as cold as death itself and watched Ulric bleed out. By the time the perverted son-of-a-bitch fell, his life gone, Constantine was laughing hysterically. Once Ulric was dead, Constantine knew he had to get as far from Greaves as possible before the body was found. There wasn't a person here who wouldn't know he was responsible for their lord's death. Though it was a fact most would be relieved that the depraved lord of Greaves had been sent to the devil, there were some who would demand Constantine's head for this.

Constantine had no intention of dying for killing a man who'd deserved to be sent to Hell.

Pushing away from the corner, his oath to Sir Walter was nothing but a fading memory in the face of the horrors Constantine had suffered here.

Constantine walked back to Ulric's body and stared down apathetically at the man who'd inflicted irrevocable damage to both his body and his mind. The things that had happened here would stay with him until the last of his days. He would see this torture chamber every time he closed his eyes. He would hear Ulric's evil laugh whenever his mind was quiet.

Dragging up a wad of spit in his mouth, Constantine spat it out on Ulric's face. "May you rot in Hell, you disgusting bastard."

He crept from the chamber on silent feet. Ulric liked his privacy when he committed his depraved acts, which was why there was no guard outside the door. On silent feet, Constantine stalked down the corridor and down the steep, narrow, steps that lead to the hall. In the hall he saw most had already taken to their pallets for the night. This was good. It would make his escape easier.

He eyed the double doors that opened out to the bailey. Beyond them lay his freedom. As he stepped off the bottom stair, someone shifted upon their pallet. Constantine's heart leapt into his throat. If anyone woke and saw him...

He was covered in blood. In his hand was the dagger he'd used to slit Ulric's throat. He'd never make it to those doors if anyone happened to wake and catch him skulking through the hall. The consequences of killing Ulric, as much as the filthy bastard deserved to die, were such that Constantine didn't dare think on them.

Someone else coughed but Constantine continued on his way to freedom. Cracking open the door, he froze when someone let out a loud snore. Sweat breaking out all over his body, he shook violently as he stepped from the hall. The frigid night air hit him, knocking the breath right out of him. Barefoot, in clothes so threadbare they would offer no protection against the brutal winter night, Constantine ran across the courtyard.

The light of the full moon lit his way as he ran around to the back of the keep. Ulric never manned the postern gate. There, he was able to escape without being seen by the guards who stood sentry atop the gatehouse.

Slipping out of the gate, Constantine didn't take the time to savor the moment of escape. Instead, his freezing feet carried him over the frozen ground as he ran all the way to Lowel Castle.

To Lady Isobel.

Once he reached the castle and was wrapped in Lady Isobel's tender embrace, did Constantine finally break. He released the tears he'd been holding back as Isobel held him, rocking him to and fro as she whispered soft words of comfort to him.

Constantine believed her. He believed her when she whispered to him that he was safe and that she would help him to get as far from Greaves as possible. She promised he would be given a new life—one that would take him to new worlds. One that would bring him glory.

But most of all, she swore to him that he would have his freedom.

And then she told him a word Constantine had ever heard before. It was a word that forever changed him and would bring him all she'd promised and more. It was a word that would ultimately lead to his damnation.

Crusade.

Chapter Twenty-Eight

Over the next weeks, time at Lowel passed as if in a dream. It all went by much too quickly as far as Lex was concerned.

Faced with the possibility that these were to be her last days as a corporeal being, Lex woke every afternoon with a prayer to God. She begged Him to prolong each night, make each one last forever. Still, they sped by, too fast for Lex to hold on to.

By day, after a shower and quick meal, Lex explored as much of the castle as she was able. There were many chambers locked off to her, but the ones she could go in were filled with treasures. Whether it be the ancients tomes in the massive library or the paintings in the gallery, Lex was awed by all that was housed within the walls of Lowel.

The weapons chamber was her favorite, much to Lex's surprise. She'd never been one who liked violence, yet something about standing amid a chamber brimming with medieval weaponry awed her. It also made it all too clear exactly how fierce these magnificent women of the Order of the Rose were.

Come the night, Lex spent most of the time locked away in their chamber with Constantine. Little by little, over the course of the nights, Constantine dropped his defenses and freely offered her his heart. To Lex, it was the most precious gift she'd ever been given, and one she'd treasure throughout time.

They never again spoke of his past. Instead, as Constantine came to accept his past, Lex accepted her fate.

Constantine however, wasn't as quick to accept it.

The closer they came to Samhain the more restless Constantine became. He may not have said it outright, but his every action proclaimed his fear of losing her. And the closer they came to the possibility of her being taken from this world—from *him*—the more scared he obviously became. Constantine, being himself, showed it through his anger.

But the night was here—Samhain—and in a few short hours Lex knew her life might come to an end. That was why, when Lex woke, she stayed where she was next to Constantine, savoring the last quiet moments with him before the world intruded.

The First was set to arrive shortly after sunset. The prospect of finally meeting the legendary vampire had Lex anxious, to say the least. That the First was a creature who gave even the Templars pause was saying much.

Constantine would be at her side, and through him, Lex knew she would find the strength to face the First and to deal with whatever came after. Which was why she wasn't giving in to her fear, letting it consume her and spoil these last hours before the ritual was to begin.

Waking as she did every afternoon, tucked against Constantine, his cool body was a most welcomed way to meet the new day. Yet Lex refused to move. She refused to acknowledge this new day. Instead, she lay in Constantine's arms wishing she could freeze this moment for all eternity.

Resting her arm across his bare chest, Lex snuggled against Constantine. He grunted in his sleep, wrapped his arms around her and pulled her even closer. His actions made her cry.

Lex didn't want this to be her last night with him. She didn't want to go to a place where she'd be nothing more than a whisper in his mind—if even that. When she imagined being able to watch Constantine, but never being able to talk with him, feel their bodies come together, be there to rejoice when the time came for him to receive the gift of his soul—and that was something Lex didn't doubt would come to be in the least— it broke her heart.

When her full bladder became painful, Lex relented and got out of bed. She walked to the bathroom on silent feet, not wanting to bother Constantine. After taking care of her basic need, she brushed her teeth and gave herself a long, hard look in the mirror.

Is this the last time I'm going to see this face?

Today wasn't merely Samhain, it was also her birthday. Lex didn't miss the irony that she might die on this day.

She'd always loved this holiday, and not just because it was her birthday. As a kid she'd loved to dress up and go trick or treating with her sister and brother. How ironic that Allie was always something dark like a witch, or a vampire. Once she'd even dressed as a shadow—something only her sister cold successfully pull off.

Christian had always dressed in a masculine costume. He would dress as G.I Joe or a medieval knight (again, Lex found this ironic). Although there was one year Allie and Lex had forced him to dress up as a girl, something that up until the day he died was a constant sore spot with him and the funniest thing ever, as far as his sisters were concerned.

Then there was her. Every year Lex added a new something to her fairy costume. Boring, yes, that she'd never changed things up, but it was what she liked dressing as, so that was her costume.

Where other people used Halloween to escape who they were, the Parker kids used it to embrace their characteristics. Visually bringing to life their personalities.

Tilting her head to the side, she saw the faint bruise that lingered over her vein. The spot was where Constantine fed from her. Often.

One good thing about being the Daystar, Constantine was able to feed from her whenever he wanted—and he wanted to often. His frequent feedings didn't weaken her. And so, like a man dying of thirst, he feasted on her, drinking her in and taking in her power as he took in her blood.

The feel of his body pumping inside of her as he pulled at her vein was so erotic it never failed to have Lex reaching an instant climax the moment his fangs pierced her.

Touching her fingertips to the bruise, Lex smiled. She'd miss him almost too much to contemplate if Isobel couldn't hold her to this plane of existence tonight. Lex could only hope that time in that other place would pass as quick as the blink of an eye. She hoped that when Constantine met her there, it would seem as if it were only a brief moment later.

Of course, that would mean he'd go on after she was gone and stay true to his oath to God. Lex had every faith in him, and that he'd join her in Heaven when his own time here was at an end.

Unable to look upon her face one more moment, Lex quit the bathroom. As soon as she stepped into the bedchamber, the light from the lamp beside the bed met her. She saw Constantine sit up in bed. His hair was in wild disarray around his face. His eyes were hooded as he watched her walk toward him.

Lex glanced at the clock that sat on the bedside table nearest Constantine. One o'clock. Way too early for him to be awake. "What are you doing awake?"

"I've slept enough."

Lex climbed on the bed and crawled up to him, laying her hands against the chest she'd been admiring moments before. "Really? Then why do you still look so tired?"

He cocked a brow at her. God, how she'd miss that arrogant look. She hoped this wasn't the last night she'd see it. "Because an insatiable wench kept me awake long into the morning begging me to pleasure her."

Well now, he had her there.

Lex and Constantine had spent the time from midnight to dawn lost in each other. By the time they'd slipped into sleep, both were drained and raw and still it hadn't been enough. With time such a precious and rare commodity for them, it was as if they loved each other enough for all the lifetimes they might never have. In truth, the coupling has been as explosive as it was heartbreaking.

"Happy Birthday, elf." Constantine gave her a searing kiss. When he moved away from her, his eyes narrowed on her. "You're afraid."

His perception astounded her, Lex thought sarcastically. She rolled her eyes. "Well of course I am."

In a swift motion, Constantine took hold of her wrists and shook her as if he meant to shake the fear right out of her. "I told you not to be afraid. I won't let anything happen to you."

Wouldn't it be nice if he were able to guarantee her that? Unfortunately, if Lex had learned anything over the years, it was that life came with no guarantees—especially when dealing with matters of fate.

"You might not have any choice in the matter and we both know it."

Constantine released her wrists and buried his hands in her hair. Lex allowed a slow trickle of her power to seep from her, making certain it filled him with warmth. "You're mine, elf. I'll not let fate have you."

The conviction in Constantine's tone helped to give Lex hope—albeit false hope. "I know I'm yours. And no matter what happens tonight, know that I'll *always* be yours." She placed a soft kiss on his mouth, loving the low growl that came from deep within him. "If the worst happens, I'll be with you whether you see me there or not."

The briefest look of utter desolation and hopelessness passed across Constantine's face. If Lex hadn't been looking as intently at him as she was, she'd have missed it. He released her hair and leaned back against the wall. "No you won't. You'll go to God."

"Not if I'm transformed into a ball of energy I won't."

No—she'd be caught between this world and the next, moving through time and space, one small part of a greater whole. Lost to the living, not quite dead and with only the other Hallowed to keep her company. That would be a fate worse than death. No wonder they hounded her inside of her mind. What else did they have to do?

Constantine's frown became downright frightening. "That's not going to happen."

"But what if it does, Constantine? What happens then?"

He left out a long, empty sigh. She was so used to his lack of breath that she no longer even noticed it. "You don't need to know that."

"Yes I do."

"Fine." He snapped, but Lex was unfazed by the outburst. "Nothing—I wouldn't do a damn thing. I'd go on as I did before, a soulless, lifeless creature."

Lex's heart broke. Dangerously close to crying, Lex swallowed down the lump of emotion that leapt up into her throat. "Swear to me you won't ever forget your oath to God. Don't give up on the hope of Heaven, Constantine. Please."

"No matter what happens, be assured that I've already seen Heaven. I see it every time I look at you."

Lex didn't even try to hold back the tears. "If things go badly and I'm—taken—know that I'll still be with you for as long as you want me around."

He pulled her head down until their lips were practically touching. "Forever, elf. I want you forever."

That was all the "I love you" Lex needed.

 C380

When Isobel came strolling down the stairs and stepped into the hall, Lex gaped in shock. She realized there was no First. Well, that wasn't exactly true. There *was* a First—it was just the last person Lex would have thought her to be.

Looking to Constantine, she saw he was just as shocked and angry. It seemed, all this time, he had no idea Isobel and the mysterious First—mother of the Order of the Rose—were one and the same.

"I'm so sorry for the deception, Lexine, but it's vital that no one know my true identity."

"You fucking bitch," Constantine growled at Isobel, obviously just as furious over the deception as Lex was.

Lex, who had hold of Constantine's hand, pulled back on it when he went to move forward. "You could have told us before now."

Isobel shook her head as she approached them. "And if someone managed to get to you ere now? Could you have maintained the secret of my identity?"

No, Lex might not have. "This is unbelievable."

Constantine pulled his hand from hers and strode up to Isobel. The twins moved in to protect her, but there was no need. All he did was sneer at her in disgust. "I should have known."

"I'm so sorry, Constantine, but you of all people know the importance of secrets."

His sneer gone, he regarded Isobel for a long, pregnant moment. During which time, Lex noticed Madeline and Lenora moved their hands to their weapons and Daria inched closer to Isobel. "If she dies tonight, so do you."

Lex's mouth dropped open in shock at Constantine's threat. She was even more shocked when Isobel gave him a slight nod. "I would expect nothing less from you, Constantine."

When Isobel looked past Constantine to her, Lex noticed that her smile was as radiant as it was tinged with sadness. The twin fangs peeking out from behind petal-pink lips had Lex pressing back into Constantine even more.

"I've waited twenty-four years for you to know me, Lexine. Please don't fear me."

"I'm not afraid of you. I just wish you would have told me the truth before now." She shook her head sadly. "I'm so tired of secrets and lies."

Part of that was directed at Constantine for his own deception.

Stepping around Constantine, Isobel walked over to her. Lex allowed her to take her hands. Isobel didn't show any outward reaction to the surge of energy Lex knew shot through her. "No more secrets, Lexine. No more lies. I swear to you I'll do everything I can to hold you in this plane tonight. Know that I'll lay down my own existence to save yours."

Lex didn't doubt Isobel's vow. The truth of her conviction was there, reflected in the depths of her eyes. It was there in the determined set of her jaw and her rigid stance. And though it gave Lex a small bit of hope, the truth was, something told her she was going to die tonight.

"Please, sit with me, Lexine."

Lex had to remind herself that this was still the same Isobel who'd showed her nothing but kindness over the last month. As she walked with Isobel toward the sofa, she was relieved to see Constantine following close behind them. She needed him near her—needed his strength tonight. As long as he was near, Lex believed she could get through this night without giving in to the terror that sat on the edge of her calm façade.

As Lex sat, Constantine came to stand beside the sofa. His hand settled on the arm, and Lex was comforted by his nearness. Daria, Lex noticed, slipped away. Lex was about to remark on this when Isobel spoke to Madeline and Lenora, now positioned near the hearth. What she said knocked all thought of Daria and the guards out of her mind.

"They've guarded you well over the years."

"Excuse me?"

Isobel motioned to the twins. "Madeline and Lenora have kept watch over you since the day you were born. They've always been there, in the shadows, protecting you over the years."

More secrets revealed. Lex didn't know how much more she could take this night without her damn head exploding from it all. The idea that those two bloodthirsty women were the ones watching out for her gave Lex a chill. "I know you had people watching over me, I just hadn't realized it was them."

"Yes, they have been your guardians over the years. Secrecy was always vital in the protection of you."

Maybe, but that didn't mean Lex liked finding out now that she had two vampire assassins shadowing her all of her life. "I wish I would have known about all of this years ago."

Isobel looked as if she regretted that Lex hadn't known as well. "If you would have known your fate it might have put you in more danger. That was something we couldn't chance."

No, of course not. Still, it was creepy that the women had never been more than a few steps behind her all these years.

"So you kept this from her all these years, even when it would have benefited us all to know she harbored the Daystar's power." Constantine's fury radiated from him, charging the very air in the hall. "Have you any idea how many women were killed in the renegades' twisted need to find the Daystar?"

"Yes, the loss of innocent souls was regrettable. Yet it was an unavoidable evil. You know how I value human life, Constantine. Look what I've risked for you. Think you it was easy for me to stand by and watch innocents die?"

"Tell that to the women who were slaughtered and had their fucking souls stolen."

"Like I said, their deaths are regrettable, but unfortunately, there was nothing we could have done to prevent it.

Lex closed her eyes and tried not to see the faces of the women on the front page of the *Damascus Herald*. Women she'd known, killed because of her. As far as Lex was concerned she was just as responsible for their deaths as the monsters who'd killed them.

A hiccup of a cry caught in her throat. Constantine sank down next to her and took her hand in his. He gave it a small squeeze and funny, but it *did* seem to help calm her enough to get Lex through the rest of this night.

"So once we do this thing and the power is neutralized, no more renegades will come after me, right?"

"The power will be useless to them. It won't be strong enough to combat the sun." There was a "but" in the way she said that. Lex was proved right a moment later when Isobel expanded on her answer. "There's no way for them to know that. So, for a while at least, you'll still be in danger."

That was *not* what Lex needed to hear.

Defeated, Lex sighed sadly and tightened her hand around Constantine's. Whenever Lex found herself faced with a challenging situation, Allie had always been there to help her through it. She looked helplessly to Constantine, whose fangs were bared in a nasty snarl. He was obviously as displeased at that bit of information as Lex was.

"This is all just too much." Lex looked to Constantine. "I can't do this, Constantine."

He knelt before her and took hold of her shoulders. "I'll be right there with you, Lex. I won't let anything happen to you. I swear it on God." Taken aback by his vehemence, Lex almost believed she'd make it through this.

Constantine stood and dragged her up with him. Lex faced down Isobel, whose eyes seemed to bore right down to her soul. "You do what you do and work your shit and get this power out of her."

Needing to get away from the hall, all Lex wanted was to be alone with Constantine. She needed his strength and his love to

272

get her through this night. "Take me upstairs, please, Constantine."

Lex swept them all with a glare that dared them to gainsay her request. No one dared.

"The twins will get you when the time comes to leave." They had to go down to the forest where a sacred henge stood. That was where the ritual would be performed. Just as Constantine and Lex turned to leave the hall, Isobel turned to the twins. "Come, we have much to do and little time to do it."

"Yes, we do have much to do."

Everyone in the hall froze and looked to the open door. There stood a tall, lean renegade flanked by six henchmen. Daria, Lex saw, hung back with a smug expression on her face.

So that's why she'd slipped away. She'd gone and invited in the devil.

Chapter Twenty-Nine

Not since his days at Chinon had Constantine been bound. His will and his body didn't know what it was to be a prisoner anymore, which was why he fought against his bindings despite the futility of doing so and the pain it caused him. From fighting against the ropes, the flesh of his wrists was raw.

Though he was being pushed through the forest at the end of Toledo steel, that wasn't what kept him moving. Julian of Harwick holding a dagger to Lex's ribs as he guided her to the henge was what prevented Constantine from taking the chance of a fight.

After Julian had come sauntering into the hall, all hell had broken loose. Constantine had managed to take out one of Julian's men before two more attacked. One had gotten hold of his arm and snapped the bone, rendering the arm momentarily useless. Another had run him through the chest with the sword now leveled at his neck.

Ian Mackenzie—one half of the Mackenzie brothers, infamous renegades who'd cut a bloody path through Scotland for centuries—looked a bit too proud of himself for having laid Constantine low. Constantine was going to wipe that smug look from the Scot's face before this night was done.

While Constantine was fighting Ian Mackenzie and his brother Malcolm, Madeline and Lenora both did their best to put themselves between Lex and Julian. Unfortunately, Madeline was ended in the struggle. Lenora grabbed for Lex as Madeline exploded to dust.

Before Isobel was able to summon her power around herself, Julian got to her and put a quick stop to whatever she'd had planned. A hard slap to her face by the large vampire sent her sprawling to the ground. Lex dove for her in a vain attempt to protect her but Julian had grabbed her and slammed her against his chest. The blade to Lex's throat ended whatever fight Constantine still had in him.

Everything in him rebelled at being a captive and led along in this macabre parade through the forest. He'd been there, done that, and didn't like history repeating itself. Yet here he was, bound like a bloody animal. If it weren't for Lex he'd have done all he could to go out fighting rather than allow himself to be bound and led around at the tip of a sword.

Once Julian had successfully brought the hall under his command, he'd led them into the forest, where he planned on taking Lex's power into himself.

With Julian forcing Lex along at the head of this morbid parade, Constantine kept his gaze focused on her. Away from the magic that surrounded Lowel, Constantine had hoped he'd be able to communicate with Lex through his telepathy. Unfortunately, whatever power veiled the castle extended out here as well. Or was it the power within Lex that kept him cut off from her? At this point, he just didn't know.

Julian of Harwick's quest for power was legendry. Constantine knew it was due to Angelina and Daria that Julian had managed to slip past Isobel's notice. Goddamn it, but he wished he had been the one to end Angelina. The bitch deserved the prolonged and painful death Constantine would have forced her to suffer her for her part in all of this.

Behind them, two renegades flanked Isobel. One held a sword to her as he roughly guided her through the trees. The other kept a sharp eye on her and made sure she didn't call on her power. Constantine knew that as long as Lex and Isobel had blades to them, none of them would dare make a move until they were out of harm's way.

Lenora brought up the rear, with an armed renegade guarding her. Not that it was necessary. She had been in a state of shock since the death of her sister, and thus far, she'd not left her catatonic state. She would not be much use to them when the time came to take down Julian and his men.

Daria, the traitorous bitch, walked beside Julian. Her animosity was a tangible thing, leaving Constantine to wonder whom she directed such hatred at. Isobel? Or Julian for his obvious attraction to Lex, which had nothing to do with the power she housed.

Though five against one weren't unbeatable odds for a warrior of his ability, Constantine wasn't about to get cocky as long as Lex's life hung in the balance of the battle. One wrong move would make the difference between victory and tragedy. The margin of error was too small for Constantine's usual arrogance, which came from lifetimes of perfecting his skill in battle, to come to the forefront. He knew he needed to wait for exactly the right moment to strike. Until then he kept on working the ropes, despite the ruination of his wrists in the process. If he damaged them too badly, his hand would be useless. As he eyed his sword dangling from Julian's hip, he knew he'd need his hands fully functional if he were to use his blade to take the bastard's head.

Giving the sky a quick glance through the crooked, barren branches of the ancient trees, Constantine remembered a night much like this one twenty-four years ago. It marked the night of Lex's birth. He'd not let this be the night of her death.

"Move, dog."

Constantine turned and bared his fangs at Ian Mackenzie. The renegade's expression went from arrogance to dread in the span of one second to the next. "Poke me again, boy, and when this shit goes down I'll make it real bad for you."

"Now, now, Dragon, we'll have none of your threats," Julian drawled over his shoulder. Lex whimpered when he ran a hand down her hair. The unspoken reminder of what Julian held was all too clear.

Though Constantine doubted Julian of Harwick was stupid enough to kill Lex before he had a chance to take her power, God only knew if he was twisted enough to do things to her that would make her *wish* she were dead.

Now that they were farther away from Lowel, his telepathy was back. From behind him, he sensed a blank mind from Lenora. Isobel's thoughts were blocked to him. When this battle went down—and it would—Constantine prayed to God Lenora would snap out of her stupor, and ready herself for the fight. The Lord knew she'd be needed.

Julian wasn't finished with his mad ramblings, since the bastard went on to taunt Constantine some more. "It's a fine night indeed to have not only the Daystar in my possession, but the legendary First and the famed Dragon as well. I'll take her power and wipe the world of the stain of you both. What say you to that?"

"I say once a fool always a fool and you, Julian, are a fool," Isobel retorted.

Julian stopped and dragged Lex around with him when he faced Isobel. "I remember you when you were naught but a cowardly bitch at the mercy of your husband. Think you you're any different now than then? If I were you, I'd watch my tongue or else I'll make your death the stuff of legends."

"I don't fear you, Julian. I never have."

"Nay, the great Isobel of Lowel fears nothing. But I assure you, *she* does." Julian leveled his dagger at the side of Lex's throat. She slammed her eyes shut. Her fervent prayers reverberated in Constantine's mind. He moved his arms against the ropes. More flesh fell from bone as they dug into him.

Julian hauled Lex around and yanked her forward as he continued on his way toward the henge. Lex tripped over a fallen branch. Julian's hold on her arm stopped her from falling face first into the dirt. Instead, he pushed her forward and snapped at her to watch where she was walking. She moved away from him when he whispered in her ear that it would be a shame for her to be damaged before he took his pleasure with her.

Daria demanded that Julian not have all the fun. She wanted to "play" with the Hallowed as well. All Julian said to that was, "we'll see."

It took everything Constantine had to keep his rage in check. He wanted to tear Julian apart and leave the prick for the sun. And he would do exactly that—once the moment was right to strike.

Lex went to say something but Constantine cut her off. *"No Lex. Not a word. Not one fucking word. Don't provoke the bloody bastard."*

"I'm scared, Constantine."

Her admission cut clean through him. *"I know, elf. Trust me when I say this night will not be your last. We'll get through this. I promise."*

He'd sacrifice himself and every member of the Order to ensure that vow.

"I trust you."

God's blood, her words brought to the forefront something in him that Constantine couldn't readily identify. He swore his heart kicked to life. That, and the oddest sensation of terror, which he'd known only one time before—when the first lick of the flames had touched his flesh.

That fear ate away at him as they neared the small henge that stood in the center of a clearing in the center of the forest. The tall bleached stones, which gave off a subtle energy all their own, bore runes running down them. Almost as if she were acting on instinct, Constantine watched Lex walk toward a stone. Her lips moved but no words sounded out. Yet he heard them in his mind. A Druid rite had replaced her Catholic prayer.

"Ah, we're here. I see you can feel it, Lexine. The magic of this place is part of you."

Julian let Lex go. Constantine tried to tell her not to run, that she'd never get away from them on her own, but her mind was closed to him. He knew it was not by her own accord. His connection to her was severed. The magic had taken over inside of her.

Isobel, Constantine noted, was moved into the henge. "Put her there, near *Ansuz*."

Constantine didn't know much about the Druids, but during their time at Lowel, he had heard certain words. *Ansuz* was one of them. It meant knowledge, wisdom, and was the rune of the First.

Lex continued to walk toward one of the stones as if she were in a trance. It was her rune. *Dagaz*. And as soon as her palms flattened against the stone her eyes closed and she threw her head back with a gasp.

Julian rushed to her and took her by the shoulders. He led her away from the stone with a tsk. "Now, now, Lexine. We'll have none of that." Then to his men, "Position them where I instructed. Lenora at *Sowilo*. Put the Templar at *Tiwaz*. He'll take Madeline's place. We'll be short Angelina, but you, Fredrick, will step in for her."

The older Mackenzie brother gave Julian a curt nod. He ushered a catatonic Lenora to her appointed stone. Daria sauntered toward her lover. She cast a long, hard glare at Lex before she draped herself on Julian.

"And me, my love? Do I stay with you until we start?"

Julian pushed her away, careful not to let go of Lex. "No. You go and take your place at *Uruz*. If I need you I'll summon you."

Given the murderous expression that passed across Daria's face, it seemed the bitch was none too pleased at being cast aside.

Julian looked at the sky and then back at Lex. By now, she seemed to have snapped out of her stupor. She looked to the others being forced into their positions for the ritual. When Julian took hold of her chin and made her look at him, a wealth of disgust emanated from her and hit Constantine like a truck.

"There is plenty of time before the ritual needs to begin. Plenty of time indeed." Julian looked Lex over. Constantine, a sword leveled at his jugular, fought against his fury. Julian's hands settled on Lex's breasts, and though Constantine saw how hard she tried to prevent it, Lex began to cry. "Watch now, Templar, as I take your woman's body and then take her blood."

Unable to hold it back any longer, blind rage had Constantine lunging for him. The renegade moved out of the way with a laugh, dragging Lex with him. Isobel yelled for him to stop, that Julian was purposely provoking him. The blade Ian held at him scraped across his neck, opening a shallow cut. He paid it no heed. He let out a battle cry and rushed Julian as he tried to bite his way free of the ropes around his wrists. He skidded to a stop when the coward placed Lex in front of him, using her as a shield.

"Constantine. No."

Constantine stopped dead at those two whispered words from Lex. Blood seeped from his neck and his wrists as he stood as still as death itself, his gaze locked on Lex. Her beautiful blue eyes were tear-filled. Her body, draped in long white robes, shook. The gentle wind lifted her cloud of black hair, billowing it around her ashen face. He knew, in that moment, that how she looked right then would stay with him for eternity.

Julian smiled at him with cool satisfaction. Constantine narrowed his eyes on the vampire, giving him a silent warning of the pain awaiting him in the very near future. "Temper, temper, Dragon. Give it free rein again and I'll hurt her."

"Hurt her and I'll make your death take centuries."

A hit with the hilt of a sword had Constantine letting out a low rumble of fury as he cast a menacing look out of the corner of his eye at Ian.

Julian tsked and cocked a brow arrogantly. "Oh, I don't think so. This night belongs to me."

Isobel went to move, but her guard lifted his sword at her. The tip of the blade ceased her movement. "I wouldn't be too cocky if I were you, Julian. This night is far from over."

In a fit of rage the renegade strode over, dragging a struggling Lex with him. His palm met Isobel's cheek in a hard

281

slap. She took the hit that snapped her head to the side with the grace of a queen. She straightened her shoulders and turned back to him, meeting his frosty glare with one of her own. Constantine now knew why Isobel had survived as long as she had. Her strength and pride knew no bounds and had caused her to endure through the ages when so many of their kind had perished.

"By the time dawn comes you'll all be dead and I'll be unstoppable."

"No, Julian. By dawn you'll be in Hell."

"We shall see, now won't we, Isobel?"

She leveled a look of cold determination at him. "The gods will protect us and you *will* fail."

Julian looked amused by that. "Where are they, then?" He stepped back into the center of the henge. He released Lex, who again, seemed to be drawn to the *Dagaz* rune. As she shuffled toward it, her arms outstretched, Julian opened his arms wide and looked around. "Why aren't they here now? And you." He grabbed Lex back. She looked at him, all of her fear in her eyes. "Where is your God? Why isn't He here to deliver you from death? He doesn't care about you, Lexine. He doesn't care you're going to die tonight. He abandons us all. Isn't that right, Draegon?"

"Fuck you, you miserable piece of shit."

Julian smiled coldly at him before he turned his attention back at Lex, who continued to fight his hold on her. Constantine watched as the vampire ran his hands down the length of Lex's arms. She shivered and tried to wrest herself away from him.

"Get your hands off of me."

He brought his face close to hers. Close enough that Constantine went to rush him again. Ian, quick as lightening despite his large size, moved in front of him and put the tip of the sword at his throat. Isobel ordered him to stop. Lex's beseeching gaze froze him in mid-step.

"I love you."

The impact of her declaration hit Constantine directly in his heart.

Julian forced Lex to look at him. Constantine watched as the fight went out of her. Just like that. It seeped from her and left her with a broken will.

"You'll do anything I want you to. Do you understand me?"

A weight crushed down on Constantine's heart when Lex nodded. Her compliance infuriated him and had him pulling at the ropes, despite how they cut into his flesh, in a bid to break free of them and take out Julian.

Whether Lex meant to do it, or if it was her body going into overdrive, Julian screamed and jumped away from her. His smoking hands told Constantine that Lex's power had surged through her and burnt him. If he didn't know Julian was going to make her pay for that, he'd cheer on her daring.

As it was, when Julian stepped back to her, Constantine knew the shit was about to hit the fan. "That was a stupid thing to do, girl."

He cracked her across the face caused Lex to stumble. Constantine roared, his fury exploding when he saw Lex's blood. He pushed past Ian when Julian sliced Lex with his dagger. Lex leapt back, out of range of the blade just as Constantine reached them. Ian tried to grab him, but Constantine sidestepped him. He fisted his bound hands together and knocked Ian to the ground.

Isobel tried to fight her way free of the renegade holding her but it was clear she was no match for his strength. Lenora finally broke out of her stupor and let out a battle cry that rivaled even Constantine's and attacked Malcolm. She jumped on the Scot's back and sank her fangs deep into his throat. He howled and tried to shake her off, but with her arms and legs wrapped around him, and the death of her twin fueling her, he wasn't about to get her off of him.

Daria made a mad dash for Lex, who gained her feet and tried to move out of the henge. Constantine saw all of this as if in slow motion. He leapt over Ian and grabbed for Julian, thinking to take the renegade down and reclaim his sword. Ian, however, wasn't inclined to stay down for very long. The Scot jumped up and caught Constantine in the back with his blade.

Daria slipped a blade from her boot, caught Lex and pressed the knife to her throat. Lex stilled instantly. Julian moved out of reach, just as Constantine was forced to face Ian. Constantine used the renegade's blade to his advantage. He waited for the perfect moment to lift his hands and have the blade cut through his ropes. Granted, the blade cut more than the ropes, but the deep gash up his right arm was a small price to pay for his freedom.

The rope hit the floor and Julian shouted out a warning as he wrested Lex away from Daria. "End him," he demanded of Ian.

"I'm going to send you to Hell, Templar."

"Come on then," Constantine taunted. "Let's get this done."

Just before Ian attacked, Constantine saw Malcolm manage to get Lenora off of him and subdue her with a well-placed punch. He drew his sword and sliced her across her stomach.

"I look forward to sending you to the devil, Templar."

"You first."

Ian must have believed he had the advantage since Constantine had no weapon. Obviously the vampire had never fought a Templar before. Besides, his lack of weapon could easily be remedied with a well-timed attack.

With his gaze locked on the dagger sheathed at the Scot's right hip, Constantine attacked. A punch to Ian's face stunned the renegade long enough for Constantine to be able to pull free the dagger. Ian stepped back, but was too late. Constantine had possession of the dagger and went on the offensive.

Though a dagger was usually no match for a sword, in Constantine's capable hand it evened the odds. A slice to the renegade's right hand had him hissing with pain and giving a pathetic jab of his sword. Constantine sneered and cut the bastard again. He would have gone for the throat and ended the fight right then and there, but Ian had obviously anticipated that and protected the area.

Constantine was about to try for the throat again when he heard Lex's scream. The bloodcurdling sound cut through the night a second before cold steel sliced down his back. It seemed another renegade had joined the fray.

Ignoring the agony exploding up his back, Constantine spun to face the renegade who'd cut him. Much to his surprise it was Daria. With a vicious growl, Constantine used his dagger on her, slicing her across the chest. She screamed and fell onto her back in a bloody mess. The dagger dropped from her hand, Constantine retrieved it and came to stand over her. Ian ran him through his upper left thigh. He paid it no mind. She attempted to get away from him but Constantine was faster than her. He impaled her throat and gave the blade a hard jerk to the right, widening the cut he'd already inflicted on her.

Daria burst into dust as Constantine went to use the daggers on Ian. As he fought the Scot, Constantine heard Isobel begin a low chant. It was followed by Lenora's scream. Lex's gasp came a second later and then silence, broken only by the sound of his fight with Ian.

Believing Lex might have been hurt, Constantine spared a sideways glance at her. It registered in his mind that she was unharmed a moment before Ian's blade pierced his chest just below his heart.

As Constantine slid slowly to the ground, Lex screamed and tried to wrest herself from Julian's bruising hold. She used her power to burn his hands and force him to release her. He did, but before she could reach Constantine, he'd grabbed her again. She was slammed against his chest and a blade poised at her ribs.

"Do that again and I'll kill you, power or no power." It was a threat Lex took to heart.

She didn't doubt he'd do exactly that.

A soft weeping had her giving a quick glance at Isobel, who lay in Lenora's lap. Her daughter cradled her as she wept tears of blood. The mother of The Order of the Rose was in much the same state as Constantine. The Viking-looking renegade had run her through the stomach to stop her chanting. It worked. Her words died on her lips as she slid to the ground in a puddle of her own blood.

"End him."

Lex screamed in protest of Julian's cold command and struggled to break free of his hold. The tip of the blade pierced her and she sucked in a hard breath.

"Please..." The Scot lifted his sword high. "Please don't do this."

"Wait," Julian ordered.

The disgruntled Scot lowered his sword. Lex's relief knew no bounds.

"Lex, no. Don't you beg that bastard for my life."

Lex ignored Constantine's voice in her head. To save him from Hell she'd do anything—risk anything—even her own soul. She'd not stand idly by and watch him be destroyed, especially not before his oath to God was fulfilled.

Julian smiled at her whispered plea. "Will you be a good girl and behave or do I have to make good on the threat and kill the Templar?"

"I'll do whatever you want. Just don't hurt him anymore."

"The bastard is going to kill me anyway, woman."

"I won't let you go to Hell," she countered.

"Lex, goddamn it, don't you do this."

Since she wasn't listening to the orders he yelled in her head, Lex didn't understand why Constantine thought she'd listen if he physically yelled them at her.

"Shut up, Dragon," Julian snapped. "We'll leave him alive. For now. After all, we do need him for the ritual."

"Thank you, God." He heard Lex silently pray.

"I told you not to beg for me."

"I love you too much to watch you die."

Not that she had a choice in the matter. Given the blood he was rapidly losing, death might come to claim him regardless of what she did to counter it.

Though it took great effort, he gained his feet. He bled past the hand he had flattened against the wound on his chest. *"They're going to kill me anyway."*

"Did they stab you...?" She didn't finish the thought and was terrified of the answer. If they'd stabbed him through the heart he was as good as dead.

"No."

Whatever Constantine might have said was cut off when Julian brought his hand to her throat. Lex knew a brief moment of fear when his hand tightened and her air was constricted. He lessened his hold and she dragged in a gulp of air.

"It's time." Lex's fear returned. "Let us begin, shall we?" Julian drawled.

Panicking, Lex didn't realize her power began to surge within her. It forced Julian to release her. Growling, be used his body to back her up until her back hit the *Dagaz* stone.

"I warned you about that."

Self-preservation kicked in and Lex threw her hands up when Julian reached for her. "I didn't do it on purpose."

His hand ran down her hair. A long moment passed before he spoke to her. "No, you didn't. The time is upon us." His smile was deadly. "How does it feel, Hallowed, to be so close to death?"

Terrified, that's how it felt, though she'd never admit as much to him. "Since I don't plan on dying, I couldn't tell you."

"Such spirit in you. Fate chose you well, Lexine." His hand caressed her check almost lovingly. "I had hoped we had more time with each other. I would have loved to sample the fire burning in your body."

Oh, she was going to make sure he'd sample it, just not in the way he thought.

Lex willed the power inside of her to rise to the forefront. The burn began deep in her core. It hurt her heart as it spread through her, burning her from the inside out. She started to sweat. It dripped from her as the power of the Daystar built to a feverish peak. She glanced at Isobel, whose blood stained the ground around her and Lenora, who still wept silent bloody tears as she held Isobel's limp body.

Calling on the powers that lay dormant in the earth, the elements awakened around her. Lex turned her face to the sky. The magic of the night flowed through her. She vaguely heard Julian call her name, demand her to look at him, but she was too far-gone in the power. She couldn't fight it back if she tried. It surged, not just by her will, but by the very nature of what this night was.

Instinctively, Lex knew there was a good chance Isobel wasn't going to survive this night.

"Don't do it, Lex."

Constantine's voice echoed in her mind, over the hum of energy and the roar of the power. She heard him past the chorus of the Halloweds' voices. It anchored her, kept her on this plane even as the power began to try to take her where she didn't want to go.

"I love you, Constantine."

Without giving it thought, Lex slammed herself into Julian. The moment their bodies collided, he tried to knock her aside. She wrapped her arms around him and held him tight, forcing the power into him. His body began to smoke she held tight. She refused to let him go even when his flesh began to blacken.

Julian's henchmen went to rush her but were stopped by Constantine. In a blur of motion he disarmed Ian, Malcolm and the Viking. Lenora stayed with Isobel as the chaos erupted around them.

By the time Constantine was done with them, the three renegades were broken and bloody. They were ended with well-placed cuts to their throats, sent to the devil in explosions of dust. And still Lex held fast to Julian. Her power burned him until Constantine pried her from him.

Constantine roared in agony when he pulled Lex from Julian. He grabbed his sword from the burnt renegade before he

289

tossed Julian away. Julian, flesh burnt raw from the intensity of the Daystar's power, faced Constantine with a sneer. The damaged renegade held the dagger out, pointing it at him. "The night may fear you, Templar, but I do not."

Constantine arched a single brow. "That's why you failed."

"You might have won this night, but you'll still serve in Hell once this world spits you back to the devil."

Constantine smiled a grin of pure evil. "Then I'll see you there, you bloody bastard."

There wasn't a hint of remorse in Constantine when he backed the renegade into a tall stone. With evil delight, he dragged the blade of his sword across Julian's neck. The vampire's eyes bulged as his blood spurted from the gaping wound. Julian exploded to dust even before he hit the ground.

The sword slipped from Constantine's blood-soaked hands. He looked at the dagger atop the mound of dust, which the night's breeze picked up and scattered across the forest.

Once again, Constantine had given the devil his due.

Chapter Thirty

Now that one threat was over, they were about to face another.

As soon as Julian turned to dust and the effects of the intensity of her power subsided, Lex ran to Constantine. The moment she touched him he hissed and pushed her away. In her need to get to him, Lex had forgotten the energy was now beyond her control. It raged within her, threatening to consume her and she was afraid. If Isobel, who with Lenora's aid was only now gaining her feet, didn't begin the ritual, Lex knew she wasn't going to survive much longer.

Though it took almost more strength than she possessed, Lex was able to pull the power back enough to touch Constantine without burning him to ash. "I thought I was going to lose you."

He wrapped his arms around her and kissed the top of her head. His tenderness brought tears to her eyes. "They're naught but flesh wounds."

Flesh wounds? He'd been nearly stabbed through the heart. As far as Lex was concerned, that was far from a flesh wound.

Through his torn shirt, Lex saw that the wound to his chest was still raw and bleeding. How his other injuries fared, she didn't know. As long as he was alive, that was all that mattered to her.

Lex looked at Isobel, cringing at the amount of blood staining her white robe. She knew the wound wasn't severe enough to end her, but Lex had to wonder if Isobel's diminished strength would hinder her from holding Lex in this realm once the ritual was underway.

When a stab of pain hit Lex in the chest, she shoved herself away from Constantine and doubled over with a gasp. Wrapping her arms around her stomach, she bit back a moan as agony sliced through her. Every breath was an effort as pain shot through her. When Constantine reached her for, she stumbled back, out of his reach and warned him not to touch her.

Through a fog of pain, Lex saw Constantine retrieve his sword and level it at the two women of the Order. There was no sympathy in his glare for Isobel, who was struggling against her own wounds. "It's killing her. Do something. Now."

The Halloweds' voices were screaming in her head, calling for her. Welcoming her to their realm. Dear God, she didn't want to go. Lex wanted to stay here, with Constantine and Allie and the other Templars. She didn't want to go where they could never follow.

"Move her into position. We haven't much time."

Moving swiftly after Isobel rasped that, Constantine took hold of Lex's arm and began to guide her to her stone. "Come on, elf, you have to walk with me."

She was trying—God knew she was, but it hurt. Yet when Lex smelled the distinct stench of burning flesh, she knew that if Constantine could bear the pain of touching her, she could damn well bear the pain of walking.

Sweating and covered in Julian's blood—and God-only-knew what else after literally melting him nearly to death—Lex began to lumber toward the stone that bore the *Dagaz* rune.

Only once she was in place did Constantine release her. The hand he'd held her with was a ruined mess of burnt flesh. When Isobel urged him to hurry, Lex slumped against the stone and watched as he raced across the henge to the *Tiwaz* rune. Isobel moved into position and leaned against her stone, too weak to stand.

Lex looked back at Constantine, who appeared as if on the verge of a great battle—not having just come from one. And maybe he was. Maybe he was preparing himself for her death, just as she was.

Another wave of pain came over her and Lex was unable to hold back her scream. It echoed throughout the forest. In answer, a hawk screeched as it soared high overhead.

When her scream died down, Lex heard the Hallowed, no longer a scream, but a whisper in her head. It soothed her as they spoke to her, telling her she wasn't alone. She was part of them now, and they would be waiting to welcome her should this be her time to leave the world behind.

A perfect calm settled over Lex and she knew she was ready to face her fate—whatever it may be. Life or death, or something else, she was ready to face it.

When Constantine sensed the calm acceptance come over Lex, he knew what true panic was. He didn't want her calm and accepting. He wanted her to fight tooth and nail for life.

Regret tore through him as all the things he should have said to her bombarded his mind. He'd never told her he loved her.

And oh God, did he love her.

He loved her with everything he was, and knew that if he lost her tonight, all that he was would go with her. Because of her, his past no longer mattered. The ghosts that had haunted him for centuries had no place in his existence as long as Lex was there to keep them at bay. The light of her being lit the dark he'd dwelled in for seven hundred years, and it had nothing to do with Daystar's power. Lex's love was a force to be reckoned with, and it broke through the darkness with an incandescence that blinded him to the horrors dwelling in the blackness of his heart.

Isobel began to chant, her voice low and strained with pain. Lex stiffened and Constantine sensed the pain that sliced through her. A brilliant light lit her, cutting through the night, making the forest as bright as day. So intense was the light that Lenora was forced to look away. Constantine and Isobel kept their gazes locked on her.

He'd make damn sure his gaze never left her. If she were to go, he wanted to see the moment the power took her. He needed her to see that he braved the pain to make sure she wasn't alone in that final moment.

When Constantine saw tears began to spill down Lex's cheeks, an unfamiliar sting irritated his eyes. A single bloody tear cut a path down his own cheek as he watched his woman weep. Never, not even when he'd burned to death, had he known such helplessness.

Here he was, an immortal warrior, a dragon, and yet he couldn't save his woman—his mate—from her fear and her pain. What good was his bloody strength if he couldn't protect his woman?

But when Lex's lips curled into a barely perceivable smile, he knew the strength of his love for her aided her more than his sword ever could.

Unable to fight it back any longer, the power burst like a raging fire. Lex bit down on her bottom lip to keep from crying out again, but even that couldn't hold in her scream. The sound was pulled from her very soul as the power pressed down on her.

Isobel called on all of the Druids who passed over to the other realms that lay just beyond a human's sight. She chanted prayers to the gods and to the elements. She prayed to the moon and to earth. Her fervent prayers charged the very ground beneath their feet.

When a vicious surge of energy shot through her, Lex's head was thrown back and her arms flung wide as if on their own volition. The pain was nearly unbearable as the incandescent light burned so bright it rendered her blind to the physical world.

Suddenly, it all vanished.

Pain, fear, and death—it was all just—gone. The weight of the last month—no, of her entire life—eased from her shoulders. A peaceful darkness surrounded her, and though Lex was able to see Constantine and the others, it was as if she were seeing into a dream. She heard Constantine in her mind, willing her to fight and watched Isobel fighting to hold her to this plane.

The voices of the Hallowed called to her, softly. And she wanted to go. Oh God, did she want to go to them. They offered her peace. Here, there was no grief. Her parent's negligence didn't matter here. Doubt and fear held no meaning in this place. Time ceased to matter. Moments could have passed or days. It all seemed the same.

Nothing mattered but the voices talking to her.

Her body seemed to float through the darkness, wherein hid the women behind the voices. They wanted her with them and she wanted to go. With a calm acceptance, Lex let go of life and began to make her journey to whenever it was those women waited.

"I'm losing her."

Isobel's voice came to her from someplace far away. Lex ignored it. It didn't matter. Nothing mattered here. Being here gave Lex a sweet relief of the burdens of life.

She stretched out her arms into the dark, reaching for something she knew lay beyond the darkness. The other Hallowed? Heaven? God? Lex wasn't sure. All she knew was that somewhere hidden in the darkness was something unknown, but something she instinctively knew she wanted to find.

Closing her eyes, Lex moved forward, further into the dark. Warmth surrounded her, wrapping around her body and taking her away from Constantine. A tinge of terror edged into her being at the thought of leaving him behind, yet something told her he'd understand her need to go in to the warmth and peace beckoning her.

Though in this place she had no breath, Lex released a pleasant sigh as the warmth engulfed her. She felt such love here. It chased away a lifetime of loneliness and neglect.

"I can't hold her much longer. She's fading, Constantine."

Constantine... His name invaded the perfect peace settling over Lex. Her need to stay with him warred with the desire to travel deeper into the blackness and come out the other end, where the promise of pure happiness awaited her.

He doesn't love you. The thought nagged at her mind. Lex wasn't sure where it came from. Whether it came from her own sub-consciousness or from the Hallowed, she didn't know. Nor did she care. She shook her head. He did love her. She was certain of it. He might not have declared it to be so, but his every action proved his feelings for her.

But the darkness pulled at her and Lex floated further away from the world. She drifted further away from Constantine. She kept on drifting until whatever she'd once been seemed to have all been a dream. Her family, her life, the Templars—even Constantine—ceased to be real to her.

"She's gone, Constantine. I lost her."

Lost? Lex smiled at Isobel's announcement. She wasn't lost. She was home.

"Bring her back, Isobel. Bring her back to me. Now."

The desperation in Constantine's tone yanked Lex back from bliss. She looked back at Constantine, who seemed a million miles away. Lex watched as he fell to his knees. When Isobel told him Lex was beyond her reach, his hoarse cry echoed throughout Lex's very being. His pain pierced her like a million knives, shattering the peace.

Oh God, how could she leave him? He was everything to her. This—wherever it was Lex found herself—wasn't real. Constantine and her love for him was what mattered. He needed her, and Lex needed him right back. Any promise of happiness couldn't be found in this realm, away from Constantine. It could only be found wherever he was.

Pushing out of the darkness, moving away from the Hallowed, Lex drifted back toward the world. Back toward the pain she knew waited for her once she stepped from this place.

Just like that, the pain returned, the forest replaced the blackness, and the song of the Halloweds' voices faded into the night.

The light around her exploded in a million points of white-hot intensity. Lex screamed loud enough to shake the night. She collapsed on the ground, her gaze fixed on Constantine as he rushed toward her. Out of the corner of her eye, Lex saw Isobel fall back. The ethereal creature who'd saved her life hit the stone and slid down to the ground. Lenora rushed to her and cradled her as Isobel was in danger of bleeding out.

Trembling violently, Lex almost couldn't believe it was over and that she was still alive. The power of the Daystar still throbbed within her, though now, it wasn't hitching a ride inside of her body. No—it was one with her. Flowing through her in time with her breathing and with the beating of her heart.

Lex wept with relief when she saw Constantine kneeling beside her. "You made it."

She laughed softly. "I know."

"You're alright?"

That was a loaded question. Her body throbbed with life. Power poured through her, and yet it was all so—natural. "I'm okay. I feel different, though, and yet the same." She shook her head in bemusement. "I know I'm not making any sense."

Constantine knelt and gathered her in his arms. "I thought I'd lost you there for a moment."

The emotion behind his words wrapped around her heart and told her how much he loved her. "I think for a moment there, you did. I fought hard to stay with you."

He pushed her away and stared deep into her eyes. He went as still and stiff as a statue. "Oh God, elf, I don't know what I would have done if I'd lost you."

"You don't have to worry about that now." She smiled weakly. "You're stuck with me for a while longer."

"Thank God for that."

"I feel strange, Constantine. I feel the Daystar power still in me. But there's something else that I can't explain."

He smoothed a hand over her hair before placing a kiss on her forehead. His lips were cool and unyielding and she loved the feel of them on her warm flesh. "You're immortal."

"That can't be. I don't feel immortal."

Whether Lex felt immortal or not, the fact remained that she was. Constantine saw the truth of it reflected in the brilliant depths of her glowing silver eyes. He'd miss the clear blue they'd been, though he had to admit the silver complemented her. With her dark hair, her now-permanently sun-kissed flesh, she looked not so much as a dark-angel come down from Heaven anymore. Now, Lex had the look of an exotic jewel he knew he was damned privileged to call his mate.

Constantine's eyes slid closed. *Thank you.* Though he knew his silent prayer of thanks would go unheard, he'd needed to say it nonetheless.

He helped Lex stand. She was none too steady on her feet and he knew if he weren't supporting her, she'd fall.

"She needs blood or else she's going to die."

The urgency that laced Lenora's voice wasn't lost on Constantine. She wiped away the bloody tears cutting a path down her cheeks and looked at him imploringly. Never would he have imagined that anyone from the Order of the Rose would look to him for aid. Nor would he ever have believed he'd be in the position to help Isobel of Lowel.

How odd that life, somehow, had come full circle.

Constantine went down on one knee and pushed aside Lenora's hands. He stared deep into Isobel's eyes and saw the acceptance of death in them. "Death won't take you this night, Isobel," he assured her. "You saved me, now I'll save you. And then my debt to you will be paid."

As he lifted her and cradled her against his chest, he was struck by how small she was in his arms. All of these centuries,

Rene Lyons

until this moment, she'd always seemed larger than life. But then he'd always viewed her through the eyes of a frightened young man.

Isobel wrapped her thin arms around his neck and held on tight as Constantine rose to his full height. "Debt? You owe me nothing, Constantine. If anything, I failed you all those years ago. I should have never sent you away with Guy. I should have..."

"You did exactly as you should have, and for that I'm grateful." He looked at Lex, who stood beside him. She was so full of life. Oh God, how he loved her. "Because of you I've finally found peace,"

The tears of blood that spilled down Isobel's face caused an uncomfortable sting in his own eyes as he carried her out of the henge. Lex walked next to him, practically glued to his side, Lenora following close behind.

When they reached the castle Lenora rushed off to call in a donor. Constantine brought Isobel up to her chamber. He laid her on her bed, and stepped away. Lex pushed past him and threw her arms around Isobel, who grimaced from pain.

"Thank you."

Isobel ran her hand through Lex's hair, though her smile was for Constantine. "I did nothing."

Lex pulled back. She came away with Isobel's blood on her. "Yes you did. You saved my life."

Isobel shook her head weakly. "No, Lexine. You saved your life. I wasn't strong enough to hold you here. You made it through on your own."

Lex looked at Constantine, frowning in confusion. "It's true, Lex. It was your own strength of will that got you through it."

"But I died. I know I did."

300

"Yes, and you came back." Isobel looked at him intently. "She came back because of you."

So she did.

His woman—his mate—was stronger even than him. Her love was a powerful force that wrapped around them both and held on when he thought to let it go. He'd been a bloody fool. Because of his past he'd almost allowed himself to push her away. That was something he'd never allow to happen again. The simple truth was, he needed Lex, and he wasn't too proud to admit that fact.

Lenora burst into Isobel's room and raced to the bed. She grabbed Isobel's hand. "A donor is on her way. She should be here soon. Can you hold on until then?"

Isobel nodded. "If Lexine can come back from death, I can find the strength to hold it off a bit longer." When Lex went to say something, Isobel held up her hand. "No. I know what you're going to offer and I won't take it. You're his, Lexine. Only his. The gift you gave him of your body and soul is for no one else."

Seeming to accept this, Lex nodded solemnly, even though Constantine sensed her need to argue the point. "Come on, Lex. Let's let her rest."

Constantine pulled Lex out of Isobel's chamber. Only once they were alone in their room did he drag her against him and hold onto her as if his existence depended on it. And maybe it did. After all, there were times over the centuries when he'd come close to veering off his path to redemption. Only once Lex came into his world, did Constantine begin to believe salvation was possible. Moreover, she made him believe in love, which was something he'd never thought to ever know.

He kissed her hard, letting all his love pour into her as he took in her energy. Her power no longer burned. Instead, it was a wonderful flow of heat that traveled through him and gave his body the momentary sense of life. What was left of his injuries healed under the loving touch of her hands.

When Lex's hands flattened on his back, Constantine sensed that she was something far greater than he realized. She was a part of the Druid magic dating back to a time before recorded history. But she was also his, and the Order had better understand that fact.

They'd want her, to protect her and keep her close to them. He'd not let her go.

Constantine broke the kiss, needing to just hold her. He placed his chin on the top of Lex's head, marveling at the pounding of her heart against his own chest. He looked out the window, out into the dark. For once, when he stared into the night it didn't stare back.

"Thank God for you."

Lex pushed away from him. The love in her smile worked its way into his heart, cleansing it of the stain of his sins. "I guess that means you love me, huh?"

"Guess?" His voice was thick with emotion. "No, elf. I *know* I love you. I've always loved you."

"It's about damn time you told me." Her hand settled on his scarred cheek. "I want to go home. Take me home to Seacrest, Constantine."

Home.

After centuries of wandering lost in the dark, Constantine found home. It was there in Lex's eyes and in her heart. But most of all, it was in the love she selflessly offered him.

Constantine remembered the wounded boy who'd left this land vowing never to return to the place where he'd suffered unspeakable horrors. This last month he'd come full circle.

Now, as he stood in the very spot where he once had, as a scared and damaged boy, he was finally the man he always should have been. After centuries of suffering, his past was put to rest.

The Dragon slept.

Epilogue

Lex stood out on the balcony, marveling at all that had happened. Was it truly only a handful of nights ago that'd she'd died and fought her way back? Or had lifetimes passed? She couldn't be certain anymore since so much had happened between that night and now.

Isobel was healing fast, the severity of her wounds far greater than anyone had imagined. Lenora hadn't left her side and others of the Order were on their way from all over England and Scotland. Lex was glad she and Constantine would be gone before they arrived. Not that she feared the women of the Order any longer. She knew none of them trusted Constantine, and after everything that happened over the last twenty-four hours, neither of them needed that tension.

Lex still couldn't believe that she'd died and had come back. Refusing to give up on her love for Constantine, she'd fought her way back to this life. Smiling into the sunset, she knew she'd never take even one moment of life for granted. She'd been given a gift and she'd live it to the fullest at Constantine's side.

How different she was from the person she'd been just a day ago. Immortal now, Lex carried the strength and glory of the sun within her. She'd share that power with Constantine, lending him life through her body and her blood. Through her, she'd make sure he knew what it was to live again and finally know peace and happiness.

As much as Lex knew Constantine's past was at rest, a part of him would always suffer for what he'd gone through in his life. All she could do was love him and be there when his memories crept up around him and threatened to pull him back down into that black pit of rage and pain.

Looking out across the Salisbury plain, Lex could almost imagine what it must have been like for Constantine to have grown up near here. Greaves and Draegon Castles had stood a handful of miles away. Both were long gone now, having succumbed to the ravishes of time. The echo of those castles still reverberated across the land. The evil they had housed stained the ground. Lex felt it now, felt the foulness of those who'd hurt Constantine move through her. She'd be glad when they were away from this place.

She couldn't imagine how hard it must have been for him to return here. Which was why they were leaving tonight. They'd been here for a month and he wanted to be gone from this place with all due haste.

Instead of flying to America, they were first going to Northumberland, to the original Seacrest Castle. Constantine had sensed—something. He wasn't sure what it was. He told her he couldn't get a fix on it, but all he knew was that he had to get to Seacrest before they returned to America. That was just fine by Lex. She was as eager to meet Edward Beaumont, Tristan's eccentric descendant, as Constantine was to get back to a place he knew of as home.

All in all, Lex had to admit that this whole Daystar thing had worked out far better than she could have ever hoped. But that was to be expected when one was facing the possibility of death and instead, came out of it not merely alive—but immortal.

Now—if only she could find a way to get his soul back...

But that was something he had to do alone.

Seeing the sun dip below the horizon, Lex smiled and waited...

She didn't have to wait long.

"Fate showed this to me."

Constantine's voice behind her had Lex smiling. She turned and laughed at the saying on his tee shirt. It read *I even scare my own family.*

She stepped into his open arms, her white robes flowing when she moved. Before they left tonight she'd change into her own clothes and leave the Druid world here, where it belonged. "It did? When?"

"The night you and Tristan saw me have that vision back at Seacrest."

She pulled back and frowned up at him. "Why didn't you tell me?"

He shrugged. "I didn't know what it meant and I didn't want to scare you."

She raised a brow at him and gave him a look that clearly said she was *not* pleased he kept his vision from her. "I'll let you get away with keeping a vision from me this time, but if you withhold information like that from me again..."

"Cease your tirade, elf." He kissed her soundly, making her forget what it was he'd done to irritate her. God, how she got lost in his kiss. Lex had the feeling he'd be using kisses to do that a lot over the coming years.

Lex wasn't the only one to lose themselves in the moment. If Constantine's senses had been honed in on the world around him and not focused on Lex, he would have detected the faint sense of death that carried on the air. Ancient death. Medieval death.

He would have sensed somewhere out there a Templar was lost in the dark. He would have felt the hunger and the pain that tore through Lucian of Penwick as he fought not to give in to the monster his brother was slowly turning him into.

It was a battle he couldn't fight forever and one he knew he was losing. It would only be a matter of time before the bloodlust overtook him and he was forced to do the one thing that could damn his soul to Hell with no hope of salvation.

He would take the life of an innocent.

About the Author

learn more about Rene Lyons, please visit http://www.renelyons.net Send an email to Rene at rene@renelyons.net or join her Yahoo group to join in the fun with other readers as well as Rene! http://groups.yahoo.com/group/renelyonsauthor/

Look for these titles

Now Available

Midnight Sun

Coming Soon:

Tempting Darkness
The Seraphim: Setheus

*Vengeance is what she sought...eternal love
is what she found.*

Fallon's Revenge
© *2006 Mackenzie McKade*

Young and inexperienced, Fallon McGregor is an immortal with one thing on her mind. Revenge. She'll do anything to destroy the demon that killed her daughter and made Fallon his flesh and blood slave. One step ahead of her tormentor, she knows her luck is running out. She needs to discover the mysteries of the dark—and fast. When she meets Adrian Trask she gets more than she bargains for in tight jeans and a Stetson.

Adrian will share his ancient blood and knowledge with Fallon, but he wants something in return...her heart and her promise to stay with him forever.

But Fallon doesn't have forever. Once her nemesis is destroyed she will seek her own death. Tormented, she must choose between a promise made and the love of one man.

Available now in ebook and print from Samhain Publishing.